THE FIRES OF BLACKSTONE

Look for these exciting Western series from bestselling authors

WILLIAM W. JOHNSTONE
and **J. A. JOHNSTONE**

Smoke Jensen: The Last Mountain Man
Preacher: The First Mountain Man
Luke Jensen, Bounty Hunter
Those Jensen Boys!
The Jensen Brand
MacCallister
The Red Ryan Westerns
Perley Gates
Have Brides, Will Travel
Will Tanner, U.S. Deputy Marshal
Shotgun Johnny
The Chuckwagon Trail
The Jackals
The Slash and Pecos Westerns
The Texas Moonshiners
Stoneface Finnegan Westerns
Ben Savage: Saloon Ranger
The Buck Trammel Westerns
The Death and Texas Westerns
The Hunter Buchanon Westerns

THE FIRES OF BLACKSTONE

A BUCK TRAMMEL WESTERN

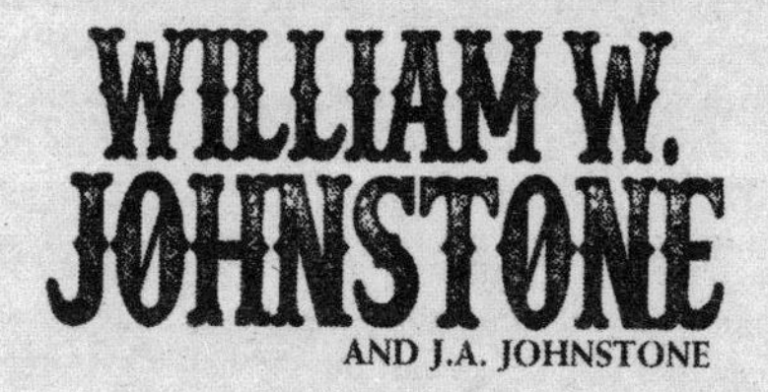

AND J.A. JOHNSTONE

PINNACLE BOOKS
Kensington Publishing Corp.
www.kensingtonbooks.com

PINNACLE BOOKS are published by

Kensington Publishing Corp.
119 West 40th Street
New York, NY 10018

PUBLISHER'S NOTE
Following the death of William W. Johnstone, the Johnstone family is working with a carefully selected writer to organize and complete Mr. Johnstone's outlines and many unfinished manuscripts to create additional novels in all of his series like The Last Gunfighter, Mountain Man, and Eagles, among others. This novel was inspired by Mr. Johnstone's superb storytelling.

First Printing: May 2022
ISBN-13: 978-0-7860-4864-9
ISBN-13: 978-0-7860-4865-6 (eBook)

10 9 8 7 6 5 4 3 2 1

Printed in the United States of America

CHAPTER 1

"Sounds like company's coming, boss," Deputy James "Hawkeye" Hauk said as the train whistle echoed through Blackstone.

"Yeah." Sheriff Buck Trammel set his coffee mug on his desk and got to his feet. "It certainly does." Unlike some residents, he found the new sound of a train whistle echoing throughout town to be charming. But he knew this particular whistle was more than just a train engine letting off steam. It was a warning that trouble was coming to Blackstone.

"Guess I'd better go down to the station to meet it." He took his Peacemaker from his desk and tucked it into the holster under his left arm. It had been a long time since he'd been a Pinkerton, but he'd never gotten comfortable with wearing a gun on his hip. "Head off whatever trouble I can." He was still getting used to the idea that Blackstone had a train station.

Adam Hagen had built a railroad spur north from the main line in Laramie so he could take his wood from the mill and his cattle to market in the city. The short line ran on a regular schedule and at his convenience. A trip that used to take half a day now took about thirty minutes. Unfortunately, the train not only served to take goods and people down to Laramie, but to also bring them up to Blackstone. Hence the reason for Trammel's concern.

The sheriff looked at the rifles in the rack by the jailhouse door but decided against taking one. It might put people on more of an edge than they already were. He figured his size and the Peacemaker would serve as suitable deterrents.

Hawkeye asked, "Want me to go with you?"

Trammel shook his head as he pulled on his hat. "Best if you stay here for the time being. But get ready to come running if you hear any trouble from the station."

If Hawkeye was disappointed, he hid it well. He took down the double-barreled shotgun from the rack and began feeding shells into the tubes. "I'll be here if you need me."

Trammel bent his head as he stepped out of the jail and onto the boardwalk. "You always are."

At six-seven and two hundred and forty solid pounds, Steven "Buck" Trammel was always conscious of his size. He'd never quite gotten used to the attention he drew whenever people saw him for the first time. Lately, he drew more odd looks than normal for there were a lot of new people in Blackstone. The railroad spur Adam Hagen had built as soon as he had gained control of the Hagen empire had brought them. The building boom he had started meant they'd stayed.

The new Hagen wood mill was almost done and a new street full of houses for the workers was almost finished. The tents the workers had been sleeping in for the past three months would soon be a thing of the past and, Trammel hoped, the disorder they'd brought would go with them. In his experience, a man tended to simmer down once he had a fixed roof over his head. It made him more appreciative of being out of the rain.

Trammel stood aside on the boardwalk as a group of ladies marched past him on the way to the new church Hagen had built at the end of Main Street. The gesture had been a small part of his plan to wipe every trace of his father from the town and remake Blackstone in his own image.

Trammel figured Adam would have to build a church twice the size of Notre Dame if he were looking to atone for all the sins he had committed in his life.

King Charles Hagen was dead. Long live King Adam Hagen.

"Good morning, Sheriff!" came a familiar voice from the balcony of the new hotel across Main Street.

Trammel stepped out from beneath the overhang and into the thoroughfare. The new Phoenix Hotel loomed larger than its predecessor, the Clifford, which had been burned in the riot the previous year. A few modest buildings had to be torn down for the Phoenix, but those inconvenienced by the construction were moved to newer, larger homes in the bargain. They had offered little complaint. Adam was a lot of things, but he knew how to treat people when he wanted something from them.

Trammel pegged the Phoenix as being more than twice the size of its predecessor. It sported a proper gaming area that rivaled even the finest gambling houses in New Orleans. Dozens of well-appointed rooms were said to put some of the nicest hotels in New York to shame. Hagen had even gone as far as to bring a chef all the way from Paris to make sure every meal was an occasion. Guests flocked to Blackstone from far and wide to see what all the fuss was about.

The large porch on the first floor featured plenty of rocking chairs where guests could lounge while they took in the bustling new Main Street. A grand balcony on the second floor served as Hagen's favorite perch from where he could see all his large inheritance had given him. He was building a town that might one day be worthy to become the capital of the territory.

"Nice to see you, Buck." Hagen toasted him with a cup of coffee. "You're looking well this morning."

Even from that distance, Trammel could see the china's intricate pattern sported a deep red design matching the fiery theme of the Phoenix Hotel.

He certainly did not feel well. Dr. Moore had pulled four bullets out of his left side after the riot. The wounds still ached whenever it was about to rain. Out of politeness, he answered, "You're looking prosperous yourself for a man with a price on his head."

Hagen threw back his head and laughed. "People have been trying to kill me for years, Buck, yet here I am."

Indeed, *here he is*, Trammel thought, but Hagen had certainly changed over the years. In the morning light, the sheriff could see the entrepreneur had aged quite a bit since they'd first met in Wichita. His fair hair had begun to turn white in places, though Trammel knew he was just past thirty. Hagen kept his beard trimmed and close to his smooth skin. He looked leaner than he used to, and his light eyes were set deeper than they used to be. Harder, too.

And since King Charles's suspicious death, Adam had changed his clothes to a more somber tone. Loud brocade vests had given way to darker colors more befitting a man of property and stature.

Hagen's smile held as he asked Trammel, "I take it you're heading over to the train station?"

"Somebody's got to go. Want to head off any trouble before it starts."

"No need," Hagen said. "Ben London and his constables are already there. They'll see to it nothing happens. Let them do their job. It's what I pay them for."

Trammel had been against the creation of a town constabulary when Hagen had first raised the matter at a town council meeting, but none of the elders saw fit to oppose him given that Blackstone was his town. The group quickly became known as *Hagen's Constables*. Their blue tunics and brass badges made them easy to spot. They existed to serve Hagen's interests, which were not always aligned with those of the town.

Trammel and Hawkeye were still the only official law existing in Blackstone, a fact of which the sheriff had to remind Hagen many times.

Standing in the middle of Main Street, Trammel saw no benefit to continuing that old argument, especially now that the second train whistle was much closer than the first. "Enjoy your coffee, Adam. I've got work to do."

"Be sure to give my regards to my family when you see them," Hagen called after him. "We're not exactly on speaking terms these days."

Trammel couldn't blame them. After all, Adam Hagen had killed their father.

The walk to the new train station at the east end of Main Street took longer than it used to. Even Trammel was impressed by all the changes made in a short amount of time. When he had first come to Blackstone, the place had been little more than a cow town. A place where miners and cattlemen who didn't work for the mighty Blackstone ranch came to find some hint of civilization. The town had been laid out as an *E* back then, with three avenues shooting off from Main Street.

Since the demise of King Charles, Adam had gone on a building spree of epic proportions. Doubled in length, Main Street featured two general stores besides the old Robertson's place, whose owner had sold out months ago and moved to Colorado. Several claims offices catered to the miners. Three banks and just as many hotels were new.

Those who couldn't afford the opulence of the Phoenix could find clean, comfortable rooms at the Occidental, the East Sider, and the Knickerbocker.

Saloons still dominated Main Street, though drunkards had ceased to wander the town per Hagen's orders. The Pot of Gold Saloon still catered to the opium trade, but the Chinese who peddled dragon smoke had taken down their canvas tents in favor of a building that fit in with the rest of the town. Hagen had also made sure a better job of keeping customers inside was done until they were sober enough to walk around on their own steam.

As he continued walking toward the station, Trammel was happy to see the shingle of Dr. Emily Downs hanging beneath that of Dr. Jacob Moore outside a two-story building. The two physicians tended to the needs of the growing town and were busier tending to colds and the flu than broken bones and gunshots.

He hoped nothing would happen at the train station to change that.

The train station on the far eastern side of the town was a small but ornate affair. Hagen had designed it with intricate wooden fixtures that gave it an elegant look. It also featured a telegraph office. The telegraph lines had followed the tracks, making it easier for Blackstone to communicate with Laramie and the rest of the country.

Modernity had its privileges.

Waiting outside the station, wagons and carriages of every sort were ready to take the arrivals or goods to their destinations.

As he waited for the train to pull into the station, Trammel looked toward the large stockyard built at the far end of the tracks for easy loading and unloading of livestock, but he was less concerned about any four-legged passengers the train might be bringing to town. It was the two-legged variety that worried him.

As it came to a halt, the locomotive emitted a large plume of steam from its great smokestack. Black porters jumped from the passenger cars and placed step stools on the ground to help passengers looking to get off at Blackstone.

Trammel walked to the end of the train where he saw the two private Hagen family cars. Their own footmen were already off the train and loading the luggage of their employers onto a waiting wagon.

Caleb Hagen was the leader of the family and looked it. He was approaching fifty and, although he had been born and raised at the family ranch in Blackstone, he could have been mistaken for a New York banker. His face had some of his late father's sharp features, but too many steak dinners and black cigars and made him thick around the middle. His dark suit had been tailored to hide his girth, but as Trammel had learned, clothes could only hide a man's true nature for so long. He had once handled the Hagen empire's investments and had been proud of his accomplishments until Adam inherited it all and replaced him.

Bartholomew Hagen was shorter than his brother and,

if the paintings Trammel had seen at the Hagen ranch house were to be believed, favored his mother. A capable looking man who lacked his brother's height and frame, the second son had been placed in charge of the family's mining interests by King Charles himself. From what Trammel had heard, he had done more than a fair job of making the family even richer than they already were.

Like her brother, Debora Hagen Forrester favored her mother's portrait except for her eyes. There she resembled King Charles, right down to the cold, casual glare. Not even the parasol or the fashionable pink hat she sported could soften her look.

Her husband, Ambrose Forrester, was at her side. He had a habit of constantly running his hand through his hair to ensure it remained in place. The fop came from the powerful Forrester family of Colorado, which counted several relatives in state houses throughout the West and one in the US Senate. Other than an impressive last name, Trammel found him entirely forgettable.

Elena Hagen Wain was the baby of the family and Adam's favorite sister. She had married a Philadelphia lawyer who Adam claimed was well on his way to being named partner in the family firm.

Where her brothers and sister were severe, Elena was gentle. Her golden hair and porcelain skin made her look like Adam's twin, though she was much younger. Trammel wondered if her siblings had told her Adam was not really their brother or if they had been uncharacteristically kind enough to hide that fact from her.

However, if there was one trait the Hagen clan lacked, it was kindness.

The family did their best to ignore Trammel as he ambled

over to them where they had clustered together on the platform outside their train cars.

"Welcome back to Blackstone," he told them.

Caleb chewed on a black cigar and scowled up at him as if he was a beggar. Bart and Debora made half attempts at smiles, but nothing more.

Elena waved and smiled. "Morning, Buck. Nice to see you again." She had still been living with her father when Trammel had brought Adam back to Blackstone. She had been a charming young woman then and he was glad some things had not changed.

Trammel touched the brim of his hat. "Nice to be seen, Elena. Hope your trip up here was a pleasant one."

Caleb took the black cigar from his mouth as he strode between Trammel and the rest of his family. "I suppose Adam sent you here to spy on us?"

Trammel had not been expecting a handshake. "Your brother and I have an arrangement, Caleb. He doesn't tell me what to do so I don't have to defy him. Makes it easier to keep the peace that way."

"My brother," the banker spat. He looked like he wanted to say more but caught himself. "What are you doing here, then?"

"Making sure your visit starts off on the right foot." Trammel inclined his head to the six men in blue tunics standing next to the station building. "I don't want anyone to make you feel unwelcome."

Caleb looked over at the six constables gathered nearby. "They look more like common thugs to me."

Trammel could not argue with him there. They were all like him, former saloon bouncers who had somehow managed to get badges pinned on their chests. Every one of the ten constables on Hagen's payroll had the same look—tall, broad, and mean. They made no effort to hide it.

Big Ben London was the biggest and meanest looking of the bunch. About Trammel's size, the silent Negro looked at the Hagens with cold indifference.

"I'm not with them and they're not with me," Trammel reminded Caleb. "They won't give you any trouble while I'm around."

"No need," Caleb said. "We can take care of ourselves against their kind."

Trammel looked at Caleb's belly and thought otherwise. "Well, with me around, you won't have to."

"That's what's always fascinated me about you, Trammel." Caleb pointed at him with the unlit cigar. "You despise Adam every bit as the rest of us, yet you always somehow find a way to save his life."

"Just doing my job."

Caleb went on. "You should've let that crowd rip him to pieces last year, but you didn't. Hell, you almost got yourself killed in the process. You're not a stupid man. That's plain for anyone with two eyes to see. Why not just sit back and let nature take its course?"

"On account of I'm not paid to let nature have its way, Caleb. I'm paid to keep the peace in town and that's what I'm going to keep on doing until they take this star from me. That's part of the reason why I came over to see you folks. I'd like to know what you're doing back here."

Caleb sneered. "So, you are scouting for Adam after all."

Trammel shook his head. "You know I'm not. Your troubles with him over your father's estate are your business so long as it stays peaceful. We've had our fair share of trouble in this town, and it's up to me to make sure things don't get out of hand."

Caleb opened his coat. "I'm not armed, Sheriff."

"Men like you never do your own fighting. I've seen some rough characters milling around town over the past couple of days. Over at the Knickerbocker and the Occidental. I figure they're yours."

Caleb shrugged. "And what if they are? What concern is it of yours?"

"None, so long as they don't step out of line."

"Does the same go for Adam's so-called constables?"

"There are only two sworn lawmen in Blackstone, Caleb. Me and Hawkeye. The constables have authority only on Hagen land and, last I checked, Blackstone is public property. They step out of line? They get stepped on same as everyone else."

Caleb Hagen took his time looking the sheriff up and down. "Is that so?"

Trammel let him look. "It surely is."

Caleb popped his cigar in his mouth and looked away. "You've got nothing to worry about from me or my family, Trammel. We're as peaceful as Pascal lambs. For now, our fight is in the courts."

"Glad to hear it." Trammel meant it. "Just make sure it stays there . . . and that your men stay out of trouble while they're here in town."

Caleb nodded toward the constables. "And them?"

"I'll be watching them like I'm watching you. They bother you or your people, you let me know."

Caleb did not look convinced, but he did not look like he wanted an argument, either. "We'll leave it at that, then. Nice seeing you again, Steven."

"Caleb." Trammel touched the brim of his hat then stood aside as he watched the family take their time loading themselves into the coaches lined up to take them to the Hagen ranch house up the hill from town.

As the family boarded the carriages, the five constables in town milled around close by but did not say a word. Only Caleb antagonized them by staring at Big Ben as they pulled away.

Trammel stayed on the platform as he watched the servants and a porter load the family's luggage—trunks and chests and boxes of all manner of size and description—onto flatbed wagons. He figured they would be staying at the house for the foreseeable future, which would only make his job even harder.

With the family gone, Big Ben slowly walked back toward town hall. The remaining five constables grew bolder around the staff.

"Would you just look at all that finery," the one named Jesse said to the others. "Why I'd bet everything I've ever owned in the world would just about fit into one of them hat boxes they've got there."

Rand, the second oldest man in the group, added, "Sure must be nice to have money. Look at all the pretty servants they got, too."

The three men Trammel assumed were footmen stopped loading for a moment before resuming their task. The black porter never stopped.

"Looks like one of them didn't like us calling him pretty, Rand," said the one called Eddie. "We're gonna have to keep our eyes on him."

The man called Smith cackled. "Be careful, Eddie. He might throw his hanky at you."

The five of them laughed, with the one called Red adding, "Now you've gone and done it, boys. They look like they're just about ready to cry."

The three servants stopped loading the wagon and squared up to the constables.

Trammel decided to step in between them before things got out of hand. "That's enough, boys. Let them work and be on your way."

The constables stopped laughing as Jesse took a step toward Trammel. "This here is Hagen property. We don't have to do a—"

Trammel decked him with a short, left hook to the jaw. He was out cold before he hit the ground.

The four remaining constables took a step backward. Only Rand found the courage to speak. "What'd you go and do that for?"

Trammel looked down at Jesse. "That man's drunk."

"Drunk?" Red repeated. "Why it ain't even noon yet. He hasn't touched a drop in two whole days."

"He has to be drunk to step up to me like that." Trammel looked at Red. "You drunk, too?"

Red held up his hands and backed farther away. "I'm sober as a judge."

"Good. You boys had best pick up your friend here and get him off the street before I run the whole lot of you in for loitering." Trammel dug the tip of his boot under Jesse's shoulder and turned him over in the dirt. "Get going."

Rand told Smith and Eddie to pick up their fallen comrade and carry him away. Red went with them, leaving Rand to bring up the rear. And he was in no hurry to move.

Trammel closed the few feet between them. "Get moving or I won't be as gentle with you."

Rand kept his hands raised as he backed up another step. "I'm moving, Sheriff. I'm moving. For now. But there's gonna come a time real soon when I won't have to move until I'm good and ready. None of us will. And that time's coming sooner than you think."

"But today's not the day." Trammel kicked dirt in his direction. "Now get like I told you."

Rand smirked as he slowly backed away until he turned and joined the other constables.

Two of the footmen went back to loading the wagon. One of them caught Trammel's eye. "We could've handled them fellas on our own, Marshal."

Trammel heard a bit of Ireland in his voice. "It's *Sheriff* and while I'm around, I'll do the handling. Get back to work." Although the constables were gone, he waited until the luggage was loaded up and on its way to the house.

No sense courting trouble as he knew there was more to come.

Chapter 2

"I'd like to thank you for taking the time out of your busy schedule to see me, Mr. Clay," said Bernard Wain, a lawyer from Philadelphia.

"So do it," Lucien Clay replied.

The younger man appeared stuck for an answer. "Do what?"

"Thank me." Clay smiled, thinking *the richer they are, the dumber they are*. "You said you'd *like* to thank me for taking time out of my schedule to meet you. I said you should do so."

Wain laughed, though it was clear he still did not understand what Clay meant. "Thank you."

"That's the spirit. Isn't it funny the way people talk these days? You say you'd like to thank me when all you had to do was cut to the core of it and thank me. English is a strange language, but it's the only one I know so I guess I'm stuck with it."

Clay watched the lawyer as he sipped whiskey Clay had personally poured from his private stock. He could remember a time when he'd enjoyed receiving visitors, especially high-born visitors who'd come to him hat in hand, but that had been in the time he thought of as *Before*. Before Buck Trammel had shattered his jaw with a single punch, causing him months of ceaseless pain and agony. Before the headaches set in and blurred his vision. Before the jaw healed crooked, ruining his face and marring his speech.

He had gone to Colorado to see a specialist who'd told him the blow seemed to have caused some damage to his brain. The same punch had also cracked his skull. At least it explained the pain and the blurry vision. The doctor said the only way for it to heal properly was to break his jaw again so it could be reset. It would require more weeks of bedrest. More endless soups and broths that had turned him into little more than the skeleton he'd become.

He thanked whatever gods existed for laudanum, the only thing that worked to dull the pain in his jaw, but not the damage to his ego. Only Trammel's corpse could cure that particular ailment.

Spending six weeks away from town was impossible. The buzzards had already begun to circle when word of his injuries leaked out the first time. It had taken a lot of killing just to preserve what he had managed to hold on to.

If he were to spend six weeks in Colorado, he knew he would return to find himself penniless and homeless. Men like Mr. Bernard Wain of Philadelphia would have no use for him then. The decision had been made for him. He would live with the pain and the deformity. And trust Dr. Laudanum to take away his agony, even at the cost of his soul.

"I heard you were quite a character, Mr. Clay." Wain smiled. "I'm glad I wasn't misinformed."

Clay decided to have some fun at the man's expense. Telling him he was gullible would be one thing. Proving it to him would make the lesson stick and remind him of his place in the matter. "What does that mean?"

Again, the lawyer came up short. He squinted his bluish eyes. His fleshy cheeks grew pink from embarrassment. "Excuse me?"

"You said I was quite a character," Clay repeated. "What did you mean by that?"

Wain blinked twice. "Your manner, sir. Your discourse. Your way of looking at life."

"And death," Clay added. "That *is* what you've come here to discuss, isn't it, Mr. Wain?"

The lawyer put his glass of whiskey on the desk. "Not in so many terms, but—"

"Of course not." Clay was glad to interrupt him. "But it's the crux of the matter, isn't it? The reason why you're really here. People like you don't come to me to loan them money or help them find workmen to build them a house or even for advice about how to run a saloon. People like you come to me when they're in trouble. When they think I can help them get out of it. And most of the time, that solution involves someone getting killed. You being an in-law of the aggrieved Hagen clan, I'd bet my last dollar you're here about Adam." Clay cocked his head to the side and ignored the nagging pain that radiated from his jaw. "You want me to kill him for you, don't you?"

Wain cleared his throat and looked away. "You're quite direct, sir."

"Killing a man's just about the most direct thing in the world, Mr. Wain. Make no mistake about that. No shame in wanting it done, either, so there's no reason to look away from me. Unless you find it hard to look at me in my present condition."

Wain still did not look at him and Clay couldn't blame

him. He caught his own reflection in the mirror on the wall behind his guest. Always a trim man, his clothes hung loose on his emaciated frame. The months of broths and brews had served to keep him alive, but barely. The swelling in his jaw decreased a little every day, but his mouth was still crooked, causing him to occasionally drool on himself. His speech was slurred as if he was on his way toward being drunk, so he compensated for it by speaking slowly. The laudanum dulled the pain, but he never drank enough to allow it to intoxicate him. That didn't mean he was not in its grip. No question he was hooked, but he told himself he had it under control.

Wain finally looked at him. "I don't avert my eyes because of your condition, sir, but for the purpose of my visit."

"No need to be bashful about it," Clay told him. "Everybody finds themselves in a tough spot at one point in their lives, even rich folks like you. I'll make it a bit easier for you. Your court case against Adam isn't going so well, is it?"

"No," Wain admitted. "It isn't."

"The judge doesn't think King Charles's signature was forged on the will, does he?"

"Two judges, actually." Wain's eyes narrowed. "How did you know?"

Clay did not grin lest it cause him pain. "I still have my sources in this territory, Mr. Wain. Adam hasn't been able to shut me out completely."

"But he has shut you out, hasn't he?" Wain persisted. "You had some kind of deal with him he has reneged on?"

"Now you're thinking like a lawyer," Clay said. "Yes, we had an agreement, a contract, even, but not the kind any court could enforce."

"But one that should be enforced between men of honor."

"Honor? No. Men of blood? Yes." Clay shifted uncomfortably in his chair. "I tried the honorable route a couple of times. All it got me was a lot of dead men. The last of them, Pete Stride, just got hung yesterday morning for his trouble." Clay drank some whiskey to dull a different kind of pain. "Stride was a good man. I hated to lose him like that."

Wain frowned at his whiskey. "May I ask why each of your attempts on Adam Hagen failed? Surely it wasn't for a lack of cunning on your part."

Clay could tell the tenderfoot was working up to something. And he would enjoy watching him do it, even though he was sure it wouldn't amount to much. "I didn't fail due to any lack of cunning or planning. Every plan I put in place to corral Hagen would've worked if it hadn't been for Trammel."

Wain took his glass of whiskey again as he sat back in his chair. "What if I knew of a way to remove Trammel from the equation? That is to say, get him out of the way, so to speak."

Clay felt a spark of hope and anger go through him. "I know what an equation is, you damned pup. And don't go thinking moving Trammel aside is an easy task. He's tougher than he looks."

"That's quite a statement," Wain said. "I've seen him, and he looks quite formidable."

Now that Clay had taken Wain's bait, he was interested in getting in the boat. He could always jump back into the water later. "What are you cooking up and what does it have to do with me? If you try to get cute about it, I'll have you thrown out of here on your ear." Clay knew they were entering his part of the forest.

Wain seemed to grow more at ease. "Adam believes he has beaten his family at their own game. We know he forged my father-in-law's signature on the will that left the Hagen empire to him. My late father-in-law hated Adam. He would've seen him dead before he left him a penny. But there are ways around that. Ways that require a pen and influence rather than guns and bloodshed. In short, Mr. Clay, you've tried to remove Adam in your own way and have come up short every time. I ask you to allow me and my family to try a different tactic. One that is more subtle and, perhaps, more effective."

Clay was interested. Only a fool wouldn't be. But he wasn't convinced just yet. "Adam Hagen and Buck Trammel aren't subtle men. Adam's not as smart as he thinks he is, but he's clever. He's used your family's money to buy him a lot of influence throughout the territory. Trammel might not like his opium and other businesses, but he always winds up backing him in the end."

Wain was not put off. "Adam has hired on his own constable force since we were here last, hasn't he?"

"Ten thugs with uniforms are still thugs," Clay told him. "And now that he's got Big Ben London with him, he's going to be even tougher to take on than ever."

Wain smiled. "Which has robbed Sheriff Trammel of some of the influence he's enjoyed in the past, yes?"

"The constables keep a tight lid on things before it gets to him, so I guess you could say that." Clay was growing tired of talking around things. "What are you working up to?"

Wain swirled the whiskey in his glass. "Perhaps the good

sheriff is discontented with his diminished role and would be amenable to a promotion of sorts?"

"Promotion?" Clay repeated. "What kind of promotion?"

Wain shook his head. "Not until you and I reach some sort of understanding, Mr. Clay."

Clay was beginning to like this young man. He was not as innocent as he looked. "What kind of understanding?"

"I'd like you to throw in your lot with my family," Wain explained. "You agree to use your remaining influence to help us, and we agree to help you. Once we get back the empire my father-in-law built, you not only retrieve all you have lost at Adam's hands but all that he has built since. I believe you're particularly interested in the opium trade he has taken over from you."

Clay shifted in his seat again, though it wasn't due to discomfort. "Since we're talking plainly here, you should know I still get a cut of everything that happens in Blackstone. Adam might've cooled to me recently, but that's one thing I have in writing."

"Thirty percent if I recall," Wain said. "A decrease from your original agreement of fifty percent. I take it that reduction was a result from his belief you had acted against him."

Clay was impressed. "I see that I'm not the only one with sources of information."

Wain shrugged it off. "My family and I are prepared to make it one hundred percent, once you help us get rid of Adam when the time comes."

For the first time in months, Clay could not feel his jaw throbbing. "That's an awfully big number to throw around. Say it again and I'm liable to hold you to it."

"The town means nothing to the family," Wain told him. "All we want is the estate, of which the town is a small and troublesome part. Agree to help us and the town is yours to do with what you like. You can keep it as it is or turn it into the biggest den of vice this side of the Mississippi for all we care. We only want the ranch and the mines, though we're prepared to allow you to keep a share of the mines in the area at thirty percent."

Clay studied this well-dressed pink man across the desk from him. He was young in years but not in spirit. His fancy clothes and elegant manners and five-dollar words aside, he knew what he was saying. And he understood the man to whom he was speaking.

"You're sure about that? You speak for the rest of the Hagen family?"

"I've already spoken to them," Wain said. "You have my word and their word as well. We can't afford to put anything in writing now, of course, but I'll gladly shake on it. And before you threaten me, please rest assured I understand the nature of our agreement. Our lives will be forfeit should we fail to live up to our end of the bargain, and none of us are fond of the prospect of dying out here in the middle of nowhere."

Clay sat back in his chair, studying the man. "You're serious."

"You're a serious man, Mr. Clay." Wain extended a pink, smooth hand across the desk to him. "Do I have to spit in my palm first or do we have an agreement?"

Clay shook his hand, embarrassed by how frail his own hand looked compared to the lawyer's. "We have a deal."

"Splendid." Wain finished his whiskey and set the glass back on the desk. "I think this calls for another drink to celebrate our new partnership, don't you?"

Clay pulled the cork out of the bottle and poured a good

amount into each glass. "When does this grand scheme of ours begin?"

Wain took his glass and inhaled the whiskey, smiling at the aroma. "That's the beauty of it, Mr. Clay. The wheels of progress have already begun to turn."

CHAPTER 3

"What's troubling you, Steve?" Emily Downs asked him.

Trammel wiped his mouth with the cloth napkin. Dinners with her were the best part of his day and he loved it when she called him by his right name. She was one of the few people in town who did. "What makes you think anything's wrong?"

"Because you haven't stopped looking out the window since we sat down. It's almost like you're waiting for something to happen."

He shouldn't have been surprised she had noticed. Dr. Downs rarely missed anything, especially when it came to him. "Sorry, Em. Guess I'm just a bit distracted is all."

She went back to cutting a piece of chicken. The Occidental didn't have the fine cuisine of the Phoenix Hotel, but it was still plenty good. "So why not answer the question?"

"Guess I'm not sure what's troubling me," he admitted. "It's like I can feel something's going on, but I'll be damned if I know what it is."

"Does it have something to do with the Hagen family coming to town today?"

"You heard about that?"

She always had a knack for finding a way to make him smile. She had thick, sandy-brown hair that she wore in a bun and framed a face of delicate features. She was taller than most women, though luckily enough, not as tall as him. She had never been heavy, but she wasn't skinny, either. She moved with a purposeful grace that Trammel found appealing, even when she was just cutting a piece of chicken.

She wasn't as fancy or as pretty as other women he had known, but he had never loved any of them as much as he loved her.

"Of course, I heard about it. A doctor's office is like a barbershop that way. People love to gossip. Takes their mind off why they're really there. My female patients most of all. Between Dr. Moore and me we have a pretty good handle on what's happening in town."

Trammel tried not to sound jealous when he said, "Sounds to me like you and Moore are pretty close."

She smiled at him as she finished chewing her food. "Why Steven Trammel. Is that a hint of jealousy I hear in your voice?"

He felt himself blush. "No. Just a guess is all. You know I don't have any claim on you."

"Nor I you." She cut another slice of chicken. "Have you heard from Lilly lately?"

"I'd have figured one of your patients would've told you she left the territory weeks ago," Trammel said. "Went back to Kansas. Seems she didn't like living under Hagen's thumb. Unlike us."

"Oh, that's right. I forgot."

"No, you didn't." He enjoyed the subtle ways she showed him she cared. "You never were good at lying."

"Guess that's why I've never tried my hand at poker." She smiled. "But I still can't understand why you're worried, Steve. The town's never been busier or quieter. Hagen's constables might be crude, but they're effective in their own brutal ways. You should enjoy the peace and quiet instead of trying to dig up trouble where there isn't any to be found. You haven't had it easy since you came to Blackstone. Why not take advantage of it?"

Trammel could not deny that the constables did a good job of sweeping a lot of trouble under the rug. He and Hawkeye still went on regular patrols, but they often went a week or so without making an arrest. He had often wondered if he was just growing bored from a lack of action, but the ache in his left side reminded him he had seen enough action to last a lifetime.

"Trouble's got a way of springing up all on its own in Blackstone," he said, "and the Hagen family being here doesn't help matters."

"It's a fight that doesn't concern you," Emily reminded him. "This one is in a court of law where it belongs. Let the lawyers figure it out. That's what they get paid for anyway."

"As long as it stays there." He found himself looking out onto Main Street again. "The town's been slowly filling up with gun hands for the past week. Caleb's men. He almost admitted as much to me when I braced him at the station today. They wouldn't be here if they were aiming to keep this peaceful."

Emily shook her head as she pushed some peas around her plate. "That's still not what's bothering you. There's something else. I can tell. Now what is it?"

He knew he should have known better than to think he could hide anything from her. He took a telegram from his shirt pocket and handed it to her. "I got this from Rob Moran this afternoon. He wants me to come see him in Laramie tomorrow."

She set her silverware down and read the telegram. "So?"

"So, I wonder why he wants to see me," Trammel said. "That telegram was awfully brief."

She rolled her eyes as she handed it back to him. "Telegrams are always brief. You pay by the word, you know."

He stuffed it back in his shirt pocket. "I know how they work, Em. I used to be a Pinkerton, remember?"

"Then you should know better than try to read something into it before you know the facts. He wants to see you. Could be for any number of reasons."

"And none of them good."

She leaned forward across the table. Her eyes wide as she looked at him. "You're the gloomiest man in the territory, you know that? Moran's a friend. He's responsible for the whole county. Maybe he just wants to talk to you about how things are going up here. You haven't been to Laramie in months."

"I send him weekly reports," Trammel said, "not that there's been much to send since the constables have started up."

"See? You've just answered your own question. There's no way of knowing why he wants to see you until you take the train tomorrow morning." She dabbed at the corners of her mouth with her napkin. "And you *will* be taking the train there and back, Sheriff Trammel. No riding for you. I've grown awfully fond of our dinners and I won't have it ruined over your refusal to take the train just because

Adam built it. It's there for a reason and you might as well use it."

Trammel smiled. She did know him so well, didn't she?

"So, you like our dinners together?"

It was her turn to blush. "I've grown used to them is all. I guess I'm a creature of habit, same as anyone."

He looked at her closely. "And that's all?"

She smiled in spite of herself. And it broke his heart when she looked at the star pinned on his vest and that smile dimmed. "Yes, Steve. For now, that's all."

He ignored the other diners in the dining room and placed his hand on the table. Her hand quivered as she took it. And when she looked up at him, he knew she loved him every bit as much as he loved her.

"We've talked about this, Steve. I won't be a widow again and I can't ask you to change who you are. You belong to the law, not to me."

No matter how much either of them had tried to avoid it, they found themselves having the same conversation about once a week since Lilly had left town. "I know that, but—" He looked up. Out of the corner of his eye, he saw a man in a blue tunic stumble past the Occidental's window.

And five of the new strangers in town were following him.

Emily pulled her hand away from his. "Go, Steve. Just go. We both know you have to."

Trammel set his napkin on the table as he got up. "I'll be right back."

Her polite smile told him she knew better than to expect it.

Chapter 4

Trammel stepped out onto the boardwalk to find one of the five strangers had the constable named Jesse up against the wall of the Black Flag Saloon and pinned by the throat. The place had only been open a month but already had a reputation for catering to a rougher crowd. The kind of crowd that did not take kindly to the presence of Hagen's constables.

"Well, would you look at this, boys?" The stranger took hold of the brass badge on Jesse's tunic and ripped it off. "Looks like we've snagged ourselves one of them constables everyone's always gassing on about."

Jesse struggled but the stranger's grip was too tight. "Keep pushing and you'll be seeing a lot more of them badges real soon."

The stranger buried a hard right fist into Jesse's gut and let him stumble forward. Another stranger gave him a boot in the backside, sending him sprawling into the muddy thoroughfare.

"Now you've gone and done it, Hank," the first stranger said. "You've gotten his fancy duds all dirty."

Hank spat at Jesse to the delight of the four other men. "A man dresses like a soldier ought to expect to be able to fight like a soldier. Ain't that right, Stan?"

Trammel figured the first man must have been Stan, for he said, "Boy's armed like a soldier, though. Just look at that sidearm he's sporting. A Colt pistol right on his hip. Be a shame if he made a play for it, wouldn't it, boys?"

"A shame for him," one of the other men said. "Not us."

Trammel pulled his Peacemaker from his shoulder holster as he stepped out into the thoroughfare. "That's enough. You've had your fun. Might as well head into the Flag and keep on drinking."

The five men on the boardwalk looked at him. As tall as Trammel was, he was eye-level with them.

Stan said, "That would be the town marshal, boys. Looks like he's come to save his friend."

"I'm the sheriff, not the marshal." Trammel stopped between them and Jesse, who was only just beginning to get to his feet. "You'd do well to move along."

"This ain't your concern, Trammel," Jesse gasped from the mud. "We'll handle this our own way."

Trammel ignored him and looked at the badge Stan was still holding in his hand. "Looks like you've got something that belongs to him." He held out his left hand. "Give it to me and you can go about your business."

Stan laughed and so did the men with him. There was bravery in numbers.

Stan held up the heavy brass badge and looked at it under the flickering light of the oil lamp. "Now why would I do that, Marshal? I worked hard for this and won it fair and square."

"It's a gift," Hank added. "On account of us not pounding your friend there into dust."

"He's not my friend." Trammel's hand didn't move. "And I'm not going to ask you again."

Stan was not laughing. Neither was Hank nor any of the men with them. "Now why would I want to go and do a thing like that?"

Trammel raised the Peacemaker and aimed it at Stan's belly. "Because I told you to."

The other four went for their guns but stopped when Trammel thumbed back the hammer. "Anyone moves and Stan dies."

Trammel did not move when he heard a round being racked into a Winchester from somewhere behind him across the street.

"He won't miss," Hawkeye said, "and neither will I."

Hank and the others stepped back with their hands raised.

Stan remained where he was but didn't hand over the badge, either.

Trammel pressed the barrel against Stan's stomach. "Brass or lead. You choose."

Stan held Trammel's glare as he slowly placed the badge in Trammel's hand. "Tonight, it's brass. There'll be time for lead later."

Trammel slipped the badge into his pocket and used his pistol to push Stan away from him. "You boys go inside and have yourselves a drink and I won't arrest you. Cause any more trouble and you'll deal with me."

Stan gave him a crooked grin as he slowly backed away. "This ain't over, Marshal. Not by a long shot."

"It's still Sheriff," Trammel told him. "Any time you want to finish, just let me know. I'm easy to find."

Stan was still grinning as he backed through the batwing

doors of the Black Flag Saloon. Hank and the others followed him inside.

Convinced it was over for now, Trammel turned his attention to the fallen constable. He had managed to rise to one knee but was cradling his sore belly.

Trammel snatched him by the collar and easily pulled him up to his feet.

Jesse thanked him by batting away his hand. "I don't need your help."

"Looked like you did," Trammel said. "What's wrong with you, anyway? Letting them corner you alone like that."

"They jumped me when I passed an alley," Jesse said. "I was on my way back to town hall when they grabbed hold of me. Spun me around, kept me off balance. Never gave me a chance to go for my gun."

"You're lucky they didn't take that from you, too. If you're going to dress like a lawman, you'd best learn how to act like one."

Jesse cringed from the effort of looking up at Trammel. "You're an odd one, you know that? This morning you knocked me out and tonight you're stepping in where you're not needed."

"You deserved it then," Trammel said. "You didn't deserve this. And if that's your way of thanking me, your manners need a bit of work."

Jesse struggled to stand upright, but the pain in his stomach kept him from doing so. "You gonna give me back my badge?"

"No."

"No?" Jesse staggered and it wasn't from the pain. "What do you mean *no*?"

"Just what I said. Tell your boss to come by the jail and ask me for it. I want him to know what happened here tonight and I want him to hear it from me. I don't want you putting a shine on it to make yourself look better than you were."

Trammel watched the pain in the constable's eyes turn to something else. "Now listen here, Trammel. We don't work for you and we don't answer to you, either. You'd best give me back that badge or I'm gonna set about taking it from you."

"I'd be careful about what you say next if I was you. You're alone." He nodded across the thoroughfare. "I'm not."

Jesse looked over and saw Hawkeye had his Winchester aimed at him. Trammel watched the fight go out of the constable.

"I forgot he was there."

"He didn't forget about you." Trammel stepped aside and pointed toward the town hall. "You said you were about to finish your shift. Go about your business. I'll be expecting your boss whenever he's got the time to spare."

Jesse eyeballed Hawkeye as he pulled himself up onto the boardwalk and slowly walked away.

Trammel also saw Emily walking across the thoroughfare and enter her office. She lived in the rooms above the place after she had sold her land to Hagen for the town hall building.

The sheriff holstered his Peacemaker. "So much for dessert."

Hawkeye lowered his rifle. "What'd you say, boss?"

Trammel smiled. "I'll tell you when you're older. You can walk me back to the jailhouse. Keep me safe from ruffians and the like."

Chapter 5

Adam Hagen pounded the dinner table, making the silverware and his guests jump. Jesse the constable hung his head while Big Ben London loomed behind him. Hagen was not really cross with Jesse, but he had to put some fear into the lad. He was a constable, not a gun hand, and he needed to act accordingly.

He circled Jesse like a wolf about to pounce on his prey. "You mean to tell me you let yourself get cornered by that rabble? In an alley? And had to be rescued by Trammel, no less?"

His dinner guests, oil men and miners, were used to the rough treatment of underlings. Their wives were not and looked appropriately embarrassed.

Hagen used the opportunity to show them another side of him. The less cultured frontier side. "Don't I pay you good money?"

"Yes, sir. You pay me fine."

"Didn't I pluck you from the gutter and put that uniform on your back? Change you from a common thug into a man of pride and purpose?"

"Yes, sir."

"And all I ask in return is for you to do your job and here you are. Muddied. Beaten up." He tapped the torn tunic where his badge had once been. "Disgraced. And not just by any men, but by the men my family has brought to town to stand against me. What do you have to say for yourself?"

"We'll get them, Mr. Hagen. We'll get them good."

"Ah, revenge," Hagen boomed. "That's your plan. Mix in a little blood with the mud and dung you're covered in, is that it? Is that your idea of progress?" He stopped circling and grabbed Jesse by the arm, pulling him closer to him. "This isn't some two-bit cow town anymore. My guests are not a bunch of drovers or snake oil salesmen or worse. These are people of standing. Pillars of their respective communities. Men and women of means and influence who wish to use their means and influence to make Blackstone a town to be admired, not only in the territory but throughout this part of the country. How do you expect them to take us or me seriously if my own constables can't defend themselves from a bunch of hired gunmen?" He released Jesse with a shove.

"Yes, Mr. Hagen. I'm sorry, Mr. Hagen."

Hagen pulled down his dinner jacket and flattened his shirt as if to compose himself. Judging by the looks on his guests' faces, they were suitably impressed. "You're right you're sorry. A sorry excuse for a constable." He looked at Ben. "Take this creature out of my sight. See that he gets a new uniform before he goes back to work tomorrow but make sure he pays for the damage to his tunic."

He stuck a finger in Jesse's face to drive home his final point. "And don't mistake my generosity for weakness, young man. One more misstep and I'll cast you back into the gutter where I found you." Hagen watched Big Ben march Jesse out of the dining room, then took a moment to compose himself before returning to his guests.

He made sure they saw him try to regain hold of his temper. "Forgive me," he said as he retook his seat. "I usually never allow business to intrude on pleasure, but this was a rare exception."

Clarence Mitchell, the oil magnate, looked more pleased than perturbed. "Nonsense, Adam. If anything, it was good to see you have such a firm hand where your employees are concerned."

"Hear! Hear!" said James Bottomley, the owner of several dozen mines throughout the West. "The troops must be kept in line lest chaos be allowed to take root. You gave that young fellow a good and fair drubbing."

"I'd have tossed him out on his ear," said Jonathan Haymes, the owner of one of the largest logging operations in the territory. "You showed remarkable restraint in allowing him to retain his position as constable, Adam. I might have been inclined to use him as an example to the others and sacked him on the spot."

Hagen hid his smile with his napkin. Their wives clearly hadn't approved of the display, but he had been seeking the approval of the men and he appeared to have it. "He will be an example, I assure you. When he gets the bill for mending his tunic, he'll bore his fellow constables with complaints over the cost."

They all laughed politely over his unfunny joke. They were his guests after all and had come to Blackstone with the hopes of joining in his recent good fortune. A polite laugh was a small price to pay for the promise of easy profit.

Mrs. Haymes cleared her throat. Adam thought her to be a hatchet-faced matron whose string of pearls she now clutched could have paid for his new mill three times over. "I must say I was rather concerned to hear of your troubles with your family, Mr. Hagen. If this territory ever hopes to become settled, family will be the bedrock upon which it is founded. I am sure I need not remind you of a verse from the Bible. 'He who troubles his own house shall inherit the wind.'"

Adam was glad the old bag had used one of the few sacred verses he had committed to memory. He responded by saying, "'And the fool will be servant to the wise of heart. The fruit of the righteous is a tree of life and he who wins souls is wise.'"

Mrs. Haymes raised an eyebrow. "Is that your aim of inviting us here to Blackstone, Mr. Hagen? To win our souls or our fruit?"

Hagen did not hide his smile. "No, Mrs. Haymes. My aim is to plant a righteous tree from which all of us can benefit." He looked at the six men and women gathered around his table. "And it is my hope, that with the help of all of you, I shall be able to do precisely that."

"Hear! Hear!" James Bottomley repeated, raising his glass. "To Adam Hagen and his righteous wisdom. May we all benefit from it for years to come!"

Adam raised his glass and joined in the toast. He had no use for their miserable souls, but he had great plans for their money.

And if all continued to go according to plan in the courts, by the end of the week, they would be begging him to take it.

After tolerating the men over brandy and cigars after dinner, Hagen summoned Ben to walk with him across the street to the jail. The large, silent black man took his gleaming Winchester with him as he escorted his employer to the jail and a conference with Sheriff Trammel.

Hagen took a moment to stop in front of the Phoenix Hotel and inhale a lungful of night air. His air. His town. The sounds of hammers and saws and wagonloads of material being moved about town had died away for the night, replaced by happier sights and sounds. Couples strolled arm in arm along the new boardwalks he had constructed. They were browsing the new shops he had built and took in the latest fashions after they'd digested a fine meal in one of the many hotels and eateries he had built.

Those of less refined tastes were enjoying the saloons catering to drinkers and gamblers of every description. Those who could not afford the high stakes tables of the Phoenix could try their luck at almost any other saloon in town. They could enjoy the company of a woman for a reasonable price and, if they were so inclined, ride the dragon's tail in the opium den he had built behind the Pot of Gold.

Another man might have taken pride in all that he had built thus far, but his time in the army had taught Adam Hagen that no battle is over until it is won. His battle with his family was just beginning. They were contesting King Charles Hagen's will that had left everything to Adam. So far, every judge who had heard the case had ruled against them. Those same judges also happened to be on his payroll.

His family was nothing if not resourceful and Adam knew it would only be a matter of time before they found an impartial jurist who was willing to hear the case if for no other reason than for the notoriety it would bring him. The promise of a healthy payday from Adam would be enough to make that judge rule in his favor. Corruption was how King Charles had built his empire and corruption was how Adam Hagen planned on expanding it. At the expense of his hated relatives, of course. The harder they fought, the sweeter it made his inevitable victory.

He pulled his coat tighter around his shoulders as he walked across the thoroughfare to the jail where Buck Trammel awaited him. The big man obviously intended on making him eat some crow before returning Jesse's badge. That was why Adam had not taken dessert with his guests. He knew the sheriff had a role to play in his family melodrama and some private humiliation was a small price to pay for it.

Adam walked up onto the boardwalk and knocked loudly at the closed jailhouse door.

"It's open," Trammel answered.

Adam nodded for Big Ben to stand watch in front of the door as Adam walked inside alone. He found Trammel at his desk, writing something by candlelight. The desk had been a massive, well-built piece he had taken from the old Clifford Hotel and donated for Trammel's use back when Trammel became the sheriff by default. It dominated the room but looked like a child's desk with the big sheriff sitting behind it.

"There he is," Adam said as he closed the door behind him. "Blackstone's champion hard at work. As diligent in his paperwork as he is at gunplay."

Trammel looked up at him and set his pen back in its holder. "Always have to make an entrance, don't you?"

"If one must make an entrance, why not make it a grand one," Adam said as he sat down. "Some things never change. Take you for instance. You've lived in this part of the world for some years now, yet you still sport that horrible Manhattan growl of yours. Put some music into your voice, man. You're a Westerner now. Make the most of it."

Trammel sat back in his chair and crossed his long legs. "This coming from the town drunk of Wichita."

"I was only a minor drunk there," Adam corrected him. "A fortunate one at that when you saved me from the clutches of my enemies, a deed for which I remain ever grateful."

Trammel shook his head. "The more you talk, the less you say."

"That's the art of polite conversation." Adam winked. "It comes in handy when dealing with prospective investors. They prefer the aroma, not tending the garden that produces the flower." He looked at what Trammel had been writing. "That a report on the unfortunate events that transpired earlier this evening?"

Trammel made no effort to hide it. "What if it is?"

"I hope you give yourself plenty of credit for saving Jesse's life. Don't spare him any embarrassment on my account."

"I won't," Trammel assured him. "I'd have expected you to pick a better class of thug as your constables. They're not too impressive from where I sit."

Hagen shrugged easily. "They serve a purpose."

"Your purpose."

"Always." Hagen grinned. "After all, what's the use in owning your own town if you don't get to have your own bully boys impose your will? And you must admit their tunics are rather dashing, aren't they? Designed them myself."

"A cheap thug in a fancy tunic is still a cheap thug, Adam."

"True, but they're my thugs. Even an old sourpuss like

you has to admit they've been most effective in keeping vice from spilling out onto the streets."

"By cracking heads and breaking noses."

"Peace is always expensive and maintaining it is never pretty," Adam said. "You know that better than anyone." He was glad Trammel did not have a suitable comeback for that.

The sheriff was a big man. A tough man, but he was no fool. Besting him in anything, even in words, was a victory Hagen cherished.

The sheriff opened the top drawer of his desk, took out Jesse's badge, and dropped it on the desk. "Your family's gun hands took that off your constable."

"As I've been told." Hagen left the badge where it was. He had designed that, too, and had them struck in Colorado at no small expense. "I'm curious, though. How many men do you think my family has seeded in town?"

"Seeded?" Trammel repeated. "You're getting fancy in your old age. Between Hawkeye and me, we've counted ten, though I'd bet there are more than that. Probably staying in your hotel over there."

"Agreed on all counts," Hagen said. "You're right about them bringing less obvious types with them. I've found three more and, for the cost of some gold, managed to convince them to work for me."

"Or so you think," Trammel pointed out. "You won't know for sure until the time comes. For all your sakes, that time better not involve gun play. Because if it does, Hawkeye and I won't be picky about our targets. Any man with a gun in his hand gets treated the same. No exceptions."

Adam had always respected and resented Trammel's sense of fairness. "If trouble starts, it won't be started by me or mine. You already have my word on that."

"For as far as it goes."

"It goes very far where you're involved, Buck," Hagen said. "I'd like to think you believe that, despite all of our differences. We've saved each other's lives enough to believe in such things." He nodded toward Trammel's left side. "I trust your wounds have healed completely."

"Only bothers me when it rains," the sheriff said, "but none of that has to do with why I wanted you to come here tonight. Jesse's badge, neither. I need a promise from you. A big one."

Hagen adjusted himself in his chair. "Then it's a good thing I ate before I came here. It'll help fortify me from the shock of knowing the great Buck Trammel is bending low enough to ask me for a favor."

"Moran sent me a telegram today," Trammel explained. "I need to go to Laramie tomorrow."

"My train is at your disposal," Hagen said.

"That's not the favor. I'm leaving Hawkeye behind to keep an eye on things. He's a good, capable kid, but with all the guns floating around town, I don't want any trouble while I'm gone."

Trammel pointed a thick finger at Hagen. "I'm telling you this ahead of time because I don't want anyone taking advantage of the fact that I'm out of town for a bit. I'll probably be back tomorrow night, but in case I'm not, I want a tight lid kept on this place until I return. No dustups with your family. Your constables either stay in town hall or they walk in pairs. No exceptions. And if your family's men try to start anything, I want your men to just walk away."

"Understood," Hagen said. He even meant it.

Trammel's finger kept pointing. "No exceptions, Adam.

If I come back and find there's been any gun play, even if it's justified, I'll lock up everyone including you. Tell me you understand that."

"I understand completely." He raised his right hand as if taking an oath. "There'll be nothing but peace and harmony until you return as far as it is mine to command."

Trammel began to interrupt him, but Hagen didn't give him the chance. "That's only fair, Buck. I can't control what my family's men do. If they start shooting up a saloon to draw out my men, I won't be held accountable for that. It just so happens I'm entertaining some important investors at the moment. Investors that could change Blackstone's fortunes forever, so the last thing I want is for bullets to fly along Main Street. But I can't allow it to happen, either. You have my solemn vow that my men will walk away whenever they can. That's about the best you can expect me to do."

Trammel lowered his finger and frowned as he shook his head. Adam could tell he did not like it, but he could not argue it, either. "I guess that'll have to be good enough."

Adam could see something more was troubling him than just the threat of violence in his absence. "You're worried about that telegram from Moran, aren't you?"

"Just don't know what he wants to see me about is all," the sheriff admitted. "I don't like walking into something I can't see the inside of. There's no good reason why he needs me to go down there, but like Emily said, I won't know that until I get there."

"Ah!" Adam brightened. "So, the rumors are true. She's taken you back and forgiven you for your dalliance with Lilly."

Trammel shot him a look that would have frozen most

men, but Hagen had seen it enough times to recognize it. "Knock it off, Hagen."

"You're actually blushing." Adam laughed. "How adorable. I for one am glad of it. She humanizes you, Steve. And if any man in Blackstone needs a little humanizing, it's you."

Hagen snatched the badge off the desk as he rose. "I know, I know. Don't push my luck. I'm going while the going's good. And good luck with Moran tomorrow."

Trammel surprised him by having one final question before he reached the door. "Why's your family really in Blackstone, Adam? I mean it. Don't kid around."

Adam turned to face him. "I don't really know and that's the truth. And since we're not kidding around, their presence here worries me. Our fight is in the courts now and there's no reason for them to come to Blackstone. Whatever their intentions, I doubt they're honorable."

Trammel ran a big hand across his chin. "I was afraid you were going to say something like that."

Adam wished he could have eased his friend's mind but hoped a word of advice would suffice. "I hear Lucien Clay's up and around again. Since you'll be in Laramie, be sure to watch your back. He still hates you for shattering his jaw and he's vengeful as hell."

Trammel did not look concerned. "Good thing so am I. But thanks for the warning."

Hagen touched the brim of his hat and left the jailhouse. It was a nice night and he decided to go for a quick stroll around town. The walk could do him good. Help him organize his thoughts and ponder his enemies, both seen and unseen.

Enemies of all sorts were easier to face with Big Ben trailing behind him, of course.

Chapter 6

The next morning, Trammel remained on the train for a bit after it pulled into Laramie. He stayed seated by the window, watching the flow of foot traffic on the platform. He wasn't worried about the passengers greeted by friends or family. He wasn't concerned about the livestock being unloaded or loaded onto the cattle cars, either.

He was looking for men who did not belong. Men who hung around while others went about their business. Men who were watching the crowd for Trammel. He was a big target and nearly impossible to miss. He looked for men who might be working for Lucien Clay, who might have been sent to kill him for the beating their boss suffered at his hand.

Seeing no one who seemed to be watching the station, Trammel got up, grabbed his Winchester from the luggage rack above his head, and stepped down from the train.

He stood alone on the platform, looking again for anyone paying him particular attention apart from the looks his size often drew. When he was reasonably certain no one was gunning for him, he moved slowly from the station to city hall where Rob Moran kept his office.

Along the way, Trammel kept a sharp eye on the crowded streets for anyone who looked out of place or might be hiding in an alley or doorway. Such things were tough to spot in a city as busy as Laramie, but he did his best. He made it to city hall without incident and found Sheriff Rob Moran waiting for him on the street.

"There you are," Moran greeted him with a handshake. "I was beginning to wonder if you might not show. Those legs being as long as they are, I figured you'd have gotten here sooner."

"Just being cautious is all."

"No harm in that," Moran said. "Come inside and sit a spell. I've got something I want to talk over with you."

At just over six feet and a few years over thirty, Moran was one of those lawmen who had not yet hit his prime and would be a formidable presence for years to come, Trammel thought. He had been brought to town from Abilene by the Laramie Businessman's Association a few years before to replace the previous sheriff who had openly been in Lucien Clay's pocket.

And like Trammel, Moran had earned a reputation for being his own man. He was as fair with the law as he was in handling a gun. He was the kind of sheriff every town wanted, but few had.

The kind of sheriff Buck Trammel hoped to be one day.

Two courtrooms dominated the first floor of city hall, and the prisoners were housed in the basement. Moran led Trammel up the stairs to his office on the second floor. The county sheriff and the U.S. marshal also had offices up there. He was sure it made for cramped quarters at times, but Laramie was the capital of the territory, so it was to be expected.

Moran opened the door to his office, which was at the

eastern corner of the building. It offered a nice view of Main Street. "Make yourself comfortable."

Trammel set his Winchester against the wall and went for one of the chairs in front of the desk.

Moran stopped him before he sat down. "Not there. Try the one behind the desk for a change. See how you like it."

Trammel didn't see why he should, but did what Moran asked. It was certainly a nicer chair—high-backed leather with plenty of padding—than the one he had back in Blackstone.

"It suits you," Moran said.

Trammel rubbed the armrests. "If I knew you had it this good, Rob, I would've asked to sit here more often."

Moran folded his arms and leaned against the wall. "It's yours if you want it."

Trammel liked it, but not enough to take it from him. "Thanks, but I don't think the porters would fit it on the train without having it dinged up some. Same as if I loaded it on a wagon. Those boys tend to be rough with fineries."

Moran grinned as he slowly shook his head. "The chair stays where it is. So does the desk. Open the top drawer and tell me what you find there."

Trammel thought it was strange for Moran to ask him to go through his desk, but when he did, he realized why. A gold star glinted up at him. SHERIFF, CITY OF LARAMIE was stamped on it.

Trammel picked it up and showed it to Moran. "What's this?"

"It's yours if you want it," Moran told him. "I got a new one just this morning." He took a star out of his pocket and pinned it on his vest. That one had U.S. MARSHAL stamped on it.

Trammel sat forward in the chair. "You quit Laramie?"

"I moved up," Moran said. "I'm in charge of the whole territory now. My appointment came in last week. I've been keeping it quiet until I found a fit replacement for my old job. And, as far as I'm concerned, I'm looking at him right now."

Trammel set the star on the desk before he dropped it. "You mean you want me to take your place? You want me to be the sheriff of Laramie?"

"It sure has a nice ring to it, don't you think?"

Trammel did not know what to think. "Rob, I'm not cut out for this. You've already got plenty of deputies who can do this job better than I can."

"Maybe," Moran allowed, "but none who can do it like you would. And that's not just me talking. The Businessman's Association and the city council all agreed with me. Hell, your name came up before I had a chance to open my mouth. Why even the mayor agrees and it's near impossible to get him and the council to agree on anything, but you're it."

Trammel had gotten on the train that morning expecting Moran to give him bad news. About Lucien Clay gunning for him or more trouble coming to Blackstone. He had not been planning on anything close to this. "This is a pretty big decision."

"Good thing you're big enough to make it," Moran told him. "Quit coming up with reasons why you should turn it down. You were a cop in Manhattan, a Pinkerton after that, and have proven yourself many times over up in Blackstone. It's high time you take on a job like this. A job where you won't be the only one doing the fighting."

"I haven't been the only one," Trammel said. "Hawkeye's lifted more than his share of the load."

"And I'm sure he'll make a good replacement for you

when you leave," Moran continued. "I've read your weekly reports, Buck. Crime is way down in Blackstone thanks to Hagen's head breakers. I don't want to see you waste the best years of your life waiting to break up the odd bar fight up there when you could be down here doing real work where it counts. Where you're actually needed."

"I'm needed up there. Trouble's brewing between Hagen and his family. The town is full up with hired guns and Adam's constables are just itching for a fight. I can't just walk away from them now, not with things being as they are."

Moran pushed himself off the wall and sat on the edge of his old desk. "Blackstone's not your town. It never was and it never will be. If the Hagen family want to tear themselves apart over that old wind scowl, let them. They're going to do it whether you're up there to stop them or not. You've almost gotten yourself killed three times near as I can figure and what did it get you? Shot up and bleeding while the Hagen clan did whatever they wanted anyway."

Moran pulled a chair closer to him and sat down. "None of that is your fault, Buck. It's the way it is when poor folks like us get caught up in rich men's games. We deserve better than that. You deserve better than that. Better pay, better roof over your head. Better men at your side to help you win the fights worth fighting."

Trammel wanted to say something, anything, that would tell Moran he was wrong. But deep down, Trammel knew his friend was right.

Moran continued. "I'm not promising you a rose garden here. Laramie's a prosperous town with plenty of trouble to keep you busy. But I think you'd rather be doing work that counts than waiting on the whims of whatever scheme Adam Hagen cooks up next. You know I'm right, too."

Trammel eased back into the chair. He had to admit it was comfortable. The sheriff's star was awfully sporty looking. And the idea of being the sheriff of a major city sounded pretty good to him. "Can I think about it?"

"You can think all you want, so long as you say yes. Chances like this don't come around often in our line of work. It could be years before something this good comes along, if ever." Moran allowed a small smile. "Besides, I've got the mayor, the city council, and half the Businessman's Association down in the courtroom as we speak ready to swear you in."

Trammel's mouth dropped open. "Damn it, Rob. I didn't even say yes yet."

"I know." Moran broke into a full grin. "I just didn't want to give you the chance to say no. That's why I've already worked out the whole deal for you. You'll have a week to finish up whatever you're doing up in Blackstone and get Hawkeye used to running things. But come next Monday, you start down here full time. That sound fair to you?"

None of this sounded fair to Trammel. He had grown used to making up his own mind. Of following his own path. The last time he had allowed himself to be railroaded into something, it meant helping Hagen escape Wichita. When it came to running a major city like Laramie, he thought it should be his idea.

"I don't like being pushed into things, Rob. You know that."

"And sometimes a man has to let his friends help make decisions for him, especially when it's for his own good. And you know I'm right."

In his heart, Trammel knew he was right. But his gut told him he was wrong. It told him he was being greedy.

"Come on," Moran said as he stood up. "Let's take that piece of tin off your vest and trade it in for a real star for a change. The mayor's waiting on us."

Trammel picked up the sheriff's star as he stood, too. He was not used to putting himself first. Maybe he deserved this after all? He knew Emily certainly did. And maybe now she would agree to marry him.

He handed the Laramie star back to Moran. "I guess we wouldn't want to keep my new boss waiting, would we?"

Trammel could not remember a time when he had shaken hands with so many people at one time in his entire life.

Mayor Walter Holm pumped his hand like it was a water pump about to run dry. The photographer kept yelling at everyone to stop moving, though the flash of the powder always made Trammel blink.

The men of the town council were next in line to greet him, led by Charles Haffey, who was also the leading haberdasher in town. "Come by my store after you get settled, Sheriff, and I'll fit you out with everything you need. At a rock-bottom cost, too."

After the council welcomed him, it was the Businessman's Association's turn. Their president, Howard Williamson, ran the cattle business in town. "We were all relieved when we heard you agreed to take the job, Buck. We hate losing a fine man like Rob, but having a man of your stature take his place puts our minds at ease. Yes, sir, it certainly does."

Mrs. Alice Smith, head of the Ladies League of Laramie, offered him her cold, gloved hand. "On behalf of the fine, upstanding women of Laramie, we wish you good fortune in your new office, Sheriff Trammel, and pray you'll continue to keep Laramie a place where women can walk our streets without fear of incident."

The whole ceremony had taken less than thirty minutes, from the swearing in until the last of the town officials left the courtroom. He still saw purple outlines of the photographer every time he blinked his eyes.

Moran sided up to him when it was over and patted him on the back. "See? That was pretty painless, wasn't it?"

"Speak for yourself." Trammel cradled his right hand. "Hope Lucien Clay hasn't gotten wind of this yet. Now would be a great time for him to take a run at me. I can't feel my gun hand."

Moran laughed. "He knows, believe me. But I wouldn't count on him taking any shots at anyone, much less you. Word is he still sees double after that whipping you gave him a few months back."

Trammel might have enjoyed hearing that if it was not for the line of five deputies standing solemnly at the back of the courtroom. "They don't look too happy about this."

"They don't get paid to be happy," Moran said. "They get paid to do what you tell them to. And, if you don't mind my saying so, now might be the best time to break the ice. The sooner you get it out of the way, the better for all concerned. Their sulking won't change things any."

Trammel had not been expecting any of this, much less confronting a room full of disappointed lawmen, but Moran was usually right. "That all of them?"

"You have ten deputies in all. Five work during the day and five work nights. They rotate every month or so, but you can change that if you want. You've got a budget for two more, but these ten seem to be doing a good enough job."

Trammel looked over the men. He had seen many of

them before on his previous trips to Laramie but had never gotten around to knowing their names. "Which one of them was expecting to get your job?"

"Sherwood Blake," Moran told him. "He's the tall, lean one in the center with the droopy mustache. Nickname's Sheriff on account of Sherwood being too tough for the drunks to say. Guess he got it in his head it was more of a title than a nickname. He'll be the toughest nut to crack, but once you get him on your side, the rest will fall in line."

Trammel flexed some blood back into his right hand. "Best get at it, then."

Moran followed him down the aisle of the courtroom to where the deputies had lined up against the back wall. None of them looked at him directly, but none of them looked away, either.

"My name is Steven Trammel and as you boys just saw, I'm the new sheriff here in Laramie. Some people have taken to calling me Buck, others just call me Trammel. I answer to either. I've seen all of you boys before, but I don't know your names. It'd help if I knew them now."

Gary Bush, a roundish, clean-shaven man, was the first to extend his hand. James Brillheart, a man of medium size and build was the second. The third was a bowlegged man named Charlie Root. Trammel pegged him as a former cow puncher who traded his saddle for a star and a gun. The fourth was a lanky man almost as tall as Blake. His name was Johnny Welch.

As expected, Sherwood Blake was the last one to give in. He made eye contact with Trammel as he shook his hand. "Name's Blake. People call me Sheriff, but my right name's Sherwood."

Trammel looked at each man in turn. "I know there's an old saying that a new broom sweeps clean. I think that's only true when there's a mess that needs to be swept up. From what I've heard and from what Rob Moran tells me, you boys have a good handle on things here and I aim to keep them that way. Any questions or complaints, you come directly to me. Same goes for the men who work nights. I don't want you talking amongst yourselves and I don't want to hear you talking about me to others, either."

He looked at each man in turn to allow his words to sink in. "The people in this city aren't your friends, no matter how friendly they might be. It always comes down to us against them. If they don't wear a star, they're strangers. I speak from experience. If we do our jobs and stick together, everything will be fine."

"That how you and your deputy handle things up in Blackstone, Sheriff?" Blake asked. "Because you're gonna find Laramie's a whole lot bigger than Blackstone."

"That's how we handled things when I was a cop in Manhattan," Trammel told him. "And how we handled things when I was a Pinkerton. Now I know some of you boys might not have been expecting me to become sheriff here. Truth is, neither was I until I spoke to Moran this morning. But what's done is done and we still have a lot of work to do. Best get back out there and be about our business."

Moran encouraged the men to leave when Trammel said, "Not you, Blake. I need you here."

The men looked at Blake before Moran ushered them out of the courtroom. He closed the door quietly behind him, leaving the two men alone.

"Something on your mind, Sheriff?" Blake made no effort to hide the contempt in his voice.

"I hear you thought you were in line to take Moran's star."

"The thought had crossed my mind, given I've been here the longest and all."

"I also hear you're first deputy around here."

"You hear a lot."

"You'll go on being first deputy for as long as you prove worthy of it," Trammel told him. "I didn't come looking for this job. The council and the mayor and the Business-man's Association picked me for it. They didn't pick you. Not Bush or one of the other men. They didn't look to bring someone in from the outside, either. They chose me and we're all going to have to live with it."

Blake sneered. "If I open my mouth, you gonna break my jaw like you done to Lucien Clay?"

Trammel was beginning to like him. "That depends on what you say and how you say it."

"I remember when you first came to this territory about three years back," Blake said. "And just about every year or so, there's been some kind of gunfight or calamity kicked up that get a lot of men hurt or killed. I don't know if you've just got bad luck, or you don't know what you're doing. I don't know and I really don't care. I just don't want the same thing happening here in Laramie. Me and the boys keep this town on a real short leash. And yeah, some of us get paid a little extra to keep an eye on things in certain establishments more than others. I don't want your bad luck following you here. And if it's more than just bad luck, I don't want you making the same mistakes you made in Blackstone costing my friends their lives."

Trammel admired the deputy's honesty. He wanted to

backhand him for being insolent, but he knew Blake and the others would be expecting that.

He tried a different tactic. "Aren't you the one who just told me Laramie's a lot different from Blackstone?"

"I surely am."

"Then it stands to reason that the same problems I faced up there will be different down here, doesn't it?"

"It surely does."

"Good. I'm going to be counting on you to help keep order in this town, just like you've always done. To show me the error of my ways in private and at the right time. And I expect you to bring your concerns to me, Deputy. You wear the same star as I do. Running me down to others won't make your star shine any brighter. Do we understand each other?"

"We surely do."

Trammel was not so sure, but the deputy's word would have to do for now. "I've got some loose ends to tie up back in Blackstone. I was planning on putting you in charge until I get back. Think that's something you might be able to handle?"

Trammel could almost feel some of the ice between them melt. "Me? Why not Sheriff Moran?"

"Because he's not the sheriff anymore," Trammel told him. "He's the marshal now and has a whole territory to worry about. Since you're the man with the most experience, I figured you should be the one to do it. But if I'm wrong, just let me know and—"

"You ain't wrong," Blake said. "I'd be happy to do it."

Trammel figured he would be. "Good. I'll try to be back on Saturday, but no later than Sunday. We'll start fresh on Monday." He extended his hand to Blake. "Thanks for helping me out. I appreciate it."

Blake seemed surprised by the hand but shook it anyway. "I'll send you a telegram each day, so you know what's happening."

"Good man." Trammel nodded toward the door. "Better let the others know what's going on. Pull one of the night men in to cover you if you need it."

Blake told him he would and walked out of the courtroom with a bit of a spring in his step.

Trammel smiled when the door swung closed, leaving him all alone in the courtroom.

His right hand still had pins and needles. "Good thing I didn't have to belt him."

Chapter 7

Trammel stepped out onto the boardwalk of the jail and felt the warm, morning sunlight on his face. He was officially Buck Trammel, Sheriff of the City of Laramie.

The streets were as bustling as he had remembered. Wagons hauling freight and all manner of goods filled the thoroughfare as carriages, coaches, and riders on horseback threaded their way through town.

People on foot had to wait for traffic to slow down in both directions before they crossed from one boardwalk to another. Some of the men and women wore the latest fashions all the way from Paris and New York. Others were more moderately dressed in suits or even work clothes.

All of them were different from the sort of men and women Trammel was accustomed to seeing each day. They moved at a different pace. They moved with purpose, the way he remembered from his time in Chicago and even during his time in the slums of Manhattan.

He was beginning to feel good about his decision.

Now, he had to find a way to break the news to Emily. She might be happy for him. She might hit him for not asking her first. Since he had no way of reading her moods lately, so no use in worrying about that until he got back to Blackstone.

Moran finished up a conversation with some civilians and went over to where Trammel was standing. "I don't know what kind of fire you lit under Blake, but he came out of that building like he was shot out of a cannon. Started barking orders to the others like he was a general." The new marshal looked up at Trammel. "What'd you say to him anyway? I know you didn't hit him because he was still alive."

"I didn't have to hit him," Trammel said. "Just gave him what he was looking for. A little respect and responsibility."

Moran joined him in looking at the crowded center of town. "That's how I always handled him. Figured you'd find your own way soon enough."

"Time will tell." Trammel pointed at the Rose of Tralee Saloon directly across from city hall. "Lucien Clay still own that dump?"

"He certainly does. Your friend Lilly ran it for him for a while before she went back to Wichita. She and Clay didn't get along and I can't say I blame her. Clay was still feeling mighty poorly from that beating you gave him, and he wasn't exactly good company."

Trammel had not liked the way he and Lilly had left things. She had felt used by Hagen in his bid to control the territory. Trammel knew she blamed him for his role in the mess. For refusing to back down despite overwhelming odds. He had prevailed in the end, but not enough to win Lilly back and now she was gone for Kansas, never to return.

"Clay's got a habit of poisoning every well he touches, don't he?" Trammel said as he looked at the Tralee Saloon.

"Wouldn't be Lucien Clay if he didn't," Moran told him. "But you can consider yourself lucky that you're out of it now. Clay doesn't give us much trouble these days. I hope that'll continue under your tenure."

Trammel watched a small crowd come out of the Rose of Tralee, followed by Lucien Clay. The way he looked astounded Trammel. He'd been a tall dandy of a man the last time he'd seen him that fateful day in Blackstone. But he was skin and bones with long scraggily hair that hung beneath a gray top hat. Even from across the thoroughfare, Trammel could see the bones of his face were sharp and his eyes were sunken.

He used a walking stick to keep his balance as he shuffled out onto the boardwalk and one of his sporting ladies handed a glass of whiskey to him.

"He looks like death," Trammel told Moran.

"Like my mama used to say, 'Eventually we get the face we deserve.' I'd say Mama was right in Clay's case."

Trammel gripped the stock of his Winchester tightly as he watched Clay take his glass and address the crowd of drunks and passersby.

"Ladies and gentlemen." His voice was weaker than Trammel had remembered. "Friends and fellow countrymen. I have an announcement to make. Sally forth and listen well for a new day is dawning here in our beloved city. The powers that be in our nation's capital have seen fit to reward our beloved Sheriff Rob Moran with a promotion to U.S. marshal of the territory with immediate effect."

The crowd of drunks clustered around him cheered and turned toward the jail where Moran stood. They raised their glasses to him. Moran acknowledged them with a brief wave and a smile.

Through clenched teeth, Moran asked Trammel, "What's he up to?"

Trammel was not smiling. "Looks like we're going to find out."

Clay went on. "Now, I know the next question you might ask is who they've named to replace this great pillar of justice. The brutal blackheart known as Blake?"

The crowd booed and jeered.

"Some hired gun from back East? Perhaps even one of the accursed Earp boys?"

The crowd booed and jeered even louder.

Trammel watched Clay hold up his stick to quiet them down before he went back to leaning on it. "Fear not my fellow citizens of Laramie for it appears fate has smiled upon us. The city elders, in their infinite wisdom have, this very hour, sworn in Moran's replacement and he is none other than the blundering bully of Blackstone, Buck Trammel!"

The crowd cheered and yelped. They shouted hurrahs and cast their filthy caps in the air.

Trammel watched Clay seem to grow stronger from the adulation and looked across the busy thoroughfare at him.

"That's right, my friends. The same man who narrowly avoided his town's destruction not once, not twice, but three times by my reckoning will now be in charge of maintaining order here in our fair city of Laramie." Clay leaned heavily on his stick as he raised his glass to Trammel. "So, I hope all of you will join me in a toast to a new era of incompetence where we will finally be able to operate in freedom without any fear of the law."

The drunkards cheered as Clay drained his glass and threw it to the boardwalk, shattering it on impact. He was still grinning at Trammel when he said, "Back inside, everyone, and the next two drinks are on the house."

Trammel stepped down from the boardwalk and began to make his way toward Clay, who seemed in no hurry to go back inside.

"Want me to go with you?" Moran asked after him.

"No."

"Don't kill him."

But Trammel was not in the habit of making promises he was not sure he could keep.

Lucien Clay grinned at Trammel as he watched the big man cut a path through the crowded thoroughfare. They had locked eyes since Clay had toasted him and had not broken contact since. Trammel did not even pay attention to the wagons and horses crowding his way. He obviously assumed they would see him and stop for him and he had been right.

Clay was glad he had managed to draw him out. Trammel was so easy to bait, it almost was not fair. He heard Delilah's boots scrape on the boardwalk as Trammel drew nearer. Without looking at her, he asked, "Where do you think you're going?"

"Nowhere," she whispered.

"Good. I'd hate to think that big oaf scared you." But he knew Trammel had scared her.

He was big enough to put the fear of God into any man who stood before him. Clay could remember a time when he had feared him, too, though he had never allowed himself to admit it. Being crippled by him had taken away some of that fear. He had taken Trammel's best punch and was still alive to tell the tale. With a crooked jaw perhaps but no one could expect to escape Trammel's wrath without paying some kind of price.

And as he watched him approach now, Clay knew the worst Trammel could do would be to kill him. If he did, it would not only alleviate Clay's suffering, it would turn him into a martyr, making him more powerful in death than he had ever been alive.

Trammel stopped at the edge of the boardwalk.

Clay used his stick to walk closer to him. What good was a challenge if he was not prepared to see it through? "The great Buck Trammel, as I live and breathe."

Trammel looked at him silently.

Clay continued to prod the giant. "I knew I could goad you over here. You've always been so predictable."

He watched Trammel's eyes move over his face. "How's the jaw?"

"Painful," Clay admitted. "Hurts all the time. When I breathe. When I try to eat. Whiskey doesn't even dull the pain anymore."

"Surprised you haven't tried any of that poison you sell," Trammel said. "I'd like to see you crawling around the gutter like some of the men your opium has ruined."

"I don't deserve all the credit. Half of that is your friend Hagen's doing."

"He's not my friend and neither are you."

"For a man who proposes to hate him," Clay said, "you sure have saved his life enough times. Speaking of which, I understand you were shot four times before Hagen pulled you from the fire. In the left side, I believe. Bet you know when it's going to rain, don't you?"

"Rain," Trammel said. "Snow. Acts up even worse when I'm around loud-mouthed idiots."

"Then you must be in agony." Clay stepped aside and motioned toward the front door of his saloon. Delilah squeaked and backed away. "I'd be honored if you'd join me inside for a celebratory drink to toast your new office."

"No, thanks, but I've got an offer for you. One you'll take me up on if you're anywhere as smart as you're supposed to be."

Clay placed both hands on his walking stick. "I'd be happy to hear it."

"When you were addressing your public just now, you forgot to mention you're the one behind each of those failed attempts up in Blackstone."

"Libelous slander." Clay smiled. "You'd never be able to prove that in a court of law."

"I don't need to prove it," Trammel said. "I know it was you or at least that you had a hand in it."

"And just how would you know that?" Clay asked.

"Because I'm still alive," Trammel said. "You've been trying to kill me in one way or another since I got to Blackstone. I don't think you'll do any better now that I'll be even closer to you. But since this is a day for proclamations, I'm going to make one of my own."

Clay bowed his head slightly. "By all means. The floor is yours."

"From here on in, everything that happens in this town is your fault. A store gets robbed, I'm blaming you. A woman gets knocked over by a wagon, it's your wagon until I prove otherwise. A drunk gets stabbed in an alley, it was one of your boys who did it. You'll get blamed for every bad turn in this city until facts prove otherwise."

Clay could tell he was not bluffing. "I believe guilty until proven innocent isn't a philosophy shared by the Constitution."

"It's my constitution you have to worry about," Trammel told him. "And the next time you take it into your head to gather a crowd and run me down, I'll make the right hand that broke your jaw look like a tap on the shoulder. Maybe I'll aim for the left side next time. Even you out a bit. You're standing a might crooked these days."

Clay gripped the silver handle of his walking stick tightly. If he swung it just right, he knew he could kill Trammel with one well-placed blow to the temple. He had seen it done. Even a big man like him was but a man.

But Lucien Clay knew he was in no shape to try it. He would only get one chance at Trammel and it was not the time. But that time would come and much sooner than the big man thought.

"Well, as much as I've enjoyed our war of words, Sheriff, I'm afraid I have business to tend to. I'm sure you do as well." Clay dipped the brim of his hat. "Best of luck in your new office. I'm sure we'll be seeing quite a bit of each other." He turned to go back inside, and Delilah linked her arm through his to steady him.

Trammel said, "You're a dead man, Clay. Never forget that."

The crime boss turned to face him, but Trammel had already disappeared into the crowded thoroughfare.

Clay smiled. Perhaps Trammel would prove to be a more worthy adversary than he had first believed. "He moves well for such a big man, doesn't he, Delilah?"

But the painted dove only nodded and urged her boss to go inside.

Chapter 8

Even though Big Ben London had not been able to speak since long before their first meeting in New Orleans all those years ago, Adam Hagen always knew what the black man was thinking. It was part of the undefined language they shared. A bond forged over countless adventures and dangers they'd faced on the infamous riverboats that traveled the mighty Mississippi River and the endless dens of inequity in the city of New Orleans, the Paris of the South.

That was why Adam saw past the scowl of the man who rode beside him and knew what was troubling him. "Don't sulk, Ben. It doesn't become you."

The big man glanced at him then returned his eyes to the road. He was riding a large bay gelding that almost looked like a pony when compared to his impressive size.

"I know you think visiting my family up at the ranch is a horrible idea," Hagen said. "And normally I'd agree with you. But you know very well all necessary precautions have been taken. After all, you're the one who put them into place."

Ben shook his head. *It's still a bad idea.*

"They've sent word they want to see me," Hagen reminded him. "I'm sure it's completely safe. Besides, how else am I supposed to learn why they've come back to town if I don't talk to them. It's certainly not for the fine food or accommodations I provide. They've been squirreled up in that drafty old ranch house since they've arrived. And it's certainly not to wish me well in my new ventures, even though they stand to benefit from them, at least in part."

Ben's horse tossed its head and readjusted itself to better carry its heavy load.

"Besides, you don't know my family," Hagen went on, speaking more for his own benefit than for Ben's. "They're not direct people. Certainly, my brother Caleb isn't. He prefers to weaken an opponent from beneath, not straight on like we do. He's a borrower. A plotter. A sneak who comes in the night rather than risk honest defeat in the light of day. And poor Bart is the very definition of a follower. He's not sure the sun will rise in the east tomorrow morning unless Caleb tells him so. Good at business, but not life. As for Ambrose Forrester, he did marry Debora, after all. Can't have much of a backbone to marry a barge like her. My only hope for any sympathy at all comes from Elena and her husband, Bernard. He's a young lawyer of some promise and I hope not too jaded to listen to reason."

Ben kept looking straight ahead as they approached the rocky outcropping known as Stone Gate that flanked the sunken road to town from the Blackstone ranch. It was a natural formation King Charles had dynamited because it was in the way of the road he had planned to build from his ranch into town. Another man might have simply gone around it or placed the road elsewhere. But King Charles was not a man to allow something so primitive as nature to stand in the way of a straight line he had drawn on a map. He had used it as a chokepoint to make a final count of the cattle he drove south to market in Laramie stockyards.

It had served as a chokepoint for other purposes, too. Adam could still see the bullet holes that pockmarked the rocks where Buck Trammel had succeeded in holding off a band of Pinkerton men sent to kill Adam and his father. Most men might have stood aside and let the ranch take its chances at the hands of the killers. But Buck Trammel was not like most men. He had saved the ranch and, as was his custom, remained the last man standing once the dust and gun smoke settled.

Adam knew neither of his brothers would have dreamed of such sacrifice. "No," he continued his thought aloud, "if there's any danger to be had, it'll come from my dear sister Debora, perhaps through the visage of her weaselly husband Ambrose."

Hagen laughed at the memory of his brother-in-law. "I wouldn't count on anything sinister or original coming from that spineless, preening fool. Debora only married him for his money and position. She's used it all to her advantage, though. And she has a growing brood to think about. They've managed to produce an heir, you know? Twice over, in fact. I didn't think Ambrose had it in him, but I suppose nature always finds a way. If he talks, his mouth might be moving but the words will belong to Debora."

They rode past Stone Gate and continued up the road to the ranch house. Hagen felt a tinge of regret for not burning it down after he had taken King Charles's life, but remembered he had left it intact for good reason. He had hoped keeping the house might have bought him some good feelings from his family once they learned they had been cut out of the will. The place was their childhood home. They had fond memories of a life spent on the ranch. He had hoped giving the home to them would soothe their jealousy.

Adam knew the resulting court battles had proven him wrong, of course. He was committed to having the damned thing burned to the ground the moment the ink was dry on their next and final appeal of King Charles's will. He might even hire a photographer to take pictures of the destruction so his siblings could relive the moment in the comfort of their distant homes. Yes, that would show them his mind in full.

Until that glorious day, Adam Hagen knew he had no choice but to play the understanding brother. The black sheep who had hidden his ram horns until the time was right.

As they drew closer to the ranch house, he felt Ben grow tense beside him . . . and soon saw why.

Standing out front on the porch of the great house, Caleb was flanked by ten hired gunmen. They sported pistols on their hips and rifle stocks resting on their belts. Dusters billowed freely in the hilltop wind.

Adam had been expecting such a reception, which was why he and Ben were carrying two pistols apiece. One on their hips and another tucked away in holsters at the small of their backs. Each man also had a Winchester in his saddle scabbard. Adam had taken the further precaution of carrying a knife on the left side of his belt. He expected Ben had done the same. Like Adam, the quiet man was good with a gun, but lethal with a blade.

"Calm down," he told Ben easily. "We weren't expecting them to toss rose petals at us. We have come prepared."

The black man barely nodded as he rode with his employer toward the great house.

Two ranch hands stood at the end of the road, waiting to take Adam's and Ben's horses from them.

Caleb stepped down from the porch. His gunmen followed close behind.

Adam smiled at his brother when he reined his horse to a stop. "Caleb. You're looking as prosperous as ever."

Caleb took an unlit black cigar from his mouth and pointed it at Ben. "I see you've brought a friend with you. My note said to come alone."

"What would be the fun in that?" Adam looked at the men standing behind his brother. "You brought friends. Why can't I bring mine? He won't be any trouble as long as there's no trouble. In fact, I can promise he won't say a word. He happens to be a mute."

Caleb looked Ben up and down as the big man slowly climbed down from his horse. "Pa never let his kind in the house. You know that."

Adam smiled. *If Caleb only knew Ben was the one who took King Charles's life.* "Well, Pa's under six feet of dirt, so I don't think he gets a say. Besides, I think we can make an exception in Ben's case. In fact, I insist." He climbed down from the saddle and shooed the approaching ranch hands away. "No need to trouble yourselves, boys. We'll ground hobble our mounts ourselves."

Ben slipped the reins under his horse's front hoof, just like Adam had taught him. Adam did the same.

The ranch hands looked at Caleb for direction.

"Those animals have had a long ride from town," Caleb said. "They could do with some rest and grain."

"No need." Adam clapped the dust from his hands. "They're used to the rigors of Wyoming life and could stand a little clean air for a change." He set his hands on his hips and breathed in deeply as he took in the view of the town. "My, it sure is pretty up here, isn't it? It's good to get away from town every so often. I find distance tends to give a man perspective." He smiled at Caleb. "Wouldn't you agree?"

Caleb dismissed the ranch hands with a wave, and they went back toward the bunkhouse. "Your horses, your way. Makes no difference to me."

"My house, too." Adam grinned as he removed his riding gloves one finger at a time. "At least until a judge says otherwise." He gestured toward the house. "Shall we? I imagine we have quite a bit to discuss."

Caleb bristled at the reminder of the contested estate. "No one's going anywhere yet. We're going to have to disarm you boys before you go inside." He pulled open his coat. "As you can see, I'm not armed, and neither is the rest of the family."

Adam looked around Caleb at the men standing behind him. "But your friends all have guns. I think we'll keep ours, too. Just to be fair."

Caleb let out a long breath and hung his head. "I figured you were going to make this difficult." He looked back at the man on his left. "Go ahead, Stan. Take their guns from them."

Stan moved out from behind Caleb.

Ben moved to block his way.

The nine men brought their rifles to their shoulders.

Stan grinned up at the big man. "You'd best get out of the way before you get yourself hurt, boy."

Adam took off his hat.

A bullet slammed into the ground at Caleb's feet, making the round man jump back. The report of the rifle shot was carried on the wind.

"And you'd best stand back and lower your rifles," Adam said. "Because if I drop this hat, you boys will lose more than your payday."

Caleb had bitten through his cigar and spat out the tobacco. "Damn you, Adam! Just how many men do you have out there?"

"Enough to cut these boys to ribbons if need be. Now, if we're done posturing, I suggest we go inside. Just you, Caleb, and me and Ben. If my men feel like I'm being threatened, well, there's just no telling how they'll respond. I'm sure it goes without saying if we're not back on our horses in an hour, they'll just start shooting out of an abundance of caution."

Adam bade the gunmen a good morning as he strode past them. Ben followed.

Reaching the door, Adam beckoned his brother to join them. "Come in, Caleb. Make yourself at home. Never let it be said I'm not a gracious host."

Ben shut the door once Caleb entered and stood watch while Adam walked into the den. Adam remembered how this room in particular had been his father's pride and joy. It was lined with dark beams and heavy furniture that conveyed the sense of power that King Charles Hagen once had over the territory. The main window offered sweeping views of rolling hills, and on a clear day, one could see the town of Blackstone from the front porch.

Every seat in the room was occupied by one frowning Hagen or another. The only empty chair was the one behind their late father's desk.

Assuming it was reserved for Caleb, Adam naturally

went and stood behind it. "My, would you just look at all of these smiling faces. Bart, you're looking well. I see Debora is as stern as ever. Glad to see some things never change." He smiled at her husband. "You're looking especially pale this morning, Ambrose. Debora must have tied your collar tighter than normal. Tell her to let up on the leash a bit. After all, you come from a prominent family, don't you? She never would've married you if you were poor."

"Demon," Debora hissed. "Father should've smothered you in your crib."

"But he didn't, did he?" Adam smiled. "Otherwise, we wouldn't be here enjoying each other's company on such a splendid morning."

His smile changed to something genuine when he saw Elena in the far corner of the room. Her husband, Bernard, held her elegant hand. "And I believe congratulations are in order. Welcome to the Hagen clan, Bernard. I hope you won't think any less of us for being an odd bunch, but these are trying times indeed. Sorry to have missed your nuptials, but I'm afraid my invitation got lost in the mail."

"You weren't invited," Debora spat.

"Then my condolences on what was surely a boring affair as a result. Debora's droll personality is matched only by her ability to host the dullest galas."

Elena hid a smile behind a handkerchief. Adam and she had always been close. He did not begrudge her coldness to him with the others in the room.

Caleb took his spot behind Debora's chair and slipped a hand into his pocket. "If you're done preening, Adam, I'd like to get down to business. None of us want to be in your company any longer than absolutely necessary."

"But of course." Adam sat in King Charles's chair, which

drew a gasp from his family. He crossed his legs and threw open his arms. "I take it we're here to negotiate terms of a settlement. I've always said I'm willing to be generous and reasonable. That still holds despite all of the difficulty you've cost me." He expected the next round of fire to come from Caleb but was surprised when it didn't.

Elena's husband, Bernard, spoke up. "Then if you'll be good enough to examine the papers on the desk in front of you, you'll be happy to see new developments at hand."

Adam did not hide his surprise. "They're actually allowing you speak? And so soon? My. Old Debora's grip must be slipping. Usually, she relies on Caleb to do her dirty work."

Debora sat forward on the couch as if she were about to spring at him. "Spare us your false piety and read it. I hope it turns your stomach."

Adam saw nothing was to be gained by goading them further and decided to read the documents on the desk. And what he read did turn his stomach, though he hid it well. "I see you've managed to get a new judge assigned to the case."

"Yes," Ambrose Forrester said. "An impartial judge this time. Not one of the cronies you have in your pocket. It seems my family's contacts you scoffed at only a few moments ago have their uses. The governor of the Wyoming Territory decided we deserved a fighting chance for our final appeal. He's allowed us to bring in someone new. From Colorado, in fact."

Adam made a show of flipping through the remaining pages of the document, though he was in no state to read them. His family had failed to shake him individually, but as a group, he should have known they would have devised a plan eventually. He decided to address Debora's husband.

"Tell me, Ambrose. Is this judge truly impartial or one of your old family friends scattered about the West like dry, old cattle bones?"

"You'll find Judge Littlejohn is as impartial as he is efficient," Ambrose said as his wife Debora squeezed his hand. "He'll see to it that justice is done."

"Your justice or mine?" Adam said.

"Justice belongs to everyone in equal measure," Bernard said from the back of the room, "though it does not always serve everyone equally."

Adam had no idea if his family could see how deeply the news of a new judge disturbed him. He thought it best if he left before he showed any reaction and held up the document. "I take it this is my copy?"

"It is," Bernard told him. "I'm sure your solicitors will find it in order."

Adam folded the documents and slipped them into his jacket pocket as he stood. "They'll undoubtedly find it interesting reading, though unnecessary. My offer to split father's holdings with you still stands. Fifty-one percent for me and forty-nine percent divided among all of you."

Debora watched him stand. Her green eyes had turned nastier than they had been when he'd first walked into the room. "Why should we settle for forty-nine percent of anything when we're on the verge of owning one-hundred percent of everything?"

Adam saw no benefit to continuing to debate her or the rest of his family. He took his hat from the desk as he bowed at the waist. "I bid you all a good morning and thank you for yet another warm, familial embrace."

As expected, Debora's words followed him from the room. "Any warmth you feel are the flames of Hell lapping at your hide, Adam Hagen!"

When he reached the front door, he beckoned Ben to follow him outside. They unhobbled their horses, climbed upon their mounts, and rode back to town under the watchful eyes of his family's hired gunmen.

If one of them had decided to shoot him, Adam doubted he would feel the bullet. What he had learned in his late father's study had left him completely numb.

And for the first time in a long time, defeat felt not only real, but quite possible.

CHAPTER 9

Later that day, Trammel stepped off the train and headed straight for Emily's office. It was only three o'clock in the afternoon, but he did not feel the news about his new position could wait until supper. He knew she would be cross with him about visiting while she tended to her patients, but he was burning to tell her his good news. He only hoped she thought it was good news, too.

He was surprised to see the streets were lined with a bawdier crowd than normal, especially so early in the afternoon. Several hours of sunlight were left in the day, but the work crews usually busy building Blackstone's future were already in the saloons. Despite being loud, everyone seemed to be behaving themselves.

He looked around the streets for any sign of Hawkeye on patrol, but the young man was nowhere in sight. He figured it was for the best, thinking he might mention his new job in Laramie and, if he did, Emily would most certainly be angry for not telling her first.

He entered the doctor's office and was glad to see only one man was waiting to be seen. Most of the men were tended to by Jacob Moore, so Trammel hoped she had a few moments to speak with him. He walked through the door that led to the examination rooms in the back. Dr. Moore's office was on the right, Emily's was on the left. He knocked on her door and was glad when she told him to come in. He found her alone, making notes at her desk.

She smiled up at him. "This is a pleasant surprise. Is it five o'clock already?"

"No," he assured her, "but I've got something important to tell you and it can't wait."

She looked worried as she got up from her chair and went on tiptoe to place the back of her hand on his forehead. "Are you feeling all right?"

He could not remember a time when he had felt better. "Of course. Why?"

"I was afraid you might be delirious from fever. You're actually grinning from ear to ear."

He laughed as he gently eased her hand away from his forehead. "I've got plenty of reason to smile. You're looking at the new sheriff of the City of Laramie."

Her mouth dropped open as she took a couple of steps away from him. "What?"

"I know. I was surprised myself. That's what Moran wanted to see me about."

She blinked rapidly as she absorbed the news. "But what about Rob?"

"He took the new U.S. marshal position that opened up for the territory. He asked me to be his replacement right on the spot and wouldn't take no for an answer. He even had the whole swearing in ceremony lined up and ready to go. The mayor was there, the city council, everyone." Trammel placed his big hands on her slender shoulders. "Isn't that great?"

But he could tell by the way she eased away from him

that she did not agree. "But what about your duties here in Blackstone?"

"I was planning on talking up Hawkeye to be my replacement," Trammel said. "He might be young, but he's more than ready for it. I'm sure I can get the mayor and the town council to agree, not that their opinion will matter much. Adam will be glad to be rid of me and, like you said last night, his constables have been doing a lot of the work lately. What's more is Laramie's got room in the budget to hire on two more deputies, so if Hawkeye wants to join me in a few months, he can."

She slowly lowered herself into her chair. "Oh. I see."

It did not sound like she did.

"They already have ten deputies on the payroll, Em. You know what that means? No more breaking up bar fights or getting shot at like I do here. I'll spend most of my time behind a desk." Her reaction began to trouble him. "I thought you'd be happy."

"I am happy for you, Buck. In a way. It's all just so sudden, don't you think?"

"Sure, it's sudden," he admitted, "but that doesn't take the shine off it any." The more he looked at her, the more disappointed he could see she was. "It's what we've always talked about. A better job. A safer job."

"There's nothing safe about being the sheriff of a city the size of Laramie and you know it. Here in Blackstone, you had only the Hagens' influence to worry about. Down there, you'll have every shop owner and town gossip banging on your door. Not to mention all the politicians that'll want your ear over something or another. It might not be as dangerous as Blackstone, but it's a different kind of danger. The kind you don't know too much about."

Trammel had been so swept up in his news he had not

thought of that. Emily was right, as usual, but for once, he was one step ahead of her. "I was kind of hoping you might be able to help me with that part of the job. The political part, I mean."

"Help you?" She laughed. "Oh, Buck. You really are in over your head, aren't you? The people up here might not say anything about you leaving my place every morning, but they won't tolerate that sort of thing down in Laramie. Why, the rumors alone would end your career before it even started."

"No need for any scandal or rumors." He took the gold ring he had bought in Laramie out of his pocket and held it out to her. "Not if you marry me first."

She gasped as she brought her hands to her mouth, looking at the thin gold band.

"I know it's not much," Trammel admitted, "but when I saw it, I thought your finger would make it look a whole lot nicer than it is on its own."

Her eyes watered as she looked at the ring. "I had one of those already, you know."

"But not from me. And I'm not him, Em. I won't get sick and die on you. And you've stitched me up enough times to know I'm a tough man to kill. I promise I won't make you a widow without putting up a hell of a fight. And with ten deputies around me, getting shot is unlikely." Holding the ring between his thumb and forefinger, he held it out to her. "So, what do you say? I think *Emily Trammel* has a nice sound to it."

The tears flowed freely as she held out her left hand. "With my luck, it won't even fit."

"It'll fit. I've lost count of how many times I've measured that finger while you slept." He slipped it on her finger, and it fit perfectly.

She held her hand up to look at it in the light. "It certainly does." She jumped out of the chair and threw her arms around him tighter than he thought she could manage. "I love it and I love you. It's perfect."

He hugged her back as gently as he could. "Guess that means you agree."

"Of course, you big dope." She pulled his face down to hers and kissed him tenderly.

When they were done, he held her close, resting his chin on top of her head. "I'm glad you didn't make me get down on one knee. Don't think I'd be able to get back up again."

She laughed into his shirt. "Think Laramie will accept a woman doctor?"

"They'll have to. We won't give them a choice."

The report of a rifle boomed from somewhere outside, and they both jumped.

Trammel pulled away from her. "That's Hawkeye's gun."

"Go to him, then," she said as he went out the door. "And be careful!"

As Trammel stepped out onto the boardwalk with his rifle in hand, he saw Hawkeye holding three men at bay in front of the Black Flag across the thoroughfare. All traffic in the street had ceased as the pedestrians stood by, watching how the faceoff would turn out.

"That first one was free," Hawkeye told the men. "The next one goes through one of you. Drop your guns on the boardwalk and do it real slow."

Trammel recognized the three men as part of the new bunch who had ridden into town before the Hagen family arrived. They weren't the men he had squared off against the previous day, but he recognized them as hired men just the same.

Trammel kept his rifle at his side as he called out, "Better listen to the man, boys. If he doesn't kill you, I will."

The gunman on the left side had a bottle of whiskey in his left hand. As he looked across at Trammel, his right hovered dangerously close to the pistol on his hip. "Well, if it ain't the new sheriff of Laramie come to stick his nose in. Get out of here, Trammel. This is none of your concern anymore."

Trammel did not know how the men had heard about his new position so quickly, but remembered the telegraph running through Blackstone. News traveled faster than ever now. "Doesn't matter if I'm the sheriff in Laramie or a drover out of Missouri. You're threatening my friend and that puts you in a real bad way. Best drop your guns like he told you."

The man sneered. "Or what?"

Trammel gripped his Winchester tightly. "Or you'll be dead before that bottle hits the ground."

The man swayed a little as he looked Trammel up and down from his boots to the top of his hat. "Never met a big man who could move that fast."

"Now you have. Just don't make me prove it."

The jagged yellow teeth the man showed told Trammel he had already made up his mind. "Well, if you think you can rack in a load and—"

The man went for his pistol.

Trammel brought the Winchester up to his shoulder, aimed, and fired in a single motion. His bullet plowed through the man's chest and into the wall of the saloon before the gunman had managed to get hold of his gun. He dropped the bottle as he sank to his knees. It did not break but rolled off the boardwalk instead.

Trammel levered in a fresh round and kept the rifle aimed

at the dying man. "Don't need to rack a load. I always keep one in the chamber." He tracked the dead man with his Winchester as he pitched forward and slid off the boardwalk into the gutter.

Neither of the remaining two men turned around. Neither of them made a move for their pistols, either.

Trammel shifted his aim to them as he quickly walked across the muddy street and pulled the gun from the dead man's holster.

They did not turn around when Trammel stepped onto the boardwalk and clubbed one of the men in the back of the head with the pistol butt. As the man fell forward, his partner turned toward Trammel, only to be backhanded by the barrel of the pistol. Hawkeye was on them, stripping them of their guns as they tried to shake the cobwebs from their heads. Trammel used his left hand to pull each man to his feet and shoved both toward Hawkeye, who pushed them in front of him and steered them toward the jail.

"What happened?" Trammel asked him as he helped push the dizzy prisoners along.

"I spotted them pushing and shoving people in front of the Flag and told them to knock it off. Said it was too early in the day for such nonsense. The three of them turned on me and looked like they were going for their guns. I fired a warning shot over their heads right before you came along. I didn't know you were back, boss. I thought you were still in Laramie."

"Got back early," Trammel told him as he booted one of the men farther along the boardwalk. "Good thing for you I did."

Hawkeye did not have to push one of the men but did anyway. "I'm grateful for the help, but I had it in hand."

Trammel was surprised by the strength in the young

man's voice. "Yeah, I suppose you did. Though be careful about shooting on the street. Bullets have a way of finding innocent people. Blackstone's not the sleepy old town it used to be."

"I will," Hawkeye assured him. "What was all that stuff the dead guy was saying about you being the new sheriff in Laramie."

"Later," Trammel said. "I'll tell you about it after we get these two behind bars."

They had just made it as far as the new town hall when three constables came out in a hurry. Pistols drawn.

Jesse was in the lead. "We heard shooting."

Trammel was disgusted. "The whole town could've been killed by the time you idiots did anything about it."

"We just got back to town. We stowed our horses and got here as soon as we could." Jesse looked at the two men wobbling on their feet. "What'd they do?"

Trammel pushed each prisoner into the crowd of constables. "Arrest them and hold them for disorderly conduct and threatening a peace officer. You'll find their friend dead in the gutter outside the Black Flag. I took care of him for you."

Jesse handed the prisoners off to the other two constables, who led them into town hall. "I don't like the way you talk to me, Sheriff."

Trammel pushed him against the wall and held him there. "And I don't like the way you do your job, constable. You're supposed to be here in town, not riding off somewhere. Where were you boys?"

"On a special assignment," Jesse said. "For Mr. Hagen, if it's any of your business. You want to know more, go ask him. I don't have to tell you a damned thing."

Trammel grabbed hold of Jesse's tunic and pulled him

off the wall. "And I don't have to save your hide the next time this bunch decides to jump you in an alley. Where's your boss now?"

"At the Phoenix. Where else would he be?"

Trammel released him with a shove toward the Black Flag. "Tend to that dead body and get it off the street. Don't come back until it's cleaned up. Hawkeye, dump off their pistols inside, then go with him. Make sure he doesn't get lost or foul it up."

Hawkeye was about to go inside, but stopped to ask, "Where are you going, boss?"

Already on his way to the Phoenix, Trammel said, "To find out what's really going on around here."

CHAPTER 10

Watching the place being built, Trammel had vowed to never step foot inside the Phoenix Hotel. But he had never expected to be railroaded into accepting a job he did not even know he wanted. It seemed to be a day for firsts.

He had no sooner shut the door behind him when one of Hagen's well-attired hosts met him at the entryway. "Good afternoon, Sheriff Trammel. How good of you to join us."

Trammel was not in the mood for conversation. "Where's your boss?"

"I assume you mean Mr. Hagen," the polite young man said. "You'll find him in the back office. I'll be glad to take you to him, but I must ask you to leave your rifle with me." He waved a hand to reveal the bustling gaming room behind him. "We don't allow rifles on the premises. It ruins the ambiance for our guests."

Trammel was not exactly sure what *ambiance* meant, but he could see a rifle had no place in the Phoenix Hotel. The gaming hall was gaudier than some cathouses he had seen. Silk draped from the ceilings. Gilded chandeliers and mirrors made the room look bigger and more dignified than it really was. Paintings of naked ladies in various modest poses were everywhere.

He handed the rifle over to the young man, who handed it to a clerk behind the front desk. "It will be well cared for and waiting for you when you leave. Now, if you'll come this way."

Trammel followed him through the gaming room that took up the entire lobby of the hotel. It was not just a poker room. Tables were also filled with people playing faro and blackjack. A couple of tables had roulette wheels and dice games of one form or another.

Having seen too many lives ruined over games of chance to put much faith in any romantic notions of winning, Trammel had never been much of a gambler. He was often the one responsible for cleaning up after Lady Luck turned a cold shoulder to men playing cards or rolling dice.

The young man led him to a door well past the cheering and moaning patrons of the Phoenix Hotel. He knocked and Trammel could barely make out Hagen's voice telling him to come in. The young man opened the door just enough to stick his head in and tell him Sheriff Trammel was there.

Hagen's voice did not sound any livelier through the half-opened door as he said, "Come in, Buck. Make yourself at home."

The young man pushed the door open and stepped aside to allow Trammel to enter.

The sheriff was surprised by what he saw. Adam Hagen's hair was a mess. His collar was not simply undone but it was off entirely. He sat behind an ornately carved wooden desk with only a bottle of whiskey and an ashtray upon it. His jacket was slung over the back of his leather chair.

"Thank you, Geoffrey," Hagen told the young man. "You may go."

Geoffrey quietly shut the door, leaving Trammel alone with the disheveled Hagen.

"What's the matter with you?" Trammel asked. "I've seen you look better after you've been shot."

"Yes, I suppose I have," Hagen admitted. "I've certainly felt better with a bullet in me than I do now. Speaking of shots"—he gestured to the bottle on his desk—"want a snort?"

"A bit early yet in the day for me." Trammel approached one of the chairs opposite Hagen's desk and sat down. "What's the matter with you? You don't look right."

"I distinctly remember you swore you'd never step foot in this place," Hagen countered. "What's the occasion?"

"Your constables, but we'll get to that. What's wrong with you?"

Hagen ran his finger along the green felt of the blotter on his desk. "Well, Buck, it goes something like this. You were here for the very beginning of my misadventures in Blackstone and you're here now for their bitter end." He forced a smile. "It seems my family are not the over-indulged simpletons I've taken them for. They're a clever bunch indeed. They're onto my ruse and I think they just might have me beaten this time."

Trammel had always known Hagen's airs of sophistication were nothing but show. Having seen him as the house drunk back in the Gilded Lily in Wichita, Trammel knew the cultured dandy the man played in Blackstone was more of an act than reality. But he had never seen Adam this low, not even in Kansas.

"What happened?"

"I'll spare you the details," Hagen said. "Suffice it to say that my family has turned the tables on me and beaten me at my own game. They have convinced the governor to allow an outside judge to come to Wyoming and mitigate our court battle."

Trammel had not bothered following the court case over the estate of the late King Charles Hagen. He just figured Adam had it tied down nice and tight, just like he always did. Probably through judges he had on his payroll, though Trammel did not want to know the particulars. "You'll find a way around it."

"Not this time. The Forrester family seems to have rallied around my siblings and used their influence for my sister's benefit. An old family friend of theirs will hear the final appeal and that ruling, I'm afraid, will be binding. They're contesting my father's signature on his will, which left everything to me. After the judge's ruling, I'll be left with nothing."

Trammel did not know about such things, but even he had always doubted the signature on the will was genuine. As it was none of his business, he did not care one way or the other. "When did you find out?"

"A little while ago while you were on your jaunt down to Laramie." He perked up a bit. "What did Moran want to see you about anyway?"

Now that Emily knew, he saw no reason not to tell him. "Moran has been named the new marshal of the territory. He offered me his old job as sheriff of Laramie. I was sworn in this morning." Trammel watched all the color rush from Hagen's face.

"You did what?"

"I had a shot at the brass ring, and I took it," Trammel said without a hint of guilt. "I figured you'd be glad to see me leave, considering I've been a thorn in your side for years."

"A thorn?" Hagen said barely above a whisper. "Good God, man. You're the only constant I've been able to rely on. The one man who held me in check when I strayed too far. You're the only friend I've got."

"You're laying it on a little thick, aren't you, Adam? We both know that's not true."

"Being at cross-purposes and being enemies are two different things," Hagen told him. "We may have disagreed, even violently at times, but I never wished you harm. And I wished you had waited to talk to me before you made such a rash decision."

"I didn't know I needed your permission." Trammel shook his head. "Leave it to you to find a way to take the good out of something that doesn't involve you."

"Sentiment has nothing to do with it." Hagen leaned forward in his chair. His eyes wide and desperate. "Listen to me, Buck, and listen to me very carefully. You got on that train this morning not knowing why Moran wanted to see you and you return as the sheriff of one of the biggest cities in the West. That's a bit sudden, don't you think?"

Trammel had thought it was all too sudden for his taste, but not enough to turn down the job. "Moran was anxious to name a replacement. Some of his boys were bucking for the job. He and the mayor didn't want to leave the spot open too long so they named me. The Businessman's Association even agreed. How's that got anything to do with you?"

"I pray nothing," Hagen said, "but you know I've never been a prayerful man. And neither have you. Don't you think it's odd that my family drops this cannonball in my lap on the exact same day you're made sheriff of Laramie?"

Trammel had not thought of it until Hagen mentioned it. Now that he had, Trammel still did not see a problem. "It's called a coincidence, Adam. The world's full of them. It happens."

"Not where my family is concerned, it doesn't." Hagen went on. "Think about it, Buck. With you, my only ally, out of the way in Laramie, I'll be left here to face my family alone. Don't sell them short. They could have arranged for Moran's promotion just to get you to take his place. They're cunning enough."

Trammel felt his temper begin to rise. "Which means I'm not good enough. Is that it? I'm good enough to save your life more times than I can count, but not good enough to run a town like Laramie?"

"Not a town," Hagen corrected. "A city. And no, you're not the first name that comes to mind. You're the bravest and toughest man I've ever known. You also happen to be the most honorable, but a city is infinitely more difficult to police than a small burg like Blackstone. That's not a slight against you. This offer didn't come to you by accident or happenstance. It came to you by *design*. Through crafty and cunning on the part of my family. And I think, with a little more thought, you'll see that I'm right."

Trammel got up before he said something he might regret later. "All I see is a half-drunk gambler scared out of his mind because, for once, things haven't broken his way. Did you really think your family would just lie down and take it in the teeth with all that money at stake? Did you think all those cronies you've been milking from Madame Peachtree's black book would stay loyal to you forever? Well, the teat has gone dry, my friend, and you're going to have to find yourself another cow. I wouldn't worry about it too much, though. You'll find another way to get around them like you always do."

Hagen called after him as he turned to leave, but Trammel only turned around when he remembered what he had come to the Phoenix to say. "And you're not alone. You've got those blue-coated idiots on your payroll. You'd better start making them earn their money. I had to kill a man before I walked in here because they were holed up in town hall like a bunch of scared mice. Said they were working on some kind of special assignment for you."

Hagen sank back into his chair. "They were covering me while I was up at the ranch house meeting with my family. I think they may have even saved my life."

"Then I guess they really were doing their job after all. Just make sure you leave one or two of them in town next time. I won't be around much longer to do their jobs for them." Trammel reached for the doorknob.

Hagen called out, "Wait, Buck. The man you shot. Who was he?"

"One of your family's gunmen drew down on Hawkeye. I killed him when he went for his gun. We didn't have time to exchange pleasantries. Count yourself lucky. That leaves nine of them now. Your constables finally have an advantage for a change."

Hagen closed his eyes. "One down. But with the promise of countless more to follow."

Trammel did not like the tone in his former friend's voice or the look in his eyes. "You heeled, Adam?"

Hagen looked up at him as if his mind had drifted a thousand miles away in only a few seconds. He patted the gun on his hip. "Always. But don't worry about me, Buck.

I'm not suicidal. It hasn't become quite that desperate. Not yet anyway."

Trammel was a bit assured by the strength in Hagen's voice. "Good, because Emily and I are getting married, and I'd appreciate it if you could avoid killing yourself until after the wedding."

Hagen smiled wearily at the news. "That's wonderful. I mean that. You two will be very happy together. I take it I'm invited to the wedding."

Trammel supposed he was. "I was kind of figuring you might be my second. Other than Hawkeye, you're about the only friend I've got, too."

Chapter 11

Trammel walked across the street to the jailhouse to find Hawkeye in the same state he had found Hagen, but for a much different reason. He was sitting at Trammel's desk with his head propped up on his chin, lost in thought.

"You and Jesse see to that body like I told you?" the sheriff asked his deputy as he put his Winchester in the rack. He would clean it after he spoke with Hawkeye.

"Dr. Moore came and took him away. Wanted me to tell you he'll have his report ready for you by the end of the day. Said he might even be able to get him planted tomorrow so long as no one comes forth to claim him."

That was good news as far as Trammel was concerned. Moore was nothing if not an efficient coroner. The quicker the burial, the more likely the man would be forgotten. "Then why the long face?"

"On account of everyone knew about your new job in Laramie except me." Hawkeye continued to frown. "Even Doc Moore knew about it."

"Someone must've sent a telegram after the swearing in ceremony."

"So, it's official, then. You're going and that's that. Why

didn't you tell me about this before you went to Laramie, boss?"

"Didn't know about it myself until I got down there this morning. And that's the truth. You can ask Emily if you want. It all came on kind of sudden. Moran's been named the new U.S. marshal for the territory."

"Good for him," Hawkeye said. "Doesn't do much good for me. Guess you won't be taking me on as a deputy with you down in Laramie."

"Why would I?" Trammel asked. "You're going to be the sheriff here."

Hawkeye picked up his head. "I'm what?"

"You heard me. I'm naming you as my replacement. I plan on talking to the mayor about it tonight. Hagen, too. Assuming you want it, of course." Trammel could not tell by the deputy's flustered expression whether he wanted it or not.

"I'm not old enough for it, boss. I just turned twenty."

"Men your age are old enough to fight and die in war," Trammel told him. "You're certainly ready to be the sheriff of Blackstone. You've learned more in the past three years than most lawmen see in their entire careers. Why I'd wager there are a couple of graybeards with stars pinned on their chests that could learn a thing or two from you."

The prospect of a new position and responsibility brightened Hawkeye's mood some, but not as much as Trammel would have expected. "I guess that would be just about the best thing that ever happened to me except that it means we can't work with each other anymore. At least not the way we do now."

Trammel cursed himself for not thinking about how the developments would affect Hawkeye and not just him and Emily. He had not thought about it because there was no question that Jimmy Hauk was ready to assume more responsibility. He had always thought the young man knew Trammel's high opinion of him, but it was clearly time for him to be plain about the matter.

"You were the first man I could trust when I came to Blackstone," Trammel told him, "and I can't think of a single time when you've let me down since. You're a hell of a lawman, Jimmy Hauk. Not just with a gun, but in how you conduct yourself. You corralled those three all on your own just now on the street. Probably would've brought them in peacefully if I hadn't stirred things up."

Hawkeye's voice was thick with emotion when he said, "I learned from watching you."

"You've learned from my mistakes," Trammel said. "And that's what'll keep you alive. It's why I can't think of a better man to replace me."

He unpinned the tin star from his vest, where he had temporarily replaced his gold star from Laramie, and looked at it. He remembered the day the town had given it to him. His first order of business had been to find the man responsible for killing the man who had worn it before him. "Sheriff Bonner disgraced this star, but I'd like to think you and I restored its honor. That's why I can't think of a better man to wear it than you."

He beckoned Hawkeye to get up and approach him. When he did, Trammel removed the deputy's star and replaced it with his own. "I don't have the power to make it official, but I'm pretty sure I can make you the acting sheriff in my place. And that's what I'm doing now." He held out his hand to Hawkeye. "Let me be the first to congratulate you, Sheriff Jimmy Hauk."

The young man shook his hand. "I'll do my best to live up to it, boss."

"It's not *boss* anymore," Trammel corrected him. "It's just Buck. Or Steve if you prefer. That's my right name."

Hawkeye looked down at the new star on his shirt. "Sheriff Hauk. I never thought I'd hear those words together."

Trammel patted him on the back. "Resume your seat, Sheriff, and let's talk about what you need to watch out for in the days to come. I just found out our town is changing and probably not for the better."

Lucien Clay had refused to use his cane as he strolled through the streets of Laramie with his guest. This man would be working for him and he did not want to appear weak or infirmed, at least in this, their first official meeting. Mercenaries had a habit of taking advantage of weakness. It was in their nature.

"You sure this is a good idea?" the taller man asked. "You and me being seen out in public like this for all the town to see."

"I prefer to conduct most of my meetings in public," Clay told him. "Or at least I did before I had my run-in with Buck Trammel. A run-in I'm hiring you to avenge."

"Given the amount you're paying me," the stranger said, "it must've been a lot more than just a run-in."

The memory and shame of several months of painful suffering flooded Clay's busy mind. One blow from Trammel's heavy fist had served to lay him lower than he had ever been. But he set those bitter memories aside for the sake of clarity. "I'm paying you to do what I tell you. I only hope you're as good with a gun as your reputation claims."

"You can rest easy on that score," the man said with an easy grin. Long gray hair flowed from beneath his plainsman's hat. His dark, deep-set eyes moved over the people they passed on the boardwalk. Clay's people had told him Major John Stanton was about fifty, but Clay was glad to see he still walked with a military bearing and moved like a man unencumbered by the effects of age.

"I can kill a man as close as we are now or from five hundred yards away with equal effect. Farther if the conditions are right and the job calls for it. My time in the army taught me that much."

Clay was glad to hear it. A man's reputation was one thing. Hearing it from his own lips always told the tale. And everything he had seen of Major Stanton thus far had lived up to his billing.

"I suppose you've heard of my reputation, too," Clay said.

"I wouldn't have made the long trip out here if I hadn't," Stanton told him. "I'm not in the habit of wasting my time before or after a job. I know who and what you are. I also know you're mighty vindictive. All I care about is the target, how you want him killed, and when. Poison, knife, pistol, or rifle, it's all the same to me. I'll take care of the rest."

Clay was glad to hear it. "A man of action. I like that."

"You didn't bring me out here for conversation and philosophy. I'm the best at what I do, just like you."

Clay was impressed by his confidence, but it was not enough. "I must make one thing absolutely clear from the very start. I am the one who brought you to Laramie. No one else."

"I took your money, so I work for you. That's how it works with me."

"That may be how it works in San Francisco, but you'll find the Wyoming Territory is a different place. I'm not the only man of influence in these parts. It's only a matter of time before others learn that you're here. Other powerful and influential men of means. Men who may wish to hire you to do their bidding. That bidding may involve betraying me."

"I've made it this long without being a turncoat, Mr. Clay. I don't aim to start now. Just about the only thing I've got in this world is my word. And I don't go back on it for anyone at any price. You mark a man and he's as good as dead. Not even you can call me off at that point. It's why my price is so high."

Clay appreciated the words, and although he only knew Major Stanton by reputation, he knew human nature. Everyone was corruptible under the right circumstances.

"Our association must go beyond the man I'm paying you to kill," Clay explained. "I'll see to it that you continue to be well compensated for your loyalty, but no matter who approaches you or what happens, you must never turn on me. That must be absolutely clear if we are to proceed. Others will undoubtedly try to convince you otherwise, but we cannot allow that to happen. Is that clear, Mr. Stanton?"

"Clear as a bell," the mercenary assured him. "Your protection is part of our agreement."

Clay was not surprised when the hired gun's curiosity came to the surface.

"Just so I know who to watch out for, who do you think would try to hire me away from you?"

"Their names are all *Hagen*," Clay said, "or in-laws of Hagen women. The family is at odds with each other over their late father's empire centered in Blackstone, a town about an hour's train ride north of here. One Adam Hagen seems to have the upper hand for now, but I've been told his advantage will be slipping in the coming days. Both sides are liable to grow desperate as hostilities increase and, once the man I've hired you to kill is dead, they will undoubtedly use all their impressive resources to find the man who did it. It will only be a matter of time before they discover you were behind it and were working for me."

"You're more concerned about them than you are about the law, aren't you?"

"I have good reason to be. I play a vital role in their schemes for now, but once my part is done, my agreement with the family may prove inconvenient. You don't need to know all the details, just that under no circumstances are you to entertain any offer of employment from them. No matter how much they're willing to pay you. Not even if their request appears to have nothing to do with me. Every action of the Hagen family and Blackstone concerns me, so even the most banal task could threaten my interests and our arrangement." He looked up at the man, ignoring the spike of pain it caused in his jaw. "Are we absolutely clear on that point?"

"Sounds mighty complicated," Stanton said. "Good thing I don't like complications. I like things nice and easy. Guess that's why I've managed to live so long."

"Me too, Mr. Stanton. Me too."

By then, they had approached the Hotel Lansdowne. Wooden planks covered the front door and all the windows on the first floor. The windows on the four floors above it were uncovered.

Stanton said, "I hope you're not putting me up in this dump. Looks closed."

"I've already secured you lodging at the Rose of Tralee. This place is closed for repairs. I should know. I own it. Which is why I also know this is the perfect location from where you can earn your money."

He and Stanton turned to face the massive city hall

building, which was about half a block up the street. "My plan is simple. The back door to the place is boarded over now, but it will not be on the day of the shooting. No one will be working inside that day, so you will be able to enter the building unseen and climb to the top floor."

"You want me on the roof?" Stanton asked.

"No," Clay told him. "You might be spotted beforehand and the whole plan would be ruined before it started. At the top of the stairs, you'll turn right and walk to the last room in the hall on your left. It faces the street. You'll find the panes of glass removed from the window, so you won't have to open it. You will have a clear view of your target once he exits city hall and, as soon as you have a clear shot, you will kill him. But you'll need to make your shot count."

Clay nodded to the busy thoroughfare clogged with wagons of every description. "The report of the rifle will be lost among the usual sounds of Main Street at first, which is why one shot is essential. More than one and you risk being marked, thus being trapped before you make your escape."

Stanton was looking over the scene. "I don't need you to tell me my business, Mr. Clay. I know how to kill a man and how to get away, too."

Clay reluctantly took the rebuke and remained silent as he looked at the top floor of the closed hotel, then back again to city hall.

When he had seen enough, Stanton asked, "Will he be alone?"

"Probably not," Clay said, "but you have the drawing I provided you. It's accurate, so you should have no problem picking him out. He does tend to stand out in a crowd. He has a very commanding presence, much like yourself."

Stanton grunted acknowledgment as he continued to examine the scene. "What about after?"

This was the part of the plan Clay was most proud of. "You will mount your horse and proceed to ride north to Blackstone. I'll provide you with a map when we're finished here. You'll find it all easy enough to follow. That part of the plan is as essential as the killing itself. You must follow my directions precisely. Once it's over, you can return here to Laramie where we will discuss what else needs to be done. Circumstances here will change drastically after the deed is done. I won't know what I'll need you to do until you return."

Stanton finished looking the scene over. "You've done this kind of thing before, haven't you?"

Clay took it as a compliment. "I've been the one who squeezes the trigger and the one who pays to have it done. I appreciate the intricacies involved. This is a most intricate plan, Major. If I simply wanted him dead, I could hire any number of thugs to walk up to him and hit him with both barrels of a shot gun. This is a more subtle way of handling things. Safer for all involved, too."

Stanton grinned. "Not for the target."

Clay grinned, too. "No. Definitely not for him. Now, if you've seen enough, let's walk over to my office. We have much to discuss."

Chapter 12

Trammel and Emily walked arm in arm along the boardwalk. Dr. Moore and Rhoades, the reporter from *The Blackstone Bugle*, trailed just behind them during an after-dinner stroll around town.

"Blackstone's loss is Laramie's gain," Moore said. "You're about to marry quite a talented physician, Buck. But I'm sure I don't have to tell you that."

"No, you don't." Trammel patted her hand. "She's patched me up enough times for me to give her a glowing reference."

"Anyone who questions her qualifications," Rhoades said, "need only to have you open your shirt and show her handiwork. You're a modern-day Lazarus if you can forgive a little blasphemy."

"It's not blasphemy if it's true," Trammel told him.

"Laramie's quite an enterprising place," Rhoades went on. "I hope you're not planning on spending your days with your feet on your desk drinking coffee and reading arrest reports, Buck. A lot of government in that city. Local, city, territorial. Why, you'll probably have lunch with the governor himself at least once a week."

"At least!" Emily added with a laugh.

Trammel was relieved she was as happy about moving to Laramie as he was. He was glad she had agreed to go with him and become his wife. He felt a certain melancholy as they walked along the boardwalk that night. When he had decided to lose himself after his stint with the Pinkertons had ended, he never dreamed he would end up in a place like Blackstone. It had been a small town back then. It was growing into a proper city, one that might even rival Laramie someday if Adam got his way.

Trammel had not felt one way or the other about the place when he had first come to town. It had been a dot on the map. The destination where he was supposed to drop off Hagen and find a new place to live. Nothing more. He had not intended to become attached to the place. The people who had lived there then had been kind to him. Most of them had either moved on or died in the years since, but they had played a part in making him think of the place as home.

He supposed that was why he had risked so much to defend it whenever it was threatened. He would like to think he had repaid their kindness in full and in blood.

Just as Blackstone had changed over the years, Trammel supposed he had changed, too. Back then, he could not have thought of a reason why he should be the sheriff of a city like Laramie. Now, he could not think of a reason why he could not do the job.

Hagen's concerns aside, Buck Trammel knew he was ready for the challenge. In fact, he was more than ready. He was looking forward to it.

Trammel was pulled from his pleasant thoughts as they approached the Occidental only to find Caleb and Bart Hagen on the boardwalk. Three hired gunmen were on the street with them, though they kept a good distance away from their charges.

Caleb noticed Trammel first. “Evening, Trammel.” He tipped his hat to Emily. “Doctor Downs.” Bart followed suit as Caleb spoke to Trammel. “I’m surprised to see you’re still here. I thought you’d be in Laramie tending to your new duties there.”

“I start on Monday.” Trammel eased Emily behind him. “Now, if you’ll excuse us, we’d like to continue our walk.”

“Just a moment.” Caleb held up a hand. “I’d like to have a word with you in private, Sheriff Trammel, if I may.”

“And if I refuse?” He looked past Hagen at the guards behind them. “You going to have them try to stop me?”

“I’d prefer to keep this civil, Sheriff. If for no other reason, then for the sake of the lady.”

Emily popped out from behind Trammel. “Don’t worry about me, Mr. Hagen. Buck has handled your thugs before. There’s no reason why my presence would stop him from doing so again.”

Trammel could feel a crackle of tension go through the Hagen brothers and their men. Emily might be up for a fight, but Trammel was not prepared to risk her safety. He looked at Moore and said, “Doctor, I’d be grateful if you and Rhoades could see her home.” He squeezed Emily’s hand. “I’ll be along in a bit.”

Emily was clearly furious but did not resist Moore’s arm when he offered it to her. And Rhoades seemed all too glad to get away from the dangerous situation. He often wrote about violence for *The Bugle*, but rarely took part in it.

Caleb Hagen had the decency to hold his tongue until Emily and the others had made it across the thoroughfare. “She’s quite a woman, Buck. I understand congratulations are in order. I hear you two are to be wed.”

"Quite so," parroted Bart. "Congratulations, Buck."

"My friends call me Buck. You two can call me Sheriff Trammel."

"I find that awfully convenient," Caleb said, "seeing how your new position in Laramie will have the same title as your current one."

"Most convenient indeed," Bart said.

Trammel hooked his right hand on his belt buckle, ready to reach up and pull his Peacemaker from his shoulder holster if it came to that. "And here I was expecting you to yell at me for killing one of your boys today."

Caleb smiled as he shook his head. "My sons are safe and sound at home in Chicago, Sheriff. They have nothing to fear from you there. Now, as for that unfortunate incident on the street earlier today, well, that was just a gross misunderstanding."

"A misunderstanding," Trammel repeated. "You're some piece of work, Hagen. One of your men lost his life and you call it a misunderstanding. A mistake." He looked over at the three guards and said, "I hope you heard that. Sounds like Mr. Hagen really values your lives."

Caleb shook his head. "My men know how much I value them. They also know how much they stand to benefit once I finally defeat my brother in a court of law. But now is not the time for such discussions. Tonight is your night to celebrate your good fortune, Sheriff. The time will come when we can talk about other, less pleasant things."

Trammel took a step closer to him.

Bart backed away. The hired guns behind them remained still.

"Why put it off?" the sheriff asked. "You've got something to say, so say it."

But Caleb would not be goaded into a confrontation.

"Another time and another place, Sheriff." He stepped aside and out of Trammel's way. "Until then, I wish you a pleasant evening and, again, my congratulations on all of your good fortune."

Trammel did not trust Caleb, but knew that if he pushed matters, he would be in the wrong. He decided to leave the matter behind him as he walked away. Even the hired guns parted to allow him to pass. He listened for a smart word or a snicker that would cause him to turn around, but all he heard was the sound of Caleb and Bart resuming their conversation as they walked in the other direction.

Trammel had no doubt he would face Caleb and his men again. He did not know where or when, but wherever or whenever it happened, he would be ready.

CHAPTER 13

"I now pronounce you man and wife," the parson announced in the main dining room of the Phoenix Hotel. "Sheriff Trammel, you may now kiss your bride."

Trammel was more than happy to comply as he took Emily in his arms and kissed her in front of half the town.

Adam Hagen cheered and was the first to throw a handful of rice at the newly married couple. Hawkeye and the others followed suit.

Trammel continued to hold Emily close as she wiped away her tears and they faced their friends for the first time as man and wife.

For his part, Trammel could not remember the last time he had been so happy. Nothing in recent memory had even come close. None of that mattered. He belonged to Emily and Emily belonged to him, and, with a new job waiting for him down in Laramie, all seemed right with the world.

Adam cut in front of the people rushing to greet them. "As the host of this blessed event, I ask to be the first to kiss the darling Mrs. Trammel." He kissed her on the cheek before getting an answer, then embraced Trammel. "While I doubt the Almighty pays much attention to anything I have to say, I pray God blesses you both with a long life of happiness and peace from this day forward."

Trammel thought Hagen was almost as happy as he was, maybe even happier. "Thanks for doing all of this for us, Adam. We weren't expecting such a big party."

"Nonsense. It's not every day my two favorite people get married. It's the least I can do. Besides, you're not the sheriff of Blackstone any longer, so no one can accuse me of trying to curry favor with you, now can they?"

Hagen stepped aside as Hawkeye and the rest of the people of Blackstone came forward to offer their best wishes for the new couple. The commotion reminded Trammel of his swearing in ceremony in Laramie. He was almost dizzy by the flurry of handshakes and slaps on the back he received from well-wishers when he noticed someone standing at the entrance of the dining room. He thought that was strange, since Adam had closed off the room for the occasion.

Caleb Hagen was standing with two of his guards at the back of the room. As if the sight of the three men was not enough to sour his mood, the two guards wore pistols on their hips.

Trammel excused himself from the well-wishers and made his way toward the intruders.

Caleb held up both hands as Trammel charged toward him. "Don't do anything rash, Sheriff. I'm just here to talk."

The guards straightened as Trammel stopped less than a foot in front of their employer. "Now's the day you decide you want to talk? On my wedding day?"

"Because it's your wedding day," Caleb said. "Please, let's talk outside where we can have some privacy."

Trammel waited for Caleb and his guards to leave first before joining them.

"Take it easy, big man," Stan said as they walked through the gaming hall to the front of the hotel. "The boss only wants to talk."

Trammel ignored him as he followed them to the area just beyond the main desk. When Caleb turned around, his hired men flanked him.

Caleb said, "Before we begin, allow me to be among the first to congratulate you on this joyful day."

Trammel did not want his congratulations. "What do you want, Hagen?"

Caleb seemed disappointed. "This is your first marriage, isn't it? It's a mighty big step getting married. It's no small thing."

Trammel could feel his neck growing redder by the second. "I already asked you what you wanted. Don't make me ask again."

"I'm here to give you a rare and invaluable gift," Caleb said. "A gift no amount of money can buy. The gift of wisdom."

"You've got nothing I need," Trammel told him. "Including wisdom."

"In this case, I believe I do," Caleb said, "because I wish to point out all of the wonderful things your future holds. I want to remind you how far you've come from the slums of Manhattan. You've not only earned yourself a reputation as a lawman, but you've become the sheriff of one of the largest cities this side of the Mississippi. I wanted to make sure you took stock of all that you have accomplished in such a short amount of time. To stop and smell the roses, if you will."

"Whatever I smell right now isn't roses," Trammel said.

"Now Buck," Caleb chided as he held his hands apart, "there's no reason for us to be enemies. Not anymore. Blackstone has served its purpose for you. You've used it as a stepping-stone to a brighter, more rewarding future in Laramie. Your future *is* in Laramie, not Blackstone. By that, I mean whatever happens in this town is no longer your concern."

"The law's my only concern," Trammel said. "Here in Blackstone or in Laramie. I don't need you or anyone else to remind me of that."

"The law in Laramie," Caleb said, "not here. You no longer have any authority here as the city limits do not extend to Blackstone. I want you to remember that as my family's trial against Adam begins in a couple of weeks."

"That trial is being held in Laramie," Trammel said. "What you do here in Blackstone is none of my business." He looked at Stan and the other guards. "But if you bring this trash to town with you, I'm going to clean it up."

"Surely you can't expect me to walk around unguarded, can you?" Caleb asked. "Certainly not with Adam lurking about. He's a stone-cold killer. Not even you can deny that."

"Why would I bother denying it?" Trammel asked. "His reputation is his business. The law is mine."

"Perhaps," Caleb allowed, "but he has gone out of his way to throw this party for you and your lovely wife. We both know he doesn't do things out of the kindness of his heart. I'd just hate for the people of Laramie to have the impression you or your deputies might be partial to him during the trial."

Trammel was beginning to see where Caleb was heading with all of this. "The only opinion that matters in that trial is the judge's. My men will be there to maintain order." He looked at both gunmen. "That goes for you, your family, and your hired hands. Anyone who steps out of line will answer to me."

Caleb looked relieved. "That's good to hear, Buck. I'm glad to hear you think of it that way. And not just for yourself. After all, there's Mrs. Trammel to consider now and—"

Trammel snatched him by the throat and pinned him against the wall.

The two guards went for their guns but a metallic click from behind them stopped them cold.

"Gentlemen," Adam Hagen said. "The sheriff and my brother are having a private conversation. It would be impolite to interfere. Hands away from your guns, please. As a matter of fact, why don't we all step outside and allow them to continue their talk in private." He wagged his pistol toward the front door of the hotel. *"Right now."*

The two guards kept their hands up as Adam marched them outside, leaving Trammel and a gagging Caleb alone.

Trammel gripped his throat tighter. "You've had your say, Hagen, now I'll have mine. I don't take kindly to threats, no matter how nice they sound. You and Adam can settle your differences between you. I do what a judge tells me to do whether it's for you or against you. But if you ever mention my wife again, if you even look in her direction, I'll choke you to death just like I'm doing now. I won't shoot you. I won't take a knife to you. I'll take you nice and slow so you feel every second of it." He released his grip on Caleb's throat a little. "Nod if you understand me."

Caleb nodded and Trammel tightened his grip again as he pulled him off the wall so he could speak into Caleb's left ear. "You think you know me? You think you know my reputation? You don't know the half of it. And you'd better pray to God you never find out." He released Caleb with a shove toward the doorway as the man gasped for air. Trammel kicked him in the backside and sent him tumbling forward toward the door.

Adam grabbed hold of him and set him upright. "My dear brother, what's the matter? Can't hold your whiskey like you used to, I see. Stumbling around in broad daylight like a common drunkard. What would dear old Pa say? I'm sure glad he didn't live long enough to see this."

Caleb clutched his own throat as he rasped his rage at Adam. "You bastard! How dare you mention his name. He'd still be alive if you hadn't killed him."

"But Father died of a heart attack," Adam said. "The coroner said so."

"*Your* coroner," Caleb said. "But you wait and see, *brother*. Wait and see what happens to you. Your end is coming and quicker than you think."

"Perhaps, but not today and not by you." He led his brother toward the door. "Now, take your friends and run along back to Debora and the family so they can tell you what to do next." He released his brother and holstered his weapon as the three men moved off to a waiting carriage.

Adam sighed as he walked back toward Trammel. "I'd offer my apologies on his behalf, but it wouldn't do any good. I'm sorry he tried to ruin your day."

Trammel still glared at the doorway. "He threatened my wife, Adam. My wife!"

"It's the Hagen way, unfortunately," Adam said. "When we can't get what we want one way, we get desperate and do something ugly instead. Besides, he wouldn't have the nerve to go anywhere near Emily. She'd lay him out flat in one punch and you know it."

Trammel laughed despite his rage. "You've got a knack for taking the sting out of a situation, you know that?"

"It's all part of my charm." Adam placed a hand on Trammel's back and urged him to join him. "Now, come back to the party. I've spent an obscene amount on champagne, and I have no intention of allowing a drop of it to go to waste due to my brother's ugliness."

Later that night, after consummating their marriage, Trammel held Emily tightly. Her warm body felt good against him.

"It was nice to be able to do that legally for once," Emily said.

Trammel felt himself blush in the darkness. He had always felt awkward discussing such matters, even with her. "Yes, it does. Can't have the sheriff be an outlaw, now can we?"

She kissed him on the cheek and laid her head on his chest. "You and Adam disappeared for a bit right after the ceremony. You didn't quarrel again, did you? He's been so generous."

He had hoped she would not ask him about that, but he should have known she would have noticed. She did not miss much. "Caleb Hagen showed up with his hired men. They tried to threaten me."

She was quiet for a moment. "They threatened me, too, didn't they?"

He did not want to tell her, but he did not want to lie to her, either. "How did you know?"

"Your pupils were the size of saucers and the vein in your neck was bulging when you came back inside." She ran her finger along the very vein she had spoken of. "I knew something had happened and knew the only thing that could've gotten you that angry was if someone said something about me. What did he say?"

"I didn't give him the chance to say it," Trammel admitted. "I might've killed him if he had. I didn't want to spend our wedding night in jail."

"But you hit him."

"Choked him." Trammel shrugged. "There's a difference."

"Not the way you do it." She sighed. "I've seen how you are when you get that angry. Did you hurt him?"

"Only his pride," Trammel said. "And his backside. I sent him on his way with a stiff kick to the pants for his trouble."

Emily seemed surprised by that. "I'm glad. Marriage has had a positive effect on you, even though it was only a few minutes old."

Trammel knew she meant it as a joke, but the memory of Caleb's words still bothered him. "I won't let anyone threaten you, Em. Ever."

She propped herself up on an elbow and gently turned his face to her. Even in the scant light that filtered into their room through the curtains, she was beautiful. "But you can't allow men to use me as a weapon against you, Steve. Caleb's not the first one who's threatened to come after me and he won't be the last. Don't let them use me to rile you up into doing something stupid. Something we'll both regret. You can't break the very laws you're paid to enforce. I know you won't let anything happen to me. I know it in my heart. I just need you to know it, too."

Trammel knew she would always be his weakness—the only way men could get to him. And while he did not mind her owning a piece of him, he knew he could never trust himself to think clearly where her well-being was in question.

But that night was not the night for such thoughts. That night belonged to them.

"How'd I get so lucky to marry a woman so smart?"

"A lack of options on my part." She laughed, then buried her face in his neck to the delight of both of them.

Chapter 14

Trammel had been glad to leave Blackstone with as little fanfare as he had received on his first day in town. He had asked that no big crowd gather to see them off. No bunting or speeches. He and Emily were just another couple boarding the morning train to Laramie.

As he sat behind his desk in his office at city hall, Trammel remembered that day.

Hawkeye said he preferred to stay in the jail out of fear he might grow too emotional. Trammel understood how he felt. They said their goodbyes at the jail, which was only fitting as that was where their partnership—and friendship—had started.

Adam Hagen was the only one who came to the station to see them off. He gave Emily a warm embrace before helping her board the train, leaving only he and Trammel alone on the platform. "This isn't the end," Adam told him. "Just the end of the beginning."

"It's time. It's just time."

"I know." Adam held out his hand. "I owe you everything,

Steve. I'll always be there for you, no matter what the future holds for either of us."

Trammel wanted nothing more than to believe that but knew better. Adam Hagen had crossed too many lines too many times over the years to think he would ever be anything more than a gambler—a man who lived life as if it were a card game, only he played with lives instead of poker chips. He poisoned men's souls with his opium and corrupted officials with his money.

Trammel supposed Adam had corrupted him, too, if only a little. He knew Hagen would go too far one day and that day might come sooner than he thought. Perhaps at the hands of his family. Perhaps in another way. Trammel was glad he would not be around to see it. He only hoped he would not be forced to play a hand in Hagen's dangerous game.

"It's been interesting," Trammel said as he shook Adam's hand. "You know where to find me." With that, they parted ways as Trammel boarded the train for his new life with his new bride in the City of Laramie.

Moran had hung around for the week since Trammel had arrived in town, showing him all the different duties that went along with his office. Hagen had been right about one thing. There was more to being a sheriff of a place like Laramie than Trammel had previously thought.

As the territorial capital, it served as the focal point for the entire territory. The U.S. marshal's office used the jail to house prisoners awaiting trial. It was also the county seat, which meant prisoners from the surrounding towns were brought there for trial and execution. The gallows in the courtyard behind the town hall had seen plenty of use in Trammel's first week in office. He hoped he would get used to the sound of the trap door opening as men dropped to their deaths at the end of a rope.

But the paperwork involved with being sheriff was more troubling than the haunting sound of the gallows. Everything had to be written down and filed away for prosecutors to use in court. County prosecutors. City prosecutors. Federal prosecutors. Murderers and thieves and rapists and drunkards all faced varying degrees of justice within these walls. And each of them had a file. Trammel was surprised to discover even records of how many records stored in the basement were kept.

And the idea of being accountable for the budget of the sheriff's department was enough to make him break out into a cold sweat. Math and numbers had never been friends of his. He found himself waiting for the inevitable panic to settle in. That feeling of being overwhelmed by the hundreds of details his new position required of him.

But a week into his duties, he had not felt the least bit worried. He saw each new requirement as a challenge to be overcome, even the budget. He could almost feel his mind becoming sharper as he took it all in.

In fact, he had never felt more alive. He was beginning to believe he might actually be good at it, too.

He looked up from a report from the night shift when he heard a knock at the door.

"Looks like you've settled in nicely." Marshal Moran pointed to the legs of his desk. "With some obvious adjustments, of course."

Trammel had almost forgotten about the old law books he had used to make the desk tall enough for his legs to fit beneath it. "It's only temporary. The mayor said he's having a carpenter come in this week and build one for me from scratch. Trouble is, they'll have to build it in here."

"A big man for a big job." Moran smiled. "That's what they're saying about you, anyway." He tossed his thumb over his shoulder. "I'm about to start my first tour of the territory. Want to come down and see me off?"

Trammel had heard that tone in his friend's voice before and knew what it meant. "Sounds like you've got something on your mind."

"Just something I heard that you might find interesting. Come on. We'll talk on the way down."

Trammel was glad to have a good excuse to leave the paperwork behind for a bit and give his eyes a rest. The two men walked down the stairs together.

"There's been a new wrinkle in the Hagen case," Moran told him. "Seems the family's gotten someone who's willing to come forward to swear Adam forged his father's signature on the will."

Trammel had enjoyed being away from Adam Hagen and his troubles in Blackstone, even if it had only been a week, but he should have known better than to think he could leave them behind forever. "Sounds like a bunch of bull to me."

Moran cocked an eyebrow. "You don't think Adam's capable of it?"

"I know he is," Trammel said. "He's just not stupid enough to let someone see him do it. Or be able to prove it, anyway."

"Well, this character claims he was part of the whole thing from start to finish. Claims old Montague ordered him to draw up the will. Don't know if there's any truth to it, but that's for the judge to decide."

Trammel remembered seeing the latest copy of the will.

"It was dated the week Charles died. I found it in Montague's office right after he shot himself. The document I saw was all stamped and legal."

"That's why I'm telling you about it now," Moran said as they reached the first floor. "I figure there's a good chance they'll call you as a witness for one side or another and wanted you to be aware of it as soon as possible. The trial's also going to draw a lot of attention, so you'll want to think about hiring on some extra deputies to handle the crowd."

Trammel had already considered it. "Thanks for the advice."

"I've heard the Hagen family has doubled the number of guns they've hired. And Adam's hired on more constables to match them. Whatever the outcome, it won't end pretty after the judge bangs his gavel."

Trammel had already known about the new men flocking to Blackstone. Hawkeye had sent him regular reports for the past week. "Thanks for the warning, Rob. I'll make sure we're ready for whatever comes next."

Together, the two men walked out onto the boardwalk in front of city hall.

"What about you?" Trammel asked Moran. "It's been a long time since you've hit the trail on your own. Hope you're up to it."

"Don't worry about me," Moran said. "I come from a long line of saddle tramps. I've got trail dust in my blood. Just because I've parked myself behind a desk for the last few years doesn't mean I'm a tenderfoot."

From the roof of the spectacle store next to the Hotel Lansdowne, Major John Stanton adjusted the sights of his

Sharps rifle. The fifty-caliber round packed enough punch to drop a buffalo with a single shot. It would obliterate whatever it struck on a human body, especially from this distance and in his hands.

The lawman's fate was already sealed. It was the manner of his death that would echo long after the man was planted in the ground. Witnesses to the gory sight would talk about it for generations to come, which Stanton supposed was Lucien Clay's desire. Stanton was not sure what this man had done to draw such hatred, but questions like *why* had never concerned him before.

Stanton was being paid good money to kill him and he intended on earning every penny of it.

He had spent the better part of the past week in Clay's saloon, sitting by the window and watching the way people moved in and out of city hall. He had tracked his target on foot, opting for different hats each time he ventured out so as not to be easily spotted by the wary lawman. Forced to spend a fair amount of time ducking into doorways and alleys as countless people stopped his target to shake his hand and wish him well in his new role, Stanton could tell affability did not come easily to him, but he had tolerated the civilians well enough.

None of them imagined they were shaking hands with a dead man. But in a few moments, they would know. And they would spend the rest of their lives telling everyone who would listen about how they had been the last man who'd shaken the great hero's hand.

It was a bright morning without a cloud in the sky and no wind to speak of. Stanton brought the rifle flush with his shoulder and fixed his target in his sights. He took careful aim on the two men as they walked out of city hall and separated just enough to give him a clear shot.

His appointment with destiny was at hand.

Stanton settled his sights across his target's shoulders and squeezed the trigger.

Trammel saw a flash from across the street just as Moran's head exploded in a red cloud of dust. The echo of a rifle shot filled the street. Wooden splinters dug into Trammel's skin as he landed on his back in the doorway of city hall.

He pulled his Peacemaker from the holster beneath his left arm and fired up at the spot of the muzzle flash. His bullet struck the ornate roof façade of the spectacles shop diagonally across the thoroughfare from city hall. He had seen something move away from the roof's edge as his bullet smashed through the plaster. It might have been a bird, but it was not. It was a man who knew he had been spotted. A man who was probably already making his escape.

Trammel looked at Moran's body as he got to his feet, ignoring the screams of pedestrians and horses rising from the panic. Nothing was left of his friend's skull and he knew Moran was dead.

Deputy Blake rushed to Trammel's side, a Winchester in hand. Welch and Root were also there with rifles of their own.

"Get over to the spectacles store," he ordered them. "I want that place surrounded. The shooter was on the roof."

Blake and the other men ran into the fray of confusion on Main Street without question. Realizing nothing could be done for Moran, Trammel ran after them. The street was a knot of wagons and horses and cursing riders trying to bring their animals under control among the chaos.

Trammel managed to duck beneath the jabbing hooves of a frightened bay as he made his way to the store from where a sharpshooter had killed his friend. He saw no sign of his deputies, and hoped they had crossed faster than he had. He pushed his way past civilians blocking the boardwalk and cut through them as he ran to the store. He knocked aside men and women alike but could not worry about such things. Moran's killer was still at the store. He had to get him before he got away.

The front door of the spectacles store was open, and he heard Blake yelling questions at the clerk inside. Trammel ducked down the alley and ran to the back of the store. A man on a black horse was already racing away, his head ducked low across the animal's neck. Deputy Root on the other side of the store opened fire on the fleeing man.

Trammel took aim with his Peacemaker and emptied the pistol in the fleeing man's direction. He could not tell if any of the bullets had struck the killer, but neither horse nor rider had not broken their stride.

"Did you get him?" Trammel called out to Root.

"Can't say," his deputy yelled back. "Don't worry. Welch is after him."

Trammel saw Deputy Welch atop a dappled gray break into the street behind the shops, digging his heels hard into his horse's flanks as he chased the assassin. Three more deputies fell in behind him and joined the pursuit of the killer.

Trammel ran to Root's side and asked, "They ours?"

"Brillheart, Bush, and Hartnett," Root told him. "Along with Welch, that boy's got a mean bunch on his heels. I wouldn't give much for his chances. They'll have him in hand soon enough. Just don't expect him to stand for no trial. Those boys won't be likely to miss when they shoot at him."

Trammel felt like a fool watching other men do his work. "Root, get me a horse. I'm going after them."

"Root," Blake called out as he stepped through the back door of the spectacle store. "We need you over at the city hall. Put something over Moran's corpse and keep the people back from him until Doc Carson shows up."

Confused by two orders he had received at once, Root looked at Trammel.

The sheriff motioned for him to go. "Blake's right. I'll find my own horse somewhere."

As Root ran down the alley and back to city hall, Trammel asked Blake, "Where can I get a horse? I need to go after them."

"No, you don't," Blake told him. "Your days of riding into the teeth of a problem are over, Sheriff. You're needed here to keep order and stop people from getting hurt in a panic. Let Johnny and the others go after him. Your place is right here in town running things."

Every part of Trammel told him to get a horse and join the chase, but he knew Blake was right. Laramie was not Blackstone, and it was not just him and Hawkeye against the world anymore.

He had men running the gunman to ground. Men who were good at what they did. They were doing their job. It was time for him to do his. He gestured for Blake to follow him back to city hall. "Let's get back there and hold back the crowd. I don't want us to have a riot on our hands."

Chapter 15

Trammel did not think his office was big enough to hold so many people. He was seated behind his desk, watching Doctor Hal Carson hold his balding head in his hands. His leather apron was smeared and filthy.

Mayor Walter Holm sat on the other side of Trammel's desk and, next to him, was Charles Haffey, head of the city council. Howard Williamson and about half a dozen other men from Laramie Businessman's Association filled the rest of the office, standing wherever there was space. Only Mrs. Smith, the head of the Ladies League of Laramie had been forbidden from attending. Mayor Holm said the details of Doc Carson's report were too gruesome for her feminine sensibilities.

All of them had filed into Trammel's office after the doctor informed them he was ready to announce his initial findings in the cause of Marshal Rob Moran's death. They all waited silently while the doctor struggled to find his voice.

No one in the office seemed to have the heart to urge him to hurry.

Doc Carson raised his head slowly only to sink lower

in his seat. "I was a field doctor in the war, gentlemen. I was at Shiloh and Gettysburg. I've seen what can happen to men in war. I've seen what a cannonball can do to a human body. But I've never seen anything like this. Maybe the subject of the examination had something to do with that."

Trammel heard something gurgle in the doctor's stomach or throat. He looked away to allow him his dignity. The other men in the room did the same.

Doc Carson cleared his throat. "Forgive me, but Rob Moran was my best friend. Stood as godfather to three of my children. Even named my oldest boy after him. This isn't easy for me to say. It was even tougher for me to see him like that."

"Take your time, Hal," Mayor Holm said. "Take all the time you need. Want something to help steady you?"

The doctor shook his head. "That would only make me feel worse." He cleared his throat again and drew in a deep breath. "Rob Moran was struck just above the neck with a fifty-caliber round at less than one hundred yards away. My guess is the assassin used a Sharps rifle. It's a common enough weapon to find in these parts and consistent with the amount of damage it caused."

One of the men in the room cursed quietly. Trammel figured most of them were familiar with the weapon and knew what it could do. If they did not know before how Moran had been shot, they certainly knew now.

"A bullet that powerful fired at such a close distance was lethal on impact. He could've scarcely done more damage if he had pressed the muzzle against poor Rob's head when he squeezed the trigger. The only blessing in all of this is that Rob never knew what hit him. He was most assuredly dead before his body began to fall to the ground." The doctor looked around the room at the men listening to him. "There are medical reasons I can offer to explain why, but all of you saw his body, so I'd appreciate it if you would allow me to avoid saying them now."

Mayor Holm held up a hand. "You can include them in your report when you're ready, Hal. You've had it tougher today than any of us here."

The doctor slowly shook his head and sat in his chair, unable to move.

Doc Carson's role was done, and Trammel knew those men would be looking to him for answers.

Mayor Holm did not disappoint. "Well, Sheriff Trammel, what do you have to say about all of this? How could a man many people in this town consider to be a hero be cut down in broad daylight with you standing right next to him?"

It was the same question Trammel had been asking himself since it happened.

He shared with them the same answers he had found on his own. "A man shot Rob from the roof of the spectacle store across the thoroughfare. I shot back and narrowly missed hitting the assassin as he ducked away. The street was a mess of horses and wagons and people. In spite of that, my deputies and I got to the store as quickly as we could and saw the shooter riding away on a black horse. Me and Deputy Root fired at him. Deputy Welch and three other deputies took off after the man on horseback. Root looked around the area for signs of blood after things calmed down a bit on Main Street."

"And?" Mayor Holm prodded.

"And they haven't come back yet, so I don't have anything more to report. As soon as I do, I'll be sure to tell you."

"You mean that's all of it?" the mayor asked as he rose

from his seat. "A brave man killed in front of the whole town and all you have to say for yourself is that you allowed him to get away? That you *almost* shot him? Is that supposed to be some sort of consolation or is that your way of shirking some of the blame?"

Howard Williamson of the Businessman's Association spoke before Trammel could. "Simmer down, Walter. Buck's not shirking anything. A Peacemaker's not much good at that distance, so it's a miracle he got close to him at all."

"Miracle?" Holm turned on him. "How dare you speak of miracles on such a dark day as this."

"Rob Moran was my friend, too, Mayor," Trammel told him. "I would've gladly traded places with him if I could, but I can't."

"Don't talk like that," Doc Carson surprised everyone. "Even if you'd been standing right in front of him, we'd have two dead men on our hands instead of one. All this bickering is accomplishing nothing. Only one man is to blame for what happened and he got away. Blaming anyone else, especially Buck, won't do anyone any good."

Trammel knew something he could do and decided it was time he got to it. "Blake!"

The deputy came to the doorway. "Yes, boss."

"How's the situation outside?"

"Almost as if nothing happened. We've got the usual critters who come out to look at a thing like this, but the boys did a good job of covering with canvas where Rob fell so no one can see anything."

"Good. Any sign of Welch or the others yet?"

"No. I'll let you know when they come back."

"They've been gone an awfully long time," Mayor Holm said. "Shouldn't they have been back by now?"

"Hunting a man takes as long as it takes, Mr. Mayor,"

Blake told him. "Ain't no rules when it comes to running down a man. I expect they'll be back soon enough." He looked at Trammel. "What do you need me to do?"

Trammel liked his deputy's spirit. "Take three men, find Lucien Clay, and place him under arrest for murder. Lock him in a cell downstairs and let me know when it's done."

Trammel's office went into an uproar as Blake went to carry out his orders. Moran had warned him Clay had friends in high places in town. He was seeing exactly how many for himself.

Mayor Holm's voice rose louder than the others. "Have you lost your mind, Trammel? Clay has barely been able to get out of bed for months after the drubbing you gave him. You said yourself the killer escaped on horseback. What could Lucien possibly have to do with all of this?"

Trammel slowly got to his feet, intentionally using his impressive height and size to his advantage. He towered over every other man in the room and was as wide as any two of them standing together. "The fact that you just called Clay by his first name is part of it. That he's got a hand in just about every dirty deed in Laramie is the other. I know he's popular with a lot of you boys for a lot of reasons. That's none of my business unless you decide to make it my business. I don't think any of you want that, so leave it alone. Leave me alone and let me do my job my way."

None of the men met his glare, least of all Mayor Holm.

Trammel continued. "I don't think Clay pulled the trigger himself, but he's more than capable of having it done. Or knowing who did it and why."

Howard Williamson asked, "What possible reason would he have for wanting Rob killed? Especially since he was no longer the sheriff. He was responsible for the entire territory, not just Laramie."

"And that's exactly what I intend on asking him as soon as Blake hauls him in here. Now I want all of you to get out of my office and let me get to work finding Rob's killer." He pointed at Holm. "That goes for you, too, Mayor. I'll come find you as soon as I have something to tell."

Trammel ignored the grumbling and dirty looks of the civic leaders as they filed out of his office. He could sense a change in them. He had gone from the bright new sheriff in town to the possible scapegoat in the death of a local hero. Someone had to be the villain. And in the absence of the real one, Trammel would have to do.

When all the men had left, only Doc Carson remained.

Trammel was happy for the company. "I'm glad you knew I didn't mean you, Doc. You can stay as long as you want."

"It's not about how long I can stay, Buck." Carson looked at him with tired eyes. "It's about how long you can stay. Throwing them out of your office must've felt mighty good just now, but it didn't win you any favors. And going after Lucien Clay like you are will only make things worse. A lot of them are beholden to Clay for one reason or another, just like some of your people up in Blackstone are beholden to Adam Hagen. Clay put Mayor Holm and a lot of the others in the positions they now enjoy. Poking Clay will only make them dislike you even more. Now is the time you need friends, not enemies."

"I need answers more than I need friends," Trammel said. "I can always make friends later."

Chapter 16

Lucien Clay hurled the glass against the wall. It was the only outward expression of rage he allowed himself to feel since learning of Moran's death. He could not yell. He could not curse. He could not even hit someone to make himself feel better. He was too dizzy from his aching jaw and his frustration to do much of anything.

Why had Stanton changed the plan? Why hadn't he done exactly what I'd told him to do?

By changing the location of the shooting, Stanton had almost gotten himself captured. The spectacle store had been too close. His getaway, even in the knotted streets following the shooting, had been too risky.

Had he been seen? Had he been shot?

If he had only followed Clay's specific orders to shoot from the hotel, he could have gotten away clean. He might have even faded into the crowd before it gathered. He had dozens of rooms to hide where he could always make his escape later.

Now, the best Clay could hope for was that Stanton had been killed by the deputies who had pursued him and had died before he had a chance to tell them anything. Of course, that would make it difficult for Clay to recover any of the gold he had given him, but such was the price of doing business.

The news was not all bad, he supposed. Stanton had done what he had been hired to do. Marshal Rob Moran was dead, thus anchoring Buck Trammel to Laramie for the foreseeable future. He would be so bogged down in the investigation into Moran's murder he would not be able to aide Adam Hagen in Blackstone even if he wanted to. All had happened just as Bernard Wain had wanted. The Hagen family could deal with Adam as they wished, and Trammel would be too busy to stop them. And in the bargain, they had a new vacancy for U.S. marshal the Hagen family could fill with their own man once the trial against Adam was settled.

But Wain's plan only worked if Moran's murderer went free. Thanks to Stanton's changes and narrow escape, that was no longer a certainty.

With everything falling apart, Clay found himself wondering where Delilah had gone off to. She should be there when he needed her. He could never count on her for anything.

Clay perked up when he heard a great calamity come from the saloon. *Had Stanton come back already? Could he have been foolish enough to do something so blatant?*

Clay fumbled for the key to his desk, where he kept a .38 revolver in the top drawer. The pain in his jaw grew worse by the second, but he hoped the mere sight of the gun would be enough to deter whoever was causing the noise outside from harming him.

He had just gotten the key into the lock when his office door burst open, and Deputy Sherwood Blake walked in. His pistol was drawn, and he had two deputies behind him.

"Nice to see you again, Lucien." Blake smiled beneath his droopy mustache. "It's my pleasure to inform you that you're under arrest."

Clay let the keys to his desk fall to the carpet. He had nothing to fear from a crook like Blake. "For what?"

"For the murder of U.S. Marshal Rob Moran." He motioned to the two men with him. "Grab him up, boys."

Even if Clay was not already dizzy from pain, he would not have fought the deputies. He was outnumbered and unarmed. He was not in the practice of fighting losing battles. As the men placed shackles on his wrists, he showed Blake he was not entirely unarmed. "Isn't it fitting that Trammel sends the most corrupt deputy on the payroll to fetch me?" He spat in Blake's direction, but missed badly. "How many saloon owners and other such people pay you off every month anyway? I've lost count."

"So have I." Blake took Clay by the collar and steered him toward the doorway. "But you're not one of them, so there's no sense in talking about it, is there?" He shoved Clay into the open door.

Pain radiated from his jaw and he screamed.

"Careful, Lucien," Blake said. "Watch your step now. Wouldn't want you hurting yourself, now, would we?"

The dank darkness of the jail cell did little to calm the throbbing pain consuming the left side of Clay's face. What he would not give for a bottle of laudanum at that moment. Even a full glass of whiskey. Anything that might give him even a moment's relief.

Relief from the pain. Relief from the worry about why Trammel had decided to arrest him for a crime they both knew he had not committed.

Or did he? Had his spies been wrong? Had they really seen Stanton escape or had that been someone else? Or had the deputies caught up with him on the trail and questioned him before he died? Clay knew if they had caught him, Stanton most certainly must be dead. He might have been insolent enough to disobey orders about the shooting, but Clay doubted any of Trammel's deputies could find a way to make him talk. Stanton was the kind of man who would hold on to something tightly if he knew you wanted it. He would use his spite to sustain him in his final moments before he allowed death to take him.

No, Clay assured himself, Trammel had nothing except suspicions and a lot of questions for which he had no answers. Questions from Clay's good friends like Mayor Holm and Howard Williamson. Men who owed him everything and had done him the favor of moving Buck Trammel from Blackstone to Laramie.

Lucien Clay heard the main cell door open at the end of the aisle and moved his feet to the floor. He had spent enough of his life in those cells to know every sound of the place. Every iron door had its own song, which was why he was not surprised to see Trammel looming outside his cell.

He was an impossibly big man, Clay decided. Big and tough and much smarter than he had any right to be. If God had cursed Clay by placing such a large obstacle in his way, why did He have to give him a smart one? Why not a big, corruptible oaf with no sense of honor, or at least no intention of acting on it? But Lucien Clay had not been that lucky and found his curse waiting for him. His jailer and nemesis.

Trammel worked the key in the lock and allowed the cell door to swing open. He made no effort to block the prisoner from leaving, though Clay imagined his own regret if Trammel tried.

Clay smiled at the empty holster rig under Trammel's left arm. "Is that for your benefit or for mine?"

Trammel ignored the question. "Your cell door is open, Clay, but this is as close as you'll ever get to freedom unless you give me some answers."

"A guessing game to pass the time? Good. I love games. Should you start or should I?"

"You can start by telling me why you ordered Rob Moran killed."

"Who said I did?"

"I'm saying it because it's true," Trammel said. "There's no sense in denying it because you're going to tell me one way or the other."

"I know this game. Heads I'm guilty and tails I'm guilty. Is this justice under the Trammel administration?"

Trammel snatched Clay by the shirt front and yanked him off the cot. The tips of Clay's feet did not reach the jail floor. The pain shooting through his body was replaced by terror of what the big man might do to him. He felt like a rag doll in his grip.

"Rob Moran was my friend," Trammel seethed. "I'd sooner put a bullet in your belly and make you beg to talk before I waste any more time on you, but I'm not going to do that. Rob wouldn't want that. So, I'm going to do something better." He tossed Clay down onto the cot.

Clay had to grab on to the bars lest he bounce onto the floor.

"I'm going to hold you for the next hour or so. I'll have my men spread the word you're not only part of Moran's murder, you know who did it. I'll tell them you won't speak until your lawyer is present."

It had been a long time since Clay had known such fear, genuine fear. "You can't do that! They'll lynch me."

"It's already being done," Trammel told him. "And once everyone in town has heard it, I'm going to open this door and set you free. Given the size of the crowd outside the jail right now, I'd say you've got a fifty-fifty chance of making it back to your saloon alive. But I wouldn't give a plug nickel for your chances of lasting through the night."

Trammel pushed him harder against the bars. "Rob Moran had a lot of friends in town besides me. You're going to meet every one of them before the sun comes up tomorrow."

Trammel released him and let him drop to his cot.

The pain returned to Clay's jaw as he sat upright. "You can't do that to me, Trammel. You don't have any proof. That's as good as a death sentence."

"That's your problem," Trammel said. "Me and my boys will do our best to get to you before the mob, of course, but you know how crowded Main Street can get. There's just no telling how long it'll take us to get from this side to the other." The sheriff cocked his head. "I'll bet you already had that figured out when you paid to have Moran killed. You were counting on all that chaos and confusion to buy your boy just enough time to ride away, weren't you?"

Clay knew Trammel was bluffing. Not about letting him loose into the arms of the mob. He had no doubt the sheriff was capable of that. But he was bluffing about having proof Clay was behind the murder. If Trammel had proof, he'd be waving it in the vice owner's face.

Now that his initial fear had settled, Clay regained his footing. It was time to turn the situation to his advantage. "Moran was sheriff here for years. He had arrested me and shut down my saloons dozens of times. Why would I want him dead now that I was finally rid of him? Revenge?" Clay shook his head, ignoring the spike of pain from his jaw. "Revenge is for suckers, Trammel. It's bad for business. It causes hotheads like you to haul me in here and let my employees and customers rob me blind. I don't even want to think about how much those lousy cheaters at my saloons are giving away right now while I'm sitting in here with you."

"You've got an angle," Trammel said. "Your type always does."

"I certainly do," Clay agreed, "when it makes me money. Which brings me back to my original question. Why would I want Moran dead now when I was finally clear of him? I hadn't so much as spat in his direction all the time he was sheriff. Look at it from my seat. Say I did hire someone to shoot him. What if they missed? What if they got caught? You think I want a U.S. marshal as my enemy, especially Rob Moran?"

Trammel continued to glower down at him. Clay could tell none of his arguments were making a dent. It was like chipping away at a mountain with a dull spoon.

"The only way you're going to save your life," Trammel said, "is to tell me why you did it. Do that and I'll give you a break. Keep lying to me and take your chances out there."

Clay was beginning to lose patience and became desperate. "Do you know how long Moran was a lawman, Trammel? A decade or more. Don't you think he managed to drum up his fair share of enemies all on his own? Must've been a couple dozen men who had a better reason to kill him than I ever did."

"And you'd know who they were," Trammel said. "Same rules apply, though I don't think it was some outlaw who wanted him dead. Moran was about to hit the trail. They could've taken him down as soon as he cleared town, and no one would've known what happened for days. Someone wanted him dead in town. They wanted to know it had been done and they paid you to make sure it was public. I want names. And not just any names. I want the shooter and I want the names of the people who hired you to have it done."

Clay found the strength to remain quiet. "Why don't you hold your water until you find the man who shot him? From what I hear, your deputies were right on his tail. In fact, I'm surprised they haven't brought him in already."

"Who says they haven't?"

Clay laughed. "Your face says it all, Trammel. Now I know why you don't play cards. If you had the killer, he'd be in here right now instead of me. You've got nothing except another dead body on your hands if you turn me loose. I'd just bet the mayor and the rest of the boys don't know you grabbed me, or if they did, they weren't happy about it. If I turn up dead because of something you did, think about what that'll do to your reputation. A local hero murdered in front of you in the morning and a lynching at night." Clay slowly shook his head. "They wouldn't even take you back in Blackstone to muck out the livery stalls, much less let you have your old job again."

Trammel grew very still, and Clay grew worried. Trammel would have made a lousy card player because he had never been good at hiding his emotions. He would tip his hand good or bad.

Just then, he appeared to figure out he was holding a royal flush. "This has something to do with the Hagen family, doesn't it? They're the ones who wanted you to kill Moran, aren't they? Why?"

Clay cursed himself. He had said too much and now the

big oaf was putting it all together. "I don't know what you're talking about. Why don't you go ask them?"

"Because I'm asking you." It was clear the more Trammel thought about it, the more it made sense to him. "They wanted Moran to die publicly. Why? To disgrace me?" A new idea seemed to come to him. "Or to keep me wrapped up here so I couldn't help Adam in Blackstone. Is that it?"

"For a dullard," Clay said, "you have quite an imagination. Why would that family hire me to do anything for them when they could hire it done themselves?"

"Because being able to pay for it and finding the right man for the job are two different things. That's where you come in. You were the middleman, weren't you?"

Clay was glad Trammel could not see the sweat that broke out along his back. "Why would I even want to do that? I make plenty of money from whiskey and games and women. More than I can spend sometimes, which isn't the happy predicament a man like you might believe it is. Why would they come to me when they could hire a Pinkerton to get it done properly?" Clay thought of something that would really push the sheriff over the edge. "You used to be a Pinkerton. Maybe they got you to do it and you're just trying to make me the scapegoat?"

Trammel started for him when Blake ran down the aisle and grabbed him. "Wait, boss. Brillheart and the others are back, and they have news. You're going to need to hear this."

Trammel reluctantly backed out and slammed the cell door shut. He turned the key in the lock and took it with him as he followed his deputy back down the hall.

Clay went to the bars and called after him, "I hope it's good news, Sheriff."

He hoped the big man could hear his laughter echo through the cells.

Chapter 17

Blake led Trammel to where the deputies were sitting on haystacks in the livery behind city hall. He was glad to see all four of them had returned.

He was not happy to see they were all cut up and bleeding. Turning to Blake, he asked, "Did you send for a doctor?"

Blake told him no. "They wanted to talk to you first. Said their cuts could wait."

Stepping closer to the men, it became obvious the deputies had chosen Deputy James Brillheart to tell their story.

"That feller couldn't just shoot, but he could ride like the wind. His mount was nothin' special, mind, but he got more out of that horse than any man could. We were on him from the beginning, but he put so much distance between us it was like he was riding a thoroughbred."

"What direction?" Trammel asked.

"North along the road to Blackstone," Brillheart told him. "Must've known the land pretty good, too, because he dodged every divot and puddle on the road. If I had to guess, I'd say he'd ridden that way before."

Damn, Trammel thought. Everything about Moran's death led back to Blackstone. Literally as well as figuratively. "Go on."

"We never got a good look at anything except his back," Brillheart explained, "but we did our best to keep up. You know that spot in the road where it bends sharply to the left? In the swamp?"

Trammel knew it well. "I do."

"We slowed down there when he rode out of sight just in case he drew up around the corner and was waiting to ambush us. As soon as we rounded the corner, that's when it happened." Brillheart's voice caught, and he looked away.

Deputy Johnny Welch took up that part of the story. "A willow tree exploded, Buck. That's the only word I can use to describe it. Damnedest thing I ever saw. Pieces of wood and bark peppered us like we was in a hailstorm. Cut us all to hell. Big blade of bark caught one of our horses right in the throat. Killed her on the spot. All of our animals reared up and threw us. Took us forever to get them out of that swamp. And when we did, the top half of the willow was blocking the road, along with a few other trees for good measure. We finally pulled the last of the horses out of the mire, and the shooter was long gone."

Still trying to get used to the idea of a tree exploding, Trammel looked to Blake for an answer.

"Saw things like that during the war," Blake told him. "Find a hollowed-out tree, put a couple of sticks of dynamite in it, and light the fuse. Turns it into one hell of a bomb." He looked at the four dejected deputies. "I know losing a horse is no easy thing, boys, but you're lucky you all made it back alive."

None of the men seemed ready to agree with him.

Brillheart finally found his voice again. "We let the shooter get away, boss. We're sorry about that. It's bad for old Rob and even worse for you." The other three deputies looked just as ashamed as Brillheart sounded.

"Knock it off," Trammel told them. "You're alive and that's more important to me than getting the shooter. That road's awfully narrow until it gets to Blackstone, so there's only one place he could've gone. I'll send a wire up there and have Hawkeye watch for strangers."

Welch said, "I already did that before we came here. Didn't want to lose any more time than we already had."

Trammel had known Moran trained his men well, but he had not expected them to be so efficient. "That was good thinking, Welch. Thanks for doing that."

Welch looked up at him with an anger Trammel knew was not directed at him. "You can thank me when we kill the man who got Rob."

"There'll be time for that, don't worry. You boys just let Doc Carson look at those cuts and bruises for you. I want you to do everything he tells you and that's an order. In the meantime, I'll send a telegram to Adam Hagen, too. Tell him to have those constables of his pay special attention to any new faces in town. Especially anyone toting a Sharps rifle."

Brillheart's mouth opened. "That the gun he used on Rob?"

Trammel nodded silently.

The men looked even more dejected. They all knew what a weapon like that could do when fired at such a close distance.

Trammel pulled Blake away from the others. "While I go send that telegram, I want you to stay here with the boys. Make sure they do what the doc tells them. Even if they need a couple of days off, they're to take it. I don't want them getting sick from any infections in those cuts. Understand?"

"I do," Blake said. "What about Clay?"

"He stays in a cell for now," Trammel said. "And under absolutely no circumstances are you to spread word about his involvement in Rob's murder to the townspeople. I absolutely forbid it. Might put Clay in a bad way if you did. Do you understand me, Deputy?"

Blake grinned behind his droopy mustache. "Sure would be a shame if people got the notion he might be involved in this somehow."

"It would be an awful shame," Trammel went on. "Especially for poor Mr. Clay."

"And we wouldn't want that, now, would we?" Blake shook his head. "I'm beginning to get awfully fond of you, Buck."

Trammel patted him on the back. "Then you're in awfully bad company. If the mayor or the others press you for answers, tell them I'll be back in a bit. They can wait. These men need tending to." He went off to find Doc Carson, then send his telegram to Hagen, hoping Hawkeye was ready to face his first real challenge as sheriff of Blackstone.

As it stood, he had a crafty killer riding straight for him.

Hawkeye made sure the Winchester and the coach gun were loaded and tucked safely into his saddle before he climbed up and took a ride out to Laramie Road. The telegram from the sheriff's office worried him.

DANGEROUS KILLER ON BLACK HORSE
RIDING YOUR WAY. BE CAREFUL.

Hawkeye had questions. Why hadn't Buck sent the telegram himself? Was he hurt? What had happened down there? Who was dead?

The telegram had not said much, but it had told him enough. Any man on a black horse would be getting extra attention from him. He thought about sharing the information with Hagen's constables, but decided against it. He'd had his share of run-ins with them before and Trammel was barely gone a week. Hawkeye did not want them thinking he would run to them every time he got a telegram.

Besides, he had gone up against plenty of hardcases before. This man on a black horse would not be his first.

Hawkeye rode over to Laramie Road and looked at the ground for signs of recent riders. As usual, the road was a mess of wagon wheel trenches and hoofprints beaten into the mud in each direction. Fresh droppings had been mingled with old, making it impossible to tell when the last rider had been there, much less what direction he might have been traveling once he reached town.

Hawkeye decided he might have a clearer picture a bit farther down the road and urged his mount in that direction. He was not sure what he was looking for but hoped he would know it when he saw it.

About a half a mile down the old trail he felt a peculiar feeling. Like he was being watched from somewhere deep within the tall reeds on the eastern side of the road. It did not feel like a bird or a mountain lion or even a bear looking at him. Something more sinister. Something human. A casual look around did not reveal anyone, but he knew someone was there.

He climbed down from the saddle and took hold of the horse's reins as he looked into the starkness of the western side of the swamp. Keeping the animal between him and whomever was looking at him from the swamp, he listened, hoping his ears could tell him what his eyes could not. He listened for anything that might tell him about the man hunting him. A snap of a reed or the sound of a boot in the mud. A horse fussing. Was he coming closer or content to remain perfectly still? Was he thumbing back a hammer, or had he already done that when he heard Hawkeye coming down the road?

Whoever he was, Hawkeye could tell he knew what he was doing. The wetlands off Laramie Road were no paradise. A man and his horse could easily get mired in the cloying muck of the swamp. And if the mud did not get you, the snakes might.

Which was why he listened especially hard for some clue of the man who had taken refuge out there. The swamp was as quiet as the grave.

It was never that quiet unless an intruder was out there. So, in its own way, the wetlands had told him something after all. And he knew what he had to do next.

He led his horse back up the road toward Blackstone. He had to get ready.

Stanton cursed his luck as he watched the young man walk his horse back toward town. He had hoped the fool would climb back into the saddle, giving him a clear shot. If he had been a normal traveler, Stanton would not have given him much notice, but this young man was clearly more than that. He had been trying to read the ground as he rode along the trail and had climbed down from his horse just as Stanton had decided to aim at him.

The young man had instincts. And while Stanton was confident the Sharps could easily punch through horse and rider from that distance, he did not want to risk another death unless he had to. Trammel's deputies had gotten awfully close to him earlier. Killing another man would only bring more attention his way. He wanted to be remembered, but in order to be remembered, he had to leave someone alive.

Perhaps the young man would serve a better purpose alive than dead.

Stanton sat low among the reeds as he watched the stranger walk his horse back to Blackstone and knew he would be seeing him again soon. In fact, he was counting on it.

Stanton tucked his Sharps back into the saddle scabbard and remained sitting on a rock in the marsh as he waited for the sun to sink a little lower in the sky. He was glad he had ridden the trail several times in the past week as he'd studied Moran's movements. He had studied the terrain, too. He could not have placed that hollowed out willow tree in a better position had he planned it. The rotted wood had made for excellent shrapnel.

He wondered how many deputies he had killed with the blast. He hoped all of them. Losing five lawmen in one day would be a horrible setback for a man in Trammel's position, which would only make Mr. Clay even happier.

Stanton was not afraid of Clay, only of what he might say about him after their business was done. A man like Stanton lived on his reputation and his reputation was only as good as his last job. Taking the Laramie position was risky. Moran was a federal marshal now, albeit a newly minted one. Stanton had not heard anything of Trammel back in San Francisco, but he had heard plenty about the man since he had come to Wyoming.

From what he had seen of him, Trammel had earned his reputation. He was not as clumsy as most men his size tended to be. He was not a bully, either. The best word Stanton could use to describe him was *self-contained*. Trammel knew what he was and how people deferred to him. He did not abuse it or take it for granted. That made people like and respect him.

It also made some smart people fear him. Stanton would not go that far in his assessment of Trammel, though he appreciated what he could do. He knew he would have to face down Trammel eventually. It was only a matter of time. He would be ready for it whenever that time came.

Trammel was not perfect. He had a temper. And Stanton knew if he played the sheriff just right, he might be able to use that to his advantage.

After an hour had passed, Stanton took his horse by the reins and led it along the rocky path he had taken into the marsh. Once on firmer ground, he climbed into the saddle and continued riding toward Blackstone to finish the one final task remaining in his contract with Clay.

The mare had given Stanton all she had and more during his mad dash north from Laramie, which was why he allowed her to move at her own pace. She had been rested and fed in the hours since, but he had been a cavalry man long enough to know the horse was his life in the field. No sense in pushing her limits unless he had to.

He rode into a clearing and got his best look at the town of Blackstone. He had only viewed the town from afar through his field glasses. He had not ventured any closer for he had not wanted to risk being remembered.

Seeing a town from afar and riding through it were two different things. Stanton had not appreciated how close the mill was to the train station, though he saw it clear enough now. The cattle pens were empty but looked about half the size of those down in Laramie. Still big enough to bring a lot of Hagen beef to market. Which branch of the Hagen family that would be remained to be seen.

He loved the smell of fresh cut wood and it was not just from the mill, but from the houses workmen were building across Main Street along the railroad tracks. He figured those would be where the men who worked the mill would live. Blackstone was no longer a tiny town in the middle of nowhere. It was going places in a hurry and Stanton had always been attracted to such towns. Maybe he would come back once his business with Clay was concluded and see what he could make of himself.

He rode past the livery and blacksmith at the edge of town when he heard a familiar *click*. It was not a blacksmith striking an anvil, but the unmistakable sound of a hammer being thumbed back.

"You'd best stay right where you are if you know what's good for you."

Stanton grinned. The boy from the road had gotten the jump on him after all. It served him right for being so deep in thought.

He made no sudden moves. "I think you've gotten me mistaken for someone else, son."

"We'll see about that and I'm not your son. Turn that horse around real slow to face me."

Stanton guided the horse until he had turned around to face the voice. It was the young man from the road. He had a Winchester aimed at the center of Stanton's chest. The sun was behind him and his face was mostly in shadow from the livery roof. But Stanton could see the star pinned to the man's vest.

Seeing the young deputy's finger was nowhere near the trigger, Stanton knew he could draw and put the boy down before he realized he was dead but the gunman decided to try flattery before firearms. "You must be Jimmy Hauk, the sheriff of Blackstone."

Just a momentary silence, then, "You've heard of me?"

Stanton laid it on thick. "The whole territory's heard of you. Why, a man can hardly mention Trammel without your name coming up right after his. It's an honor to meet you, Sheriff. The boys back home won't believe me when I tell them."

"You call Laramie home?"

"No sir," Stanton said as affably as he could manage. "San Antonio, Texas. Train stopped in Laramie, though. Got off there last night and decided to ride up here this morning. Pretty country you've got. I'm glad I took my time riding through it." He hoped the flattery would be enough to make Hauk lower his rifle.

But Hauk didn't move a muscle. "Train comes up here, too. Why'd you ride instead?"

Stanton acted embarrassed. "Well, I know that, Sheriff, but you see, a man my age gets sort of set in his ways and it just so happens I fancy a young lady in Laramie. It's not exactly admirable, but a man can't live on bread alone. Her schedule didn't exactly jibe with the train's, so I've been left to ride my horse."

"What brings you to Blackstone?"

Stanton had an answer ready for that, too. "Business, though I'm not at liberty to say more than that. And I'm afraid I'm late for that appointment, so if you'll excuse me,

I'll be on my way." He began to slowly move the mare backward . . .

Until Hauk said, "I'll be having a look at those rifles you're toting."

Stanton drew his belly gun—a Colt—and aimed it at Hauk's head. He would have fired if the fast movement had not made the young sheriff flinch and lower his rifle.

"I've had just about enough polite conversation to suit me for one day, boy. Best drop that rifle before I put one through your head. Go on, now."

Hauk did not drop the rifle as much as he allowed it to fall from his hands. It was close enough for Stanton's needs. "Kick it away from you nice and slow."

Hauk complied and toed the Winchester a good ten feet away from him along the hard-packed dirt of the livery.

"Good boy. Now unbuckle your gun belt with your left hand and let it drop. And if you think an old graybeard like me isn't fast enough to plug you, remember who got the drop on who."

Again, Hauk did as he was told and kicked it over toward where the rifle had landed.

"You're good at following directions, Sheriff. I like that in a lawman. Most of them are just stupid enough to get themselves killed. You keep on doing what I say, and you'll be fine." He nodded toward the horse tied up to a roof post. "Climb up on that sorrel and ride out ahead of me. Don't do anything dumb, like signal your friends or call out for help. I'll plug you before you make more than a peep. And ignore those fancy constables while you're at it. We're just two friends taking a nice ride up to the Hagen ranch."

"The Hagens?" Hauk said as he sat in his saddle. "You're working for them."

"That's the appointment I told you I was late for," Stanton

lied. "Now, I know this town a lot better than you think I do, so let's stick to the edge out here and I'll leave you at Stone Gate. By then, I'll be up at the house and about my business and you can raise all manner of ruckus then."

Stanton watched the young man's smooth face grow scarlet as he brought his horse around to the side road that led up to the Hagen place. He could almost hear his mind turning like the wheels under that locomotive that had taken him from San Francisco, not Texas. As soon as Stanton let him go, he had no doubt Hauk would head straight for the telegraph office to let Trammel know the man they were looking for was working for the Hagen family.

Just as Lucien Clay had wanted the world to believe.

CHAPTER 18

After sending the telegram to Adam, Trammel took his time walking back to his office in city hall. For the past week, he could barely take a step without running into someone eager to shake his hand and wish him well in his new position, but an uneasiness had settled over the city. He wanted to get a feel for the town in the aftermath of Moran's death.

People clustered together on boardwalks were quick to look away as he passed. It was as if they were afraid they might be drawn into some kind of danger simply by looking at him. He had been expecting that. People tended to wish a sheriff well until they saw what being sheriff was all about.

It was not just about being seen and threatening force. It was a bloody, violent business most people liked to ignore as they went about their lives. It was why they hired sheriffs in the first place. Enforcing order often came at the cost of a human life, and they had seen just how bloody enforcing the law could be.

Trammel would mourn the loss of Rob Moran as much as any of them, perhaps more because he knew what the man had sacrificed. He knew who had been behind it, too. Lucien Clay. And before the sun set on another day, he would know why.

Trammel saw Deputy Blake running toward him from across the thoroughfare and knew something was wrong. Blake held up his hands like he was trying to ease a spooked horse.

"What happened?" Trammel asked him.

"First, I'm going to need you to promise you'll stay calm."

"I can't promise that until I know what it's about, so talk."

Blake let out a heavy breath. "The mayor cut Clay loose."

Trammel felt his temper spike. "He did what?"

"He got Judge Weatherly to sign the order releasing him on account of a lack of evidence," Blake said. "Technically, Clay's lawyer did it, but it was Mayor Holm who helped it happen and quick, too."

Trammel knew there was nothing he could do about it. "Weatherly's a federal judge. Murder's not a federal case."

"Weatherly and Holm are old friends," Blake explained. "They sprung him while I was watching Doc Carson patch up the boys like you told me." The deputy toed at the ground. "There's something else, too. Something I've got to tell you, but don't want to."

Trammel already had a pretty good idea what Blake was about to tell him. "Let me guess. He asked you to take my job."

Blake looked up at him. "How did you know?"

"I've been fired enough times to see it coming. What did you say?"

"I told him no and that the rest of the boys were with me," Blake said. "I told him what happened to Rob was nobody's fault except the man who killed him. Told him if he fired you, the rest of us would quit on the spot. And we will, too."

Normally, Trammel might have appreciated the gesture, but nothing was normal that day. "Thanks for the vote of confidence."

"Confidence has nothing to do with it," Blake said. "What's right is right. If it makes you feel any better, one of the men from the Businessman's Association heard him make me the offer and almost tore his head off. You've got them on your side too, boss."

"For now." Trammel sighed. "Give it a couple of days and I might not even have that." He decided holding on to his job should be the last thing on his mind. "Doc Carson fix up the boys?"

"He did and every one of them refused to go home. Said they were getting paid to do a job, not sit home. They're back in the hall now, waiting for orders."

Trammel knew he might not have much going for him, but at least he had the loyalty of his ten deputies. More than something, it was everything. "Let Brillheart and the others take a few hours to rest. Where's Clay now?"

"Holed up in the Rose of Tralee," Blake said. "I managed to tell a few people he had a hand in Rob's murder, but not as many as I'd have liked. Word will spread, though. That much I can promise you."

Now that the shock of Clay being free had passed, Trammel saw a way to use the event to his benefit. "I want two men posted outside his saloon at all times. I want them checking everyone who goes inside. Haul in any man with a Sharps or a big bore rifle for questioning. I want Clay to know just because he's not in jail, he's not free. If he kicks up a fuss, tell him it's for his own safety. There's a rumor going around town he paid to have Rob killed, isn't there?"

"There certainly is, thanks to us." Blake walked with him back to city hall. "Yes, sir. I have a feeling you and me are going to get along just fine."

Adam Hagen enjoyed a brandy as he watched over the town from his balcony at the Phoenix Hotel. It was just another day as far as Blackstone was concerned. He was sure word had already begun to spread about Rob Moran's murder, but it was little more than grist for the rumor mill in his town. Something to talk about over the dinner table or in the saloon over a glass of beer. A topic discussed over a game of cards while players decided to up the ante or fold.

Hagen new better. Upon receiving Trammel's telegram, he had ordered all his constables out on patrol. All thirty of them, even Big Ben, were fanned out across Blackstone looking for a rider with a Sharps rifle on his saddle.

Despite being out on his balcony, Adam was not concerned for his safety. Both Colts on his belt were loaded, as was the Winchester he kept behind him against the balcony doorway. He'd had men try to kill him before. He knew what precautions to take.

He was concerned about other things. He had found Trammel's telegraph troubling at best. Terrifying at worst.

Rob Moran had been *assassinated*. He did not think the word was too big for what had transpired in Laramie earlier that morning. Clues were sparse, but he had no doubt Lucien Clay was involved. He had either organized it or allowed it to happen. No one would dare attempt something so big without informing him about it first.

Adam knew his family must have been involved in it. Clay and the Hagen family were working together. That much was certain, and he cursed himself for not seeing it coming.

He had kept his siblings on their heels long enough. They were going on the offensive by bringing in an outside mediator to settle the contested will of King Charles Hagen. Since Adam did not trust his own telegraph office to keep such requests secret, he had sent letters far and wide for information about Judge Carlisle Littlejohn from Colorado. It would take time for his sources to write back to him. A week at the earliest. A month would be considered a speedy reply if any replies came at all.

His contacts were not foolish. They would sense the desperation in his request and take their time in responding. Continuing to make money off the Hagen empire, they could afford to sit back and wait until the dust settled to see which side ultimately won the family squabble.

He had no doubt Moran's death was part of the family's plan. Probably one of his in-laws. His relatives were not above murder to win control of the Hagen empire, but it would not be their first choice. Not even Debora was that ruthless. But one of his brothers-in-law might be that cunning. Neither Ambrose Forrester nor Bernard Wain had married into the family purely for love. After all, it was just as easy to fall in love with a rich woman as it was a poor one. Elena was a beauty, but her fortune had only made her more appealing to the Wain family of Philadelphia. Wain was also a lawyer, which only diminished him in Adam's eyes.

Moran's murder was a masterstroke. The Hagen family infighting would have been the talk of the territory as it moved its way through the court system. Now, every resource possible would be dedicated to finding the killer of a local hero. And Buck Trammel, often Adam's only ally, would be bogged down in the resulting efforts. He would be unable to come to Adam's aid, even if he were inclined to do so.

With his best friend out of the picture and his contacts cautious, Adam was all alone. Just as his family had wanted.

They had even taken the threat of violence off the table. They had brought gunmen to town to match his constables. When they had not proven to be enough, they hired more, forcing Adam to increase the size of his constabulary force. At a stalemate, it was clear each side was in a position to hire more men if needed. Another smart move on his family's part. A way to keep war at bay while the fight remained in the legal system. Bullets would do neither side any good there.

His family had proven to be colder and more calculating than he had thought. But they had made one mistake. They knew only the Adam of his youth. The youngster who was always at odds with their father. The rebel. The willful spirit. The black sheep of the family.

They did not know the Adam who had been forged in the fire of years spent in the wilderness of their father's affections—the man who had been forced to fend for himself. The man time and tribulation had made him.

Their cunning had dealt him a serious blow, but as in any fight, one had to expect to be hit. How one responded made the difference between victory and defeat.

Hagen set his mounting troubles aside when he noticed

young Sheriff Hauk riding along Main Street. Adam knew he could count on the young man if the time came. As for what help he could provide, well, that remained to be seen.

But Hagen saw something else. The sheriff was usually polite but ignored greetings from various townspeople he passed along Main Street. Usually he did his best to emulate Trammel by riding tall in the saddle and looking people in the eye, but he was riding with sagging shoulders and his head down.

Something had happened.

Hagen bolted from the balcony and raced downstairs, through the gaming room, and out the front door of his hotel.

Hawkeye had just finished tying his horse to the hitching rail and was about to walk into the jail when Hagen called out, "Sheriff Hauk. A moment, please."

But Hawkeye did not stop unlocking the jailhouse door. "Not now, Adam. I've had about enough of you and your family for one day."

Sometimes Adam hated being right. He followed him into the jail anyway. "Jimmy, please. What's wrong?"

"You want to know what's wrong?" he yelled as he put his Winchester in the rifle rack on the wall. "I'll tell you what's wrong. You and your whole family is what. You people fight over this town like a bunch of wolves over a carcass and don't care who gets hurt. You forget this place isn't just some property you own, Adam. People live here. They work here. The things you see in one of your ledgers might just be numbers to you, but they mean everything to us. And who pays for your fighting? We do. Men like me and Buck and Rob."

Adam saw more than anger in the younger man's eyes. He saw fear. "You'll get no argument from me, Jimmy.

I'm not here about that. Something happened to you. What is it?"

Hawkeye walked over to his desk too angry to sit down.

Adam knew whatever had happened must have been bad. "I hope you know better than to be ashamed of anything around me. God knows you've seen me at my lowest and I doubt whatever happened today could be that bad."

"I'd have preferred a bullet," Hawkeye yelled. "I let an old man get the jump on me, Adam. I had him dead to rights and he pulled on me anyway. And what did I do? I just stood there like a deer. I was too scared to move. I had my finger right near the trigger, but it wouldn't budge. I had a round racked and everything. All I had to do was move that finger less than half an inch and squeeze. But I let him take my guns and march me off like I was a prisoner."

Adam could feel the shame burning deep within his young friend, but he needed to know more. "Where did he take you?"

"He rode me out to Stone Gate at gunpoint, then just rode off toward your ranch house without a word. I didn't have anything on me but a knife, so he knew I couldn't do anything about it." Tears welled in Hawkeye's eyes. "If it had been a throwing knife, I would've buried it in his back when he turned away."

"It was the man Buck warned us about, wasn't it?" Adam asked. "The man on a black horse."

"Damned right it was." Hawkeye pawed at his eyes with his sleeve. "Long gray hair. Old guy, too. About fifty or more, I'd say. I should've taken him easy, but I let him back me down. It was his eyes. Cold, dead eyes. I . . . I . . ."

Adam looked down at the floor to allow Jimmy Hauk

time to compose himself. "You never saw eyes like that before, did you?"

Hawkeye's voice was thick when he said, "Never. And I don't ever want to see them again."

Adam understood every mangled emotion coursing through Hauk just then. "Do you think I'm a tough man, Jimmy?"

"You?" The sheriff's eyes were red. "Of course. You're the deadliest man I've ever seen, except maybe for Buck."

"No." Adam slowly shook his head. "I'm no tougher than you are. I've just had more practice at killing than you is all. Do you think I was born with a gun in my hand? Do you think I got good at killing men by shooting at targets? Son, I've been where you were more times than I can remember because when you're in our line of work, there's always someone faster and meaner than you are. This man got the drop on you because he's probably been killing men since before you were born. Men like that get old for a reason."

Hawkeye stiffened a bit. "He said something like that to me. Almost those very words."

"Because it's true. There's a reason why your finger didn't hit that trigger. Instinct. He would've killed you if you had. There's no honor in dying. I'd wager Rob Moran would agree with you if he could. You didn't just let the man pass. You didn't come running for me or the others to find out what to do. You saw what needed doing and had the guts to do it. You didn't drop your gun and run away. He disarmed you and kept you at a distance. That means he respected you. I know it doesn't feel like that right now but give it time to scab over. You'll see I'm right."

Hawkeye blinked away his tears. "If he'd killed me, at least I wouldn't have to go around feeling like this."

"If he'd killed you, all you'd be is *dead*," Adam told him. "Dead men aren't much good to anyone except grave-diggers and worms. This man made a mistake in letting you live and we're going to make him pay for it. You and me. Together."

Hawkeye's eyes were not as red and he was standing a little straighter. "You know this man, don't you?"

"Not based on the description," Adam admitted. "I can think of about a dozen or so men who sound like the man who let you go. The fact that he rode up toward the ranch house tells me something, though not what our friend probably thinks."

Hawkeye's brow furrowed. "Huh?"

"My family's ruthless," Adam explained, "but they're not stupid. This man let you live so you'd tell someone you saw him riding toward their house. I'd bet every cent I have he rode on past the house only to double back later. They wouldn't bring a man like that to their doorstep, but some-one wants us to think they did. Someone who paid him to kill Rob Moran."

Hawkeye went around the desk and slowly lowered himself into the chair. "When we figure out who did that, we'll find the man who killed him. The man who did this to me."

Adam smiled. "Yes, we will. And when we do, we'll make an example of him. You and me together like I said." He was glad Hawkeye was in better spirits than he had found him.

Doubt could cripple a lawman and the sheriff was no good to anyone in such condition.

As he turned to leave, Adam offered a final bit of advice. "No one else needs to know what happened to you today. Don't wire Buck about it, either. We'll tell him when we see him in person."

"What'll we do until then?"

"We'll do what I do best. Plot and execute." Adam threw him a wink as he opened the door. "Stay close, Jimmy. I'll be back soon."

Chapter 19

Lucien Clay could not take the shouts from the street any longer. It was bad enough Trammel had staked two men in front of his saloon for the past ten hours, searching anyone who tried coming into the place. When he had tried to run them off, the deputies were only too happy to remind him that they were in a public street and were searching every man for the Sharps rifle that had killed Rob Moran that morning.

It put Clay in a bad position. If he raised too much of a fuss, he would be blamed for not caring about finding Moran's killer.

As word spread that he had been questioned about his role in the murder, the town had begun to turn against him. An angry mob had formed outside the Rose of Tralee Saloon, calling for Clay to come out and answer questions. As night fell and people got off work, they had lined up in front of the saloon with lighted torches.

More deputies arrived to slow the number of people who came into the saloon, only they did it under the guise of protecting Clay from an angry mob.

Clay had no choice but to call in bouncers from his

other saloons to keep an eye on things inside and keep order. Two men had come in as common cow pokes only to try to kick in his office door and drag him out to the waiting crowd. Fortunately, his men stopped them and doled out sufficient beatings. It would be a month or more before either of them was fit to sit in the saddle again. Clay had even ordered his men to throw the two anarchists out to the mob to show them what happens to anyone with similar intentions. The crowd had gotten smaller after that, but the chants only grew louder.

By torchlight, "We want Clay. We want Clay," sounded particularly menacing.

With a sparse crowd in the saloon and nothing more to be accomplished in his office, Clay decided to go upstairs to his rooms. He hoped to stuff a couple of cotton balls into his ears to drown out the noise until the fools got tired and went home. Maybe his regular patrons would come back after the ruckus died down.

One of his men followed him upstairs to make sure no one was waiting for him along the way. The crowd had proven to be crafty enough to slip two of their number inside, so it stood to reason they could have done it again.

"Have you seen Delilah around?" Clay asked the bouncer. "I haven't seen her all day."

"Me neither, boss," said the bouncer as he waited for Clay to unlock his door. "I can go look for her if you want."

With already enough to worry about, he decided one of the other girls could tend to him if he needed it. "I want you here. She'll turn up eventually and, when she does, I'll tan her hide."

With the door unlocked, the bouncer insisted on going in first to check his rooms. He had no sooner stepped inside when Clay saw him go for his gun.

"Don't do it, son," a man said from somewhere inside. "I don't think Mr. Clay would appreciate your guts decorating his fine carpet."

Clay pushed past the bouncer and saw Major Stanton sitting in a parlor chair. A glass of Clay's best whiskey was on the table at his elbow. A Havana cigar smoldered in his left hand. His right hand aimed a Colt at the bouncer.

"It's all right, Elroy," Clay told the bouncer. "I was expecting him. Just make sure you don't tell anyone I have a visitor."

"Whatever you say, Mr. Clay." Elroy backed out of the room and pulled the door shut behind him.

Now that it was just the two of them, Clay asked Stanton, "How'd you get in here?"

"Climbed to the roof of the building next door and down the stairs," Stanton told him. "You'd better hope the townsfolk don't get the same notion or you'll find yourself at the end of a lynching rope."

"I'll take my chances." Clay went to the bar to fix himself a drink. "After that stunt you pulled today, I have half a mind to call Elroy back in here and finish you off."

The mercenary laughed as he set the pistol on the table. "The only thing finished would be poor Elroy. Same goes for any of the rest of those fools you've got on your payroll."

Clay poured himself a healthy glass of whiskey and put the plug back into the decanter. He turned a bit to block Stanton's view of the bar as he produced a bottle of laudanum from his pocket and added a few drops for good measure.

"I seem to be in the practice of hiring nothing but fools these days. You cost me a lot of trouble today, Stanton."

That drew another laugh. “What did you think would happen? A parade? One of their heroes got killed before their very eyes. You can’t expect them to throw roses in your path.”

“No, but I can expect the man I hired to do the killing the way we agreed.” He tucked the laudanum back into his pocket and faced his guest. “I don’t think that’s too much to ask.”

“In my experience,” Stanton said, “doing something someone else’s way is suicide. Your plan had flaws. I decided to make some changes.”

“Changes that almost got you caught and put me in more trouble than I already am.”

“Changes that assured I wouldn’t get caught if you grew a conscience,” Stanton argued. “Or suddenly decided I was expendable. What you didn’t know couldn’t hurt me.”

Clay wished he could have argued with him, but drank his whiskey instead. The man made sense. “Next time, don’t deviate from the plan.”

“Come up with a sound plan next time and I won’t have to, assuming there is a next time.”

Clay swirled his drink and sat behind his desk. “I understand you managed to evade Trammel’s deputies.”

As if doing Clay a favor, Stanton turned slightly in his chair. “That bunch of townies never knew what hit them when that tree exploded. How many did I get with that blast, anyway? I didn’t bother to stop and take count.”

“One of their horses got it in the neck,” Clay told him. “The deputies were cut up pretty bad, but they’re all back at work standing in front of my place right now.”

Stanton winced as he took a long pull on the cigar. “Tough luck about the animal. I hate it when a horse gets killed." He watched the dark smoke trail up toward the ceiling. "Couldn't be avoided, though. At least I got them off my trail."

Clay could feel the laudanum-laced whiskey begin to do its work on his aching jaw. "What about the rest of our plan? Did you follow that part of it, at least? Or did you simply decide to have lunch at Hagen's hotel?"

"Had a run-in with that brash young sheriff you warned me about," Stanton said. "Tough kid."

Clay stopped his glass halfway to his mouth. "Did you kill him?"

"Didn't have to, though I probably should have. Disarmed him and hurt his pride a little, but he's alive. Got a feeling he won't forget about me or where I went any time soon. Made sure he saw me heading to the Hagen spread."

It was the best news Clay had heard all day. "Good. Any trouble once you got up there?"

Stanton shook his head. "Rode the trail long enough for junior to see me go, then cut off when I hit the rise. Never got close to the place and no one saw me. I doubled back, grabbed the train just after it pulled into the station, and came back here." He grew quiet as he looked Clay over. "Sounds to me like you've had quite a day. Trammel pulled you in, didn't he?"

Clay almost gagged on his drink. "Who told you?"

"You did. You've got worry written all over your face. What happened?"

"Nothing. Mayor Holm got a judge to have me released, but the town's got it in its head I had Moran killed. That's Trammel's doing. That big man's smarter than I expected."

"I could've told you that." Stanton sipped his whiskey. "Spent the last week watching the man come and go about his business. Dangerous for a man that big to be that smart. Dangerous for you and me."

Clay was not so sure. "He overplayed his hand by running me in today. The mayor and my friends on the council are furious with him. Williamson at the Businessman's Association is none too pleased, either, but he's positioned himself as the voice of reason. They'll keep Trammel tied up here while the Hagen family pulls Adam apart in court. Once they swindle the empire away from him, I'll own Laramie and Blackstone lock, stock, and barrel."

Stanton toasted him with his glass. "Bully for you, but I'm not in the empire business. I'm in the money business. What do you need me to do for you next? And don't ask me to kill Trammel. That would just be your pride and the laudanum talking."

Clay felt his temper stir. "Laudanum is for housewives and lunatics."

"And for saloonkeepers with busted jaws," Stanton told him. "That stuff stinks to high heaven, but the only people who can't smell it are the men who drink it." He nodded toward Clay's glass of whiskey. "You'd best be careful with that stuff or you'll wind up on a pillow next to your customers out back."

"Don't worry about me." Clay swirled his drink and sipped it. "The only place I intend on laying my head is in the lap of luxury. Come this time next month, that's exactly where I'll be. Now, if you're finished doling out advice, I have another job for you."

Trammel tried to enjoy the sliced ham dinner Emily had brought to his office in a picnic basket but could only manage a few bites.

"You have to eat," Emily told him from the other side of his desk. "You won't do anyone any good by starving yourself to death."

"I lost a good man today, Em. Happened right in front of me." He set his fork on the plate. "Could've even been aiming for me and hit Rob instead."

"At that distance? I don't know much about guns, but any man who uses a rifle like that isn't apt to miss. I'm just glad it wasn't you." She set down her fork, too. "And here I was thinking Laramie would be safer for us."

"I thought it would be," Trammel said. "I wasn't counting on anyone taking a shot at Rob or me. It's Clay who's behind this. It's just got to be."

"And what if it is?" She checked to make sure the office door was closed. "The mayor's already pinned your ears back once. You can't go after him again unless you've got a good reason. And suspicion isn't a good enough reason. Clay's got too many friends in the right places."

As usual, he knew she was right, but that did not make the truth any easier to take. "Seems like everywhere I go, everyone's got friends in the right places except me." He shut his eyes and rubbed his knuckles into his temples. "First real day on the job and I've got a dead U.S. marshal and four wounded deputies on my hands."

"And a dead horse," Emily added. "Don't forget about that. The poor thing."

He opened his eyes to see her smiling at him. "For a doctor, you've got a knack for gallows humor, Mrs. Trammel."

"I learned it from you. I know Rob was your friend, but he knew the risks of this line of work same as you. And I'm sure if he was here right now, he'd be telling you to keep your strength up for the fight ahead."

"Yeah." Trammel sighed. "I guess there is a fight coming after all, isn't there? Just don't know yet, from where."

The sounds of the townspeople across the thoroughfare chanting, "We want Clay. We want Clay," picked up again.

"At least you're causing Clay a sleepless night," Emily offered.

"If I can't sleep, neither will he," Trammel said. "The mayor's already been in here twice tonight demanding I send that crowd on their way. I told him we don't have enough deputies to enforce it, but he's more than welcome to try if he wants. That idea didn't sit too well with him."

"It wasn't meant to, was it?"

"No," Trammel admitted. "It wasn't." He looked up when he heard a knock at his door and saw it was Haid, one of the night deputies.

Trammel beckoned him to come in.

"Sorry for the interruption, Sheriff"—he nodded to Emily—"Ma'am. I know you're eating supper and all, but I've got a telegram for you. Envelope says it's urgent."

Trammel took it from him and thanked him for delivering it. As he opened it, he was surprised to see Haid still standing there. "There something else, Deputy?"

"Just wanted to let you know all the boys from the night crew are with you, boss. Same as Blake and the others. Anything you need doing, just let us know. And I do mean anything. We all looked up to Rob."

"So did I, Haid. And thank you."

Haid bowed his way out and closed the door behind him.

"Well, that was nice, wasn't it?" Emily said.

"As far as it goes." Trammel opened the envelope. "If I don't catch Rob's killer in a week, they might start blaming me, too. But I'll worry about that when it happens."

He pulled the telegraph from the envelope and saw that it was from Colorado. He read the contents and tossed the telegram on his desk. "Judge Carlisle Littlejohn from Colorado will be arriving on the morning train. The trial over the Hagen estate will start at noon tomorrow."

Emily picked up the telegram and read it for herself. "That sounds kind of rushed, doesn't it?"

"Convenient, too," Trammel said, "seeing as how we're in the middle of a manhunt for Rob Moran's killer." The gravity of the situation landed on him all at once and he dropped his head into his hand. "Damn it."

Emily got up from her chair and came around the desk to him. "Steve. What's wrong?"

"The trial's in city court," he told her. "That means my boys will have to serve as bailiffs. And with the amount of attention this case will get, I'll have to use every man on the day shift to keep order. Those are five fewer men I'll have ready to ride the trail looking for Rob's killer."

"And the longer he goes free, the more pressure that'll put on you." She stroked his head, and his headache went away. "It all does seem awfully convenient, doesn't it?"

He was glad Emily understood. "Yeah. Too convenient."

She kissed his forehead and went back to her chair. "You can always quit and come to work with me and the other doctors at the office. We've always got room for one more smiling face to greet folks."

He appreciated her attempt to make him feel better. "No thanks. I've got a feeling you and every other sawbones in town is going to have their hands full in the days to come."

Chapter 20

The next morning, Trammel stood in front of city hall, checked the Bank of Laramie clock tower, and saw it was just a minute or so before nine o'clock. Judge Carlisle Littlejohn's train was due to arrive any moment. Although he wanted to be available when it did, he had no intention of meeting the jurist at the station. He did not require that kind of deference.

His presence making sure no one tried to shoot the man, Trammel could feel an uneasiness had settled over his adopted city, though he could not tell what. The Clay protestors had given up their vigil in front of the Rose of Tralee around midnight, but he could still hear the echo of their cries in his mind . . . *"We want Clay. We want Clay."*

Some of those same people were trudging along the boardwalks as they hurried off to work by the time the clock struck nine. Other townspeople moved about the boardwalks, too. The Morning Birds, as he had come to think of them. Those early risers and insomniacs who were on the street each morning to not simply go about their business, but also to gossip with their neighbors. They usually huddled in close groups, sharing whatever secrets they had with each other.

Trammel imagined he had been their topic of conversation the previous week.

Something appeared different on that particular morning. Those same people stood in open groups with their backs against buildings. They looked around at who was coming and going as if they were afraid someone might be listening.

Watching, Trammel felt it was about more than just the memory of the Moran killing. It was as if they were waiting to see what happened next. He knew how they felt.

Blake cleared his throat as a way of announcing himself. "Morning, boss."

"It sure is," Trammel agreed. "Don't know whether it'll be a good morning or bad."

Blake looked up at the clock tower. "Guess we'll find that out as soon as the judge gets here. You boys ever have a spectacle like this up in Blackstone?"

"Only when shooting started," Trammel said. "Either nothing happened or everything happened at once. Not much middle ground up there. Still isn't, last I heard."

Blake let out a long breath and watched the plume disappear in the cold Wyoming air. "Guess you'd have Hawkeye standing with you at a time like this. Sorry you'll have to make do with me."

"I'm glad to have you." Trammel meant it. "But Hawkeye wouldn't be next to me. He'd be set up somewhere across the street with a rifle to cover me."

"Take a look up at the rooftop of the hotel," Blake suggested.

Trammel squinted in that direction and saw Brillheart on

the roof with a Winchester. He felt like a fool. "I should've seen him up there."

"He just got up there about five minutes ago," Blake told him. "Got Welch up on the roof here at city hall. They've got a good view of the town from up there."

It was nice to not have to do all the thinking for once. "Thanks for doing that."

"It's my job. I also got a view of something else this morning over at the train station. Some of those gunmen from Blackstone you were talking about made their way down here last night. Looks like they're waiting for the judge's train to come in."

Trammel had been expecting that. "They're bought and paid for by the Hagen family. It only figures they'd be here to protect their personal judge. How many of them are there?"

"Five," Blake told him. "They weren't breaking any laws, so I let them go. We don't allow guns in court except for us, so it'll be mighty interesting to see what happens then."

"Guess it's our job to make it boring, isn't it?"

The train whistle blew in the distance and he knew Judge Littlejohn was close by.

The people milling about the boardwalk turned their attention to the station as the train slowly rolled in. Trammel and Blake watched quietly as passengers and wagons began to filter into town.

Judge Carlisle Littlejohn would have been easy to spot even if he had not been surrounded by five Hagen guns. He was a tall, pear-shaped man with a black top hat and a black silk vest. A pair of eyeglasses were perched at the end of his hawkish nose and he looked as if the smells of the busy thoroughfare were far from his liking.

A smallish man in a brown suit lugging two large valises

struggled to keep up with him. Trammel took him to be a clerk or manservant for the judge.

As the contingent drew closer to town hall, Trammel recognized Stan and Hank among the men surrounding the judge. The other three looked familiar, but he did not know their names.

The guards hung back as the judge and his follower approached the hall.

Judge Littlejohn peered up at him. "I take it by your size and stature you must be Sheriff Trammel."

"And I take it by your friends here you must be the Hagen family's judge."

Littlejohn bristled at the insinuation. "I am no one's judge except for the law, Sheriff. You'd do well to remember that, especially since you've already gotten off on the wrong foot with me."

"That so?"

"Indeed. I was expecting to be met at the station and escorted over here to city hall this morning. Instead, I had to find my own way."

"And I expected to own my own railroad and sleep on a bed of money by now, Your Honor. Looks like we both have our disappointments to bear." Trammel looked at the Hagen men lined up behind Littlejohn. "Besides, you seem to have brought an escort of your own."

"For my protection. It's unfortunate such steps are necessary in what is supposed to be a civilized city, but given the events of yesterday, one can hardly blame me for taking precautions." The judge glanced over at the canvas still covering the spot where Rob Moran had died. "Rob Moran was a good man. I hope you have made progress in finding his murderer."

Trammel made sure he looked at Stan when he said,

"We're getting closer by the second, Your Honor. Now, if you'd like to get situated before the trial, Deputy Blake here will be glad to take you inside and show you your chambers. He'll be serving as chief bailiff for the trial this afternoon."

The judge grunted his approval as he walked up the stairs past Trammel. He had not bothered to introduce his assistant and Trammel had not bothered to ask about him.

As the gunmen began to climb the stairs, Trammel moved to block their way. "Sorry, boys. Only the judge for now."

Stan spoke for the others. "We're being paid to keep the judge safe."

"So am I and all of my deputies," Trammel told him. "If there's room in the gallery, you'll be allowed in, but without your guns."

Stan slowly shook his head. "You never learn, do you, Trammel? You just keep pokin' and pokin', expectin' no one to poke back."

"Plenty have tried, and I'm still here. Now, you boys find a hole to crawl into until noon."

Stan looked back at the others and motioned them to follow him. Trammel watched them walk away toward the center of town. He wondered if they might find themselves in one of Clay's saloons. If he had enough deputies, he might have had one of them follow the Hagen men. But he was stretched thin enough and could not spare anyone.

About to go inside, he heard Mayor Holm call his name. Trammel thought about acting as though he had not heard him but knew the man would only corner him in his office. It was best to get it over with.

Holm skipped the pleasantries. "What progress have you made in finding Moran's killer?"

"None, since you won't let me question the chief suspect.

Now that some of the shops have begun to open, I plan on having a couple of my boys go around and ask if anyone saw the shooter or anyone who looked suspicious."

"Suspicious?" Holm mocked. "This is Laramie, not Blackstone. We're a city, not some backwoods outpost. This place is filled with suspicious looking characters. You'll be wasting city resources and valuable time chasing around a bunch of harmless drunks and poor old fools who had nothing to do with the killing."

Trammel kept his temper at bay. "Since you won't let me work my way, that's the best I can do. Damn it, Walter. Poor Rob hasn't been dead a full day yet. These things take time."

"Time is the one thing you don't have, Trammel. And if you consider harassing an innocent man like Lucien Clay as part of your job, I might start thinking we made a mistake in hiring you in the first place."

"Clay is a lot of things, but innocent's not one of them," Trammel said. "And this star comes off just as easily as it pins on. You can have it back any time you want. But whether or not I'm wearing it, I'm still going to find Rob's killer. Not you or all your stonewalling is going to change that."

Trammel had expected the mayor to continue the argument, but Holm held up his hands. "I'm sorry, Buck. I really am. This whole thing has thrown me for a loop, and I haven't been myself since it happened." He glanced at the canvas where Moran had died and quickly looked away. "I just can't get over the fact that Rob is dead. He was such a . . . a presence. I didn't mean to threaten you. I don't know what I was thinking."

Trammel may have been quick to anger, but he was glad to put all of that aside for the sake of progress. "Then why won't you let me question Clay? I know you probably owe him for something, and I don't care about that. I'm not looking to bother him about a bar fight or loud music or even his opium business. This is important, Walt."

Holm took off his bowler hat and ran his hands over his graying hair. "I know it is, but Clay didn't do it. He's been laid up for months with that busted jaw you gave him, so he can't have killed Moran."

Trammel never thought he did. "No, but he could've paid to have it done and you know it. He's done it before in Blackstone and I know he's done it here in the city, too." He watched Holm struggle with what he knew was right and with what he could not do. He watched in earnest, wondering which side would win out.

Holm put his hat back on his head, his mind made up. "Clay's got more friends in town than just me. You know that. I can't let you lock him in a jail cell, and I can't allow you to bother him without a solid reason." He held up a finger. "But you have my blessing to treat him as if he's involved. Just not in person unless you have rock solid, iron clad proof."

Trammel would have laughed if it had not been so tragic. "That's not helping me much, Walter."

"I'm afraid it's all I can offer for now." The mayor rested a hand on Trammel's arm. "I'll support you as much as I can, but since it's Clay we're talking about, all of us need to tread lightly."

"Treading lightly has never been my strong suit."

Holm patted his arm and walked into city hall.

Alone on the boardwalk, Trammel rubbed his eyes and shook his head clear. His conversation with the mayor had gone around in so many circles, he almost felt dizzy. Once again, he was reminded of Adam Hagen's warning about being sheriff of Laramie was much different from being sheriff of Blackstone.

Up there, everything was straightforward. The lines of right and wrong were blurry sometimes, but they were there. In Laramie, the truth was as crooked as its streets and just as marked with wheel ruts, divots, and dung. A few hours in a cell with Clay would give him all the answers he needed, but Holm and the other men who ran the city could not allow that. The man was just a few yards across the thoroughfare in the Rose of Tralee, but as far as Trammel was concerned, he might as well be the man in the moon.

Holm had said a lot but given him little. Trammel supposed that was the way it was in cities. He had seen it when he had worked in Manhattan and in Chicago.

But he had not been the sheriff of those cities. He was the sheriff of Laramie. He was not just a copper or a Pinkerton, but the one with true authority. It was up to him to find out who had killed Rob Moran and that was exactly what he planned on doing.

Along with keeping order during the Hagen trial and having his men keep order like they did every day.

He patted the star pinned to his chest. It seemed to get a bit heavier by the day.

Again, he turned to walk into city hall when he heard a woman call out his name. He closed his eyes and hung his head. It had already been a long day and it was just after nine in the morning.

"Sheriff Trammel, please wait," the woman repeated.

Trammel slowly turned to see Mrs. Alice Smith, the head of the Ladies League of Laramie, rushing toward him as fast as her black skirts would allow. She was pulling along a gaunt, pale woman in a plain black dress who looked young enough to be her daughter.

Trammel touched the brim of his hat, wishing he could just find a moment's peace in his office. "Morning, Mrs. Smith."

"We have a matter of great urgency to discuss with you," Mrs. Smith said. "It's about the murder of poor Marshal Moran."

Trammel had been afraid of that. "I know you're concerned, but we're doing everything we can to find out who was behind it. Now, if you'll excuse me . . ."

Mrs. Smith's bony hand latched on to his arm, holding him in place. "Presumptive and dismissive. Just like a man. We're not here to gossip about what happened, Sheriff. I've brought this young lady here to tell you she knows who the killer is."

Once he had ushered them up to his office, Trammel offered the ladies some coffee, but they politely refused. He poured himself a cup, sat down behind the desk, and leaned forward to make himself appear as small as possible. The young woman was about a quarter of his size and he knew how intimidating some people found him to be.

Now that he had a good look at her, Trammel recognized her as one of Lucien Clay's parlor girls. She had been there right after he had been sworn in as sheriff . . . when he'd confronted Clay.

"Why don't you start off by telling me your name and what you saw," he encouraged her. "Take your time. No one's rushing you and I'm not writing anything down.

Just tell me what you came here to say, and we'll take it from there."

The young woman looked at Mrs. Smith for encouragement and the old widow gave her a curt nod.

"My name is Delilah Harper and I used to work for Lucien Clay."

Although he knew the answer to his next question, he had to ask it anyway. Mrs. Smith had already given a lesson in the dangers of assuming things. "What kind of work did you do for him?"

"I wasn't a working lady if that's what you're asking. I cleaned up around the place and looked after the girls, but I never spent any time upstairs. Not like they did, anyway. I guess that's why Lucien took a liking to me. I wasn't all used up and pox-ridden like the rest of the girls. He and I became a couple, you might say." She glanced at Mrs. Smith and looked down at her hands, ashamed. "We knew each other in a biblical sense. I'm not proud of that."

A biblical sense, Trammel thought. Mrs. Smith was already trying to reform her. "What does that have to do with what happened to Marshal Moran?"

Delilah would not be distracted from her story. "I tended to Mr. Clay's wounds after that beating you gave him. His jaw never did heal quite right, and it's given him awful pain since. A doctor in Colorado told him he'd have to break it again to set it proper."

Trammel would gladly do it for him but kept that part to himself. "Go on."

"Well, I was with him almost every minute of every day and night," she said, "on account of him needing so much care. For the pain, you see. He's been at the laudanum something awful, though he doesn't want anyone to know that. Between the pain in his jaw and the headaches from the laudanum, he's been right ungodly to live with."

Trammel imagined she was getting to the point, so he struggled to seem interested and keep quiet.

"He's been in a dark mood all these months," Delilah said, "except for a couple of weeks ago when a stranger sent him a message that he'd like to have a word."

Suddenly Trammel was interested. "What stranger?"

"I don't really remember his name. I kind of got a taste for the laudanum myself, so my brain is a bit foggy. I remember he was younger than Mr. Clay's usual customers. Much better dressed, too. He looked fancy, like he came from back East. I think he had a lot of money or else Mr. Clay wouldn't have taken the time to meet with him. He had an odd name, but I'm sorry I can't remember it."

Trammel figured they could come back to that later. He wanted to keep her talking. "What did they meet about?"

Delilah shook her head. "I wasn't there, so I don't know. I remember what he looked like, though. I know I'd recognize him if I saw him again."

It was something, but not much. "Do you remember what happened after Clay met with this man?"

"I sure do." A hint of a smile. "I don't know what they said, but Mr. Clay was almost back to his old self again. He wasn't as short with me as he usually was. He didn't—"

Her voice caught short, and Mrs. Smith placed her hand over Delilah's. "You can forget that part of the story, child. Tell the sheriff what happened next."

"Right after the fancy man left," Delilah told him, "Mr. Clay wrote out a telegram and had me deliver it to the telegraph office for him. He knows I never got around to learning how to read, so he knew I wouldn't be able to understand what it said. I remember he told me to wait until he got a response. I had to sit in that drafty old telegraph office for almost three hours until the reply finally came. I took it to Mr. Clay, and he got even happier. I didn't know why until a few days later when I saw him meet a stranger at the train station."

Now they were getting somewhere. Trammel did his best to remain calm. "Did you see what he looked like?"

"I did, but I got a better look at him when Lucien brought him back to the saloon," Delilah told him. "He was an older man. Tall, though not as tall as you. He had long gray hair and his face had a lot of wrinkles. They stopped talking whenever I came in the room, but the Major Stanton was always nice to me otherwise."

Trammel had to stop her. "You said 'Major Stanton.' Was that the stranger's name? The man Clay had telegraphed?"

"I don't know that for certain," she admitted, "but I know his name was Major John Stanton. He introduced himself to me, even though Mr. Clay told him not to bother. He had nice manners, that man."

Trammel grabbed a pencil and wrote the name on the corner of a report before he forgot it. "What else do you know about him?"

"Nothing," she said. "Like I said, he was kind to me. Gave me a hundred-dollar gold piece. Genuine, too. Believe me, I checked. It was more money than I'd ever had at one time in my whole life. As soon as he gave it to me, I knew I had my chance to get away from Mr. Clay, so—"

"So she came to me," Mrs. Smith said for her. "The poor thing was half frightened out of her mind. I've been harboring her for the past week or so in my cellar. She was terrified Clay would find her, so I kept her safe until I thought enough time had passed and it would be safe to get her on a train out of town. But when we heard about the description of the man who killed poor Marshal Moran, Delilah told me it sounded like a man Clay had met with. I knew it was worth the risk to bring her here to talk with you, despite the proximity to Clay's saloon."

A lot of ideas and questions and details flooded Trammel's mind. He forced himself to slow down and take things in order. Too forceful, he might scare Delilah and he did not want that. The first thing he had to do was find this Major Stanton. "Do you know where Stanton is staying?"

"Last I knew he was staying in the upstairs of the saloon on the top floor, same as where Mr. Clay's rooms are, just down the hall. He might have moved since then. I don't know."

Delilah might not know where he was, but Clay certainly would. Either way, it was worth finding out for himself.

Trammel checked the clock on the wall. It was just before ten o'clock. The Hagen trial would not start until noon. Most of his deputies would be tied up after that, but until then, they were ready.

The hard part came next. "Delilah, I know you said you can't write, but I'm going to have to ask you to let Mrs. Smith here write down everything you've just told me so I can use it against Clay. You can make your mark at the bottom of it, but it needs to be in writing for me to do anything about it."

Mrs. Smith opened her bag and handed him a folded sheet of paper. "We've already done your work for you, Sheriff. Delilah insisted on doing it before we left the house, lest one of Clay's thugs tried to grab her. Or worse."

Trammel kept his hands steady as he sat back in his chair and read over the letter. It was a full account of everything she had just told him. Not only had Delilah made her mark, but it had also been notarized by one Andrew Solomon, Attorney-at-law.

Trammel felt his gut grow cold and asked Mrs. Smith, "You've already been to an attorney. Can he be trusted?"

Mrs. Smith stiffened in her chair. "I should hope so. He's my grandson."

Trammel allowed himself to breathe again. He could not believe it. After all these years, he just might be holding the end of Lucien Clay in his hands. He looked at Mrs. Smith. "Do you have money?"

"Enough to make Croesus blanche," she told him. "And we already have two tickets for the eleven o'clock train heading west, hence the need for the urgency this morning."

Trammel was all smiles as he locked the statement in his desk. "And I've got an entire squad of deputies at your disposal to make sure you get on that train safely. Just wait here and Deputy Blake will be here in a moment to tell you what to do next."

He got up from his desk and took a knee beside Delilah. "I know this isn't easy. You've been very brave."

Her pale, sunken eyes watered, and she silently shook her head. "Mr. Solomon said I'd have to come back to testify in open court. I . . . I don't know if I could do that."

Trammel rested a large hand on her slender shoulder. "If I know Clay, it probably won't come to that." He got to his feet and went to open the door.

Delilah stopped him. "Mind the bartender at the saloon. There's an old bell behind the bar. He rings it loud if there's any sign of trouble."

Trammel had not known that, but he knew it now. "Thank you. Deputy Blake will be here in a moment." He opened the office door and shut it behind him. Calling out for Blake, Trammel heard his own voice carry throughout the building.

A few of the deputies in the other room jumped at the sound.

"Here, boss," Blake responded from the first floor as he ran up the stairs. "What's going on?"

Trammel pointed at the closed door. "Two ladies in my office need to get on the eleven o'clock train. I want every man we've got at that station watching everyone who gets on the train. No one gets on without a ticket. Talk to the conductor and see if they've got a detective on board. They probably do for a long haul like that. Make sure the man keeps a close eye on them the entire time. You stay with them until the train leaves the station and not a second before."

"We've got the Hagen trial at noon, but we'll be back before then." Blake looked around Trammel at the closed door. "Who's in there?"

"Mrs. Smith and Delilah."

"Who'd want to hurt them?"

"The same man who killed Rob Moran," Trammel told him. "And I'm about to bring him down. Personally."

CHAPTER 21

Trammel knew time was of the essence. The best way he could make sure Delilah and Mrs. Smith got to the train safely was to create a meaningful distraction. And he could not think of anything more meaningful than getting the jump on the man who had killed Rob Moran.

Trammel knew any number of Clay's men would notice him as soon as he stepped outside, so he left city hall and walked across the thoroughfare to the telegraph office. Instead of going inside, he took a left on the boardwalk and headed straight for the Rose of Tralee. The cover of the boardwalk would prevent anyone eyeing the street from the saloon windows from seeing him until it was too late.

Pulling the Peacemaker from the holster beneath his left arm as he reached the saloon, he pushed through the batwing doors and found a large bouncer named Oates dozing in a chair by the door. The man snorted awake as he heard the doors being pushed open, but the blow of a gun barrel across his temple sent him sprawling and back to sleep.

Trammel aimed the Peacemaker at the bartender, who was already more than halfway to the brass bell hanging behind the bar. Paying attention to Delilah's warning, he told the barman, "Don't move. Come around on this side. Climb over if you have to."

The bartender was flustered. "I can't do that, Sheriff. My legs are mighty stiff these days."

"Seemed to be nimble enough to run for that bell." Trammel thumbed back the hammer to show he was serious. "Climb over the bar or die where you stand."

The barman pulled himself up onto the bar and rolled across it until he dropped to his feet in front of the bar.

The sheriff kept his pistol leveled at him. "Run away and don't come back until it's over."

The bartender stepped over the bouncer on the floor and reached the batwing doors. "How will I know it's over?"

"You'll know. Now get moving."

The bartender pushed through the doors and ran off. As soon as Trammel heard his footfalls on the boardwalk, he began to walk upstairs to Clay's rooms and, he hoped, to Major John Stanton himself.

The stairs were surprisingly well constructed and did not creak beneath Trammel's weight. He took them two at a time until he reached the top level where Delilah had told him he would find Clay and Stanton. Remembering Clay's room was at the top of the stairs on the left, it stood to reason the hired gun had the large room on the right. Trammel held his pistol ready as he placed his ear against the right-hand door in hope of hearing something on the other side.

He heard a type of scraping. Not from inside the room, but quieter than that. He did not know what might be causing the sounds, but it sounded like Stanton was inside.

Trammel took a few steps back and rammed his shoulder into the door. The lock gave way and the door swung inward. He swept the room with his Peacemaker and saw a pair of legs on the balcony disappearing toward the roof. Stanton must have heard him coming, climbed atop a table, and was trying to get away.

The Rose of Tralee saloon was one of the few buildings in his new city Trammel knew fairly well. He ran down the hall, climbed out the window and onto the fire stairs outside, letting his pistol lead the way as he inched his way steadily up to the roof. Stanton was trying to leap up to the roof of the hotel next door, which was a good six feet taller or more than the saloon, meaning he needed a running start to scale the wall successfully.

He was mid-stride when Trammel aimed at him and yelled, "Stop right where you are, Stanton. Throw up your hands and turn around real slow."

Stanton did not halt. Continuing to run toward the wall, he jumped just before he reached it. His boots made contact with the brickwork, propelling him even higher up the wall. He managed to reach the top of the wall and began to pull himself up when Trammel fired. His bullet missed, though just barely, and took a large chunk out of the brickwork of the hotel.

The shot seemed to give Trammel's quarry renewed energy for he scrambled up and over the top with ease.

Trammel ran to the wall. Due to his height, he did not need to leap but jumped up and grabbed hold of the top of the wall with his left hand while swinging his right hand still holding his pistol over the top.

As he began to pull himself up, his head was rocked back by a hard boot heel to the face. Trammel could feel the deep cut the blow had opened along the right side of his nose to the top of his forehead. It stung, but it only took a second or two before blood began to flow into his eyes.

A second, frantic kick missed his face, but connected with the left arm holding him in place on the wall. His arm held, but he could feel his grip beginning to slip. Although blinded by blood, he could hear Stanton's boots scraping on the roof as he prepared to let loose with another kick.

Trammel used all his strength to swing out wildly with his right hand. His Peacemaker connected with Stanton's ankle and sent the fugitive sprawling onto the roof.

Ignoring the blood flowing into his eyes, Trammel dug his elbow over the top of the wall and pulled himself up and over to the other side. He heard Stanton curse as he got to his feet.

Trammel used his sleeve to wipe away the blood from his eyes in time to see Stanton limping away along the roof. Blinking away the blood, he took aim and fired. His bullet sailed wide but close enough to get Stanton's attention.

The gunman turned as he drew the pistol from his hip but fell as he fired two bullets at Trammel. Both bullets struck the roof well short of the sheriff.

Realizing he was too blind by blood to see and Stanton was too hobbled to move, Trammel forgot about trying to shoot Stanton and decided to charge at him in a crouch instead.

As he closed the distance between them, Trammel sensed, rather than saw, the gunman aim at him and he dove for the rooftop. He tumbled toward Stanton as a shot rang out but did not feel the familiar sting of a bullet.

Close enough to see Stanton about to bring down the pistol on the back of his head, Trammel buried a left hook deep into the gunman's belly. The blow was hard enough to stagger Stanton and make him drop his gun.

As Trammel got his feet beneath him and began to stand, he left his own gun at his feet as he brought up a blind uppercut, connecting more with Stanton's throat than his jaw. The blow knocked the assassin backward.

Trammel wiped his sleeve across his eyes again, ready to throw another punch when he saw Stanton had fallen from the roof and landed on top of the spectacle shop. The same perch from where Trammel figured Stanton had killed Rob Moran. Trammel picked up his gun and turned when he heard a man calling out his name from somewhere behind him. He saw the blurry outline of Deputy Gary Bush running toward him along the roof.

"What are you doing here?" Trammel yelled. "I told Blake to have everyone guard the women."

"He sent me for you when he heard the shots," Bush told him. "Damn it, boss. You're bleeding mighty bad."

Trammel did not care about himself as his eyesight grew blurry again. He pointed down at the roof below. "What about Stanton? Is he still there?"

The deputy chanced a look over the side. "Don't look like he's going anywhere, except maybe to Hell, boss. He looks mighty dead to me."

Trammel did not care about looks. He cared about facts. "Keep an eye on him. If he moves, shoot him. I'll get Doc Carson and some others to pull him off there. Don't move until we get back." He lurched across the roof back toward the saloon.

"You sure that's a good idea?" Bush called after him. "You can't hardly see with that cut being so bad."

No, Trammel was not sure it was a good idea. But under the circumstances, it was the best one he had.

Chapter 22

As Doc Carson tended to Trammel's wound in the doctor's basement office, the sheriff asked, "What time is it?" He almost cried out as the doctor applied something that made the cut feel like it was on fire.

"It's time for you to keep your mouth shut and let me work."

Emily looked on from behind Carson. "That's as deep a cut as I've seen, Buck. We can see right down to the bone."

Trammel's eyes watered from the pain as Carson used forceps to dab at the gash with gauze. "Guess this means I won't be pretty anymore."

"Means more than that." Carson frowned. "This is a mighty bad cut that runs from your right check, along your nose, and up over your left eye. There's an excellent chance it could become infected. If that happens, you might lose your nose or an eye. Maybe even both eyes."

Trammel pulled away from him and lowered Carson's hands. "That's impossible."

"It's more likely than I'd care to admit." The doc pulled his hand free and went back to work. "If you're lucky, all you'll have for your trouble is a nasty scar across your face.

But if infection sets in, and that is highly likely, no one can tell what might happen." He glanced back at Emily. "Do you concur, Doctor Downs?"

She quietly nodded. "He's not exaggerating, Buck. You'll need to spend a good amount of time at home to cut down on the likelihood of infection."

Trammel did not doubt they were telling him the truth. He had seen how even the smallest flesh wound could fester into an infection that could cost a man a limb or his life.

But the City of Laramie was not paying him to take it easy. They were paying him to enforce the law and bring Rob Moran's killers to justice. And that was exactly what he was going to do for as long as he could do it.

"What about Stanton?" Trammel asked. "What happened to him?"

"He's just about the only man in town worse off than you," Carson said as he continued to treat Trammel's wound. "He's still alive, but don't ask me how."

"Alive?" Trammel yelped from another sting from the doctor's medicine. "How?"

"I said he's alive," Carson said. "I didn't say he's in good condition. He's got a fractured skull and he's paralyzed from the waist down. His entire rib cage is either fractured or broken in several places. Even if he regains feeling in his limbs, his right knee is shattered. Even if he lives, he'll never walk properly again. If I didn't have him pumped full of morphine, he'd probably die from the shock of his injuries. Still might."

The news was the only thing that made Trammel's face hurt a bit less. "Good."

"Blake told me you think he's the one who killed Moran," Carson said.

"That's what Delilah told me. Got it in writing as a sworn statement, too." Then he remembered telling Blake about getting Delilah and Mrs. Smith on the train. "Get Blake in here. I need to ask him about something."

Carson continued working. "You're in no shape to talk to anyone, Sheriff. Even if you were, I doubt Blake has the stomach to look at you. He told me he delivered the ladies to the train and they're safely on their way out West to parts unknown. There's nothing more you can do for them."

"But the Hagen trial is starting up at noon," Trammel said. "I have to be there for it. Trouble's bound to break out between the two sides."

"Trouble that Blake is more than capable of handling," Emily told him. "You're not. Please be reasonable, Buck. There's no sense in putting your health at risk when you've got plenty of men to help you."

Trammel knew he had plenty of men who could help him, including one who might not know it yet. "How many people know Stanton is still alive?"

"Doctor Kelly and two townspeople helped me haul him down off the roof," Doc Carson said as he worked, "but we could hardly tell if he was dead or alive at that point. He's in the other room now, being tended to by Doctor Kelly. Why?"

"Kelly someone you can trust?"

"He's a competent physician," Emily said. "Helps Doctor Carson from time to time when he's busy. Why?"

"Because I need him to do something for me."

Doc Carson shook his head. "Everything that can be done for you is being done right here by me."

"Not for me, then," Trammel clarified. "But for the town. I need him to tell people that Stanton is dead."

"Dead?" Carson lowered his forceps. "Why on earth for?"

"Because I want to keep him alive," Trammel explained. "And the best way I can do that is if people think he's already dead."

Carson and Emily traded looks before the doctor went back to dabbing Trammel's wound. "You just sit here quietly and let me clean this thing for you. After I finish stitching it up, what you do is your business."

No, Trammel thought. *It's the city's business.*

As he pulled his gray gloves tighter, Adam Hagen waved to the crowd of citizens lined up to be allowed into the courtroom. He walked up the stairs of city hall, where Deputy Blake stood with two other deputies waiting to inspect him. The deputies had the stocks of Winchesters resting on their belts.

"Good morning, sirs." Adam grinned as he held open his coat. "As you can see, I am unarmed. I shall gladly allow you to pat me down if it'll make you feel any better."

"Anyone going into that courtroom gets patted down whether they like it or not."

Adam had left his pistols with Big Ben back at the hotel. Knowing a weapon would not be found, he held his hands up while Blake conducted a thorough search of his person. "I'm surprised to see you here, Deputy. I'd have thought Sheriff Trammel would've wanted to oversee security personally."

"The sheriff's laid up for a bit," Blake told him. "Move along."

Adam had no intention of going anywhere. "Laid up? What happened?"

"I'm not sure. Just that he got hurt pretty bad. Now move along like I told you."

Adam resisted when the deputy tried to move him aside. "Wait just a minute." He was not expecting Blake to shove him against the wall.

The two deputies aimed their Winchesters at him.

Blake glared at him as he pinned him to the wall. "Listen to me, you dandy. You might be a big deal up in Blackstone, but down here, you're just another mouthy civilian. You do like I told you and either go into the courtroom or get out of here. No more questions, got it?" Blake grabbed a handful of Adam's lapels and shoved him toward the courtroom.

Deciding nothing was to be gained by arguing with Blake, Adam fixed his coat and walked to the only courtroom doors that were open.

He had enjoyed the awkward train ride down from Blackstone with his family. He had taken pleasure in watching them shift in their seats and avoid looking at him during the brief ride to Laramie. He liked to think his presence had put them at a disadvantage somehow. Anything that put them ill at ease, even a little, could only help his cause.

But news of Trammel's injury spoiled the feeling. He had worried about his friend since learning of Moran's death. He knew Buck had enough deputies at his side to help him, but Laramie was a far cry from Blackstone. Moran's assassination had proven that. He would have to wait until the trial was in recess before he inquired further about Trammel's condition. For now, the sheriff had to focus on saving his own life.

Adam removed his hat as he strode into the courtroom. His brother-in-law, Bernard Wain, and his brother Caleb were already sitting at the table to his left. He made sure his smile held as he walked past his family seated in the gallery, pushed through the swinging door between court and spectator, and sat at the same table.

Wain and Caleb looked over at him strangely.

"What do you think you're doing?" the attorney asked.

"Taking my rightful place in court." Adam began removing his gloves one finger at a time. "I know you're young, Bernard, but I would've expected you to know how these things work by now."

"Where is your attorney?" Wain asked.

"I'll be representing myself in these proceedings. I've read a good bit of the law and am more than equal to the task. And please spare me that old saw about fools and clients. I've heard it before and haven't lost yet."

His brother-in-law looked as if he wanted to say more, but a tug on his arm from Caleb made him think better of it. The three of them remained seated in silence as the court began to fill with spectators.

Blake and five other deputies fanned out around the courtroom as every available seat was quickly filled. Adam looked around for signs of his family's hired guns, but none of them was present. He heard a rustle of activity from behind the judge's bench before a door opened and a small, bespectacled man in a plain dark suit toddled out and took his seat beside the elevated judge's chair.

"All rise!" Deputy Blake called out.

Everyone in the courtroom complied. Judge Littlejohn came out of his chambers. His black robe and somber expression seemed appropriate for the occasion. Once he sat down, he bade them all to sit down, and everyone but the deputies did so.

"This court is now in session," Littlejohn announced.

"We are here today to deliberate the contested last will and testament of one Mr. Charles Hagen. Who will be representing the petitioner in these proceedings?"

Adam's young brother-in-law quickly rose to his feet. "Bernard Wain of Philadelphia, Pennsylvania, Your Honor."

Littlejohn's clerk immediately took notes.

"And who will represent the respondent in this matter?" the judge asked.

Adam stood and bowed dramatically at the waist. "Your humble servant Adam Hagen, Your Honor."

The judge peered down at him from the glasses perched on the end of his long nose. "You mean you're representing yourself in this matter?"

"Yes, Your Honor. Contrary to popular legal wisdom, I believe I have a genius for a client. I have argued cases before judges before and am confident this matter can be cleared up with a simple presentation of the facts."

Littlejohn frowned. "You are aware you will not be allowed to use self-representation as grounds for an appeal should this court rule against you?"

"I am well aware, Your Honor. I don't believe that will be necessary."

The judge motioned for him to sit down and he gladly did so.

"I'll now hear opening statements in this matter," Littlejohn said. "Mr. Wain, as you are the plaintiff, I will allow you to go first."

Wain stood at the table and folded his arms behind him, impressive that he spoke without the benefit of notes. "If it please the court, on behalf of the Hagen family, I intend to prove beyond any reasonable doubt the signature on the document in question was forged by none other than

Mr. Adam Hagen for the sole purpose of gaining control of the late Mr. Hagen's interests and leave his siblings destitute."

"Objection," Adam said as he got to his feet.

Judge Littlejohn sighed heavily. "One cannot object to an opening statement, Mr. Hagen."

"One can if said statement is patently and factually false," Adam said. "While my late father's will clearly lists me as the sole heir to his fortune, I have constantly sought to settle the matter with my siblings at a fair price."

"Which is?" Littlejohn asked.

"I have offered them forty-nine percent of the family interests while I retain fifty-one percent. I believe this arrangement preserves my father's intent while softening his attitude against his other children. I wish to repeat that offer here and now in open court and am prepared to do so in writing at this very moment."

Wain said, "Why should the family agree to a fraudulent forty-nine percent when they are legally entitled to a full one-hundred percent? We are prepared to call a witness who will testify the signature on that will and testament is, indeed, a forgery."

Adam said, "A witness, Your Honor, who did not come forward in two previous trials but has miraculously appeared now." He held out his hands. "Can we expect Mr. Wain to multiply loaves and fishes next?"

The gallery laughed and he was glad when Debora got to her feet. "You'll get more loathing than loaves from us, you heretic!"

Adam smiled in victory as Littlejohn banged the gavel. "I'll have order in this court. One more outburst like that and I'll have the bailiff remove you for the rest of these proceedings."

Adam used the interruption to his advantage. "I ask the

court to forgive my dear sister, Mrs. Forrester, Your Honor. This matter has placed her under an amazing strain."

Littlejohn pointed the gavel at him. "And I've heard just about enough from you, sir. Take a seat and refrain from making any further objections until the first witness is called."

Adam resumed his seat and kept his eyes on the table while Wain tried to regain his composure.

"This court has a copy of the fraudulent last will and testament of Mr. Charles Hagen," Wain said. "The Hagen family will produce a witness who is willing to testify the signature has not only been forged, but said witness saw the forgery take place."

Adam could hardly believe what he heard. He knew no one had seen him forge the signature except for Frederic Montague and he was dead. Unlike King Charles, Fred had the good sense to take his own life when he saw the die had been cast against him.

When Wain sat down, Littlejohn looked over at Adam. "I take it you plan on making an opening statement that the signature is genuine and two previous courts have so ruled?"

Adam got to his feet again. "I couldn't have said it better myself, Your Honor."

"Good," the judge said. "For the sake of brevity, I'll waive your opening statement and ask Mr. Wain to call his first witness."

Adam decided not to object, for he was eager to see how all of this played out.

Wain said, "We call Mr. Charles Grimm to the stand."

Adam had never heard the name before, but when he turned to see the witness walk into the courtroom, he recognized him. He was one of the forgettable clerks who had worked for Montague at the bank. Adam had seen the balding little man dozens of times but had never bothered to know his name.

He had a feeling he would not be forgetting it any time soon.

Once Littlejohn's clerk swore Grimm in, Grimm took his seat in the witness chair. Wain asked him to say his name and spell it for the record.

When that bit of business was completed, Wain asked, "What is your profession, Mr. Grimm?"

"I was Mr. Montague's clerk at the Bank of Blackstone," the man replied.

"And who was Mr. Montague?" Wain asked.

"The president of the Bank of Blackstone," Grimm answered.

"And would you say you were Mr. Montague's chief clerk, Mr. Grimm?"

"I worked with him more than anyone else in the bank, so I suppose you could say that. I enjoyed the privilege."

Wain continued. "In addition to serving as the president of the Bank of Blackstone, did Mr. Montague also serve as Charles Hagen's confidant?"

Adam thought about objecting but decided to wait to see what Grimm said.

"Mr. Hagen was one of Mr. Montague's closest friends and advisors," the clerk testified. "Also an attorney, Mr. Montague conducted a significant amount of business for Mr. Hagen over the years."

"I see," Wain remarked. "And did Mr. Montague conduct any business for Mr. Adam Hagen by chance?"

"Reluctantly, yes." Grimm frowned.

Adam stood. "Objection. Calls for speculation."

"Sustained." Littlejohn spoke to Grimm. "You will omit any opinions or adjectives from your answers, Mr. Grimm."

Wain remained on track despite the judge's admonition. "How would you describe Mr. Montague's interactions with Adam Hagen? Was Mr. Montague as friendly with Adam as he was with Charles?"

"Mr. Montague was terrified of Adam Hagen," Grimm said.

"Objection!" Hagen shouted.

"Overruled," Littlejohn said. "You'll have a chance to ask the witness plenty of questions of your own in a while, Mr. Hagen."

Wain continued. "And why do you say Mr. Montague was terrified of Adam?"

"Because Adam was blackmailing him," Grimm said.

A ripple of murmurs went through the gallery. Adam was about to object, but Littlejohn pointed at him and shook his head. "Continue, Mr. Wain."

"With what information was Adam blackmailing Mr. Montague?"

Grimm seemed reluctant to answer. "Mr. Montague was a good man, but he had his flaws like anyone else. He enjoyed the company of young ladies. Ladies far younger than himself. Adam Hagen learned Mr. Montague had ruined the virtue of several of these young women who were beneath the age of consent. One of them happened to be related to a senator, though I'm not sure which senator it was."

How did Grimm know all this? Adam got to his feet. "I must object, Your Honor. I had no such knowledge."

"I'll allow it for now," Littlejohn said, "but I caution you to come to a point very quickly, Mr. Wain."

"I will do that with my very next question, Your Honor."

He looked at Grimm. "Assuming Mr. Montague wanted to keep this matter a secret, what did Adam ask Mr. Montague to do?"

Grimm cleared his throat and said, "He forced Mr. Montague to draw up a new will from Charles Hagen that left everything to him in the event of his death. He also made Mr. Montague forge Mr. Hagen's signature on the document."

"Objection!" Hagen thundered as he got to his feet over Littlejohn's warning. "That is an outright lie. I never did such a thing." Adam knew Grimm was lying, for it was Adam who forged the signature, not Montague.

"Sit down," the judge warned him, "or you will leave me no choice but to have the bailiffs restrain you."

Adam was going to protest but did not want to give Littlejohn the satisfaction of having Blake cuff him to the chair. He sat down again, marveling at Wain's cunning. He was smart. Calling in experts claiming the signature had been forged had failed twice before. Now, they had gotten Grimm to pin it on a dead man beyond questioning or the reach of the law.

Wain hid a smile as he continued. "How do you know Mr. Montague forged the signature?"

"He had me draw up the revised will and I saw him trace Mr. Hagen's signature onto the new copies from documents in his possession already having Mr. Hagen's signature. In Mr. Montague's defense, he did it with tears in his eyes."

Wain took a document from the table and took it over to Grimm. "Is this the document you prepared, Mr. Grimm?"

Grimm barely looked at it. "It is."

"And is that Mr. Montague's forgery at the bottom of it?"

Grimm closed his eyes and nodded. "Yes, it is."

Wain handed the copy of the will to the judge's clerk.

"This document is already in evidence, Your Honor. We resubmit it for the court's review. No further questions of this witness."

Adam Hagen sat quietly while he tried to figure how he could possibly question Grimm. Wain had painted him into a delicate corner. Adam could accuse Grimm of lying under oath, but not without admitting he had forged the signature. He had not counted on his brother-in-law for being cunning enough to find a clerk to perjure himself. The young lawyer had the makings of a Hagen after all—if the facts fail to suffice, create your own.

The ends had always justified the means. It was the best lesson Charles Hagen had ever taught him.

Adam knew he not only had to overcome a biased judge, but a mousey clerk who would look even more pathetic should Adam begin to thunder away at him with facts. He would look desperate, which is exactly what Adam imagined his family had been hoping for. How could he get at the truth without turning the hapless Grimm into more of a martyr than he already appeared?

"Mr. Hagen," Judge Littlejohn yelled. "Are you still with us, sir? I said it's your turn to question the witness."

Adam snapped back to the present. "Yes, of course, Your Honor. Forgive my delay in responding, but I've always had a weakness for losing myself in tall tales. And Mr. Grimm's is among the tallest I have ever heard."

The gallery laughed as Wain got to his feet. "Objection. Argumentative."

"Sustained," Littlejohn said. "Mr. Hagen, although you may not be a trained lawyer, I expect you to conduct yourself as though you are one. One more outburst like that and I'll hold you in contempt."

Oh, I'm sure you would, Hagen thought as he got to his

feet and approached Grimm. He had a strategy, but it was risky. Fortunately, he had nothing to lose except everything. "Mr. Grimm, how long did you work for Mr. Montague?"

"Five years."

"That's a fair amount of time. And you say you were his chief clerk at the bank?"

"I said I worked with him more than any other clerk," Grimm stated, "so I think it's fair to say that I was, in fact, his chief clerk."

"Do you have any proof of that?"

Wain looked like he might object but stopped himself.

Grimm squinted. "Excuse me?"

"It's a straightforward enough question," Adam explained. "You claim you were close with Mr. Montague. Can you prove that?"

Grimm stammered and Adam pressed on. "For example, you say you worked with Mr. Montague to produce the revised will. Do you have any proof of that?"

"Well, not with me," Grimm admitted. "I suppose I have my notes back at the bank that I could refer to, but—"

"But those haven't been submitted into evidence," Adam pointed out. "Not in this trial or the two trials that preceded it. For the moment, all we have is your word, is that correct?"

Grimm pulled at his collar. "Well, I suppose, but I did take an oath just now."

"Yes, you did," Adam agreed. "To tell the truth, the whole truth, and nothing but the truth as I recall. Tell me, Mr. Grimm, how well did you know the late Frederic Montague?"

Grimm looked confused. "I just said we worked closely together."

"Yes, we all remember what you said. That wasn't my question. Allow me to put a finer point on it. Would you say you were personal friends? Did you dine together often? Did you see each other socially?"

Grimm seemed to search his memory. "No, I can't say that I did. I suppose our relationship was more of a professional association."

Adam feigned surprise. "Is that so? Then why would Mr. Montague discuss his inner most personal concerns with you?"

Grimm adjusted his glasses. "I didn't say he did."

"You most certainly said that very thing only a few moments ago when you claimed he told you I was blackmailing him over his indiscretions with a young lady. A daughter of a senator, no less. That is quite a secret to share with a clerk in his bank, don't you think?"

"Objection," Wain said. "Argumentative."

Adam appealed to the judge. "Your Honor, aside from Mr. Grimm, I am the only one in court today who actually knew Mr. Montague. And despite his friendship with my late father, I considered him a friend. I did not know him to be a trusting man, so I must be permitted to question why he would share a personal matter with a clerk who admitted his relationship with the deceased was a purely professional one."

Littlejohn seemed taken by the flurry of words. "I'll allow it. Objection overruled."

Adam turned to face Grimm. "Did Mr. Montague really tell you his concerns about the senator's daughter? Or did you surmise that?"

Grimm adjusted himself in his seat. "It was well-known that Mr. Montague had an affection for—"

"Objection," Adam said. "Hearsay is irrelevant, Your Honor. Idle town gossip cannot be submitted as evidence."

Wain got to his feet. "It can, Your Honor, if it speaks to Mr. Montague's state of mind at the time of the forgery."

"Alleged forgery," Adam corrected.

Wain continued. "The blackmail Mr. Grimm said Adam Hagen was using to pressure Mr. Montague into drawing up a phony will is more than hearsay, Your Honor. It is a fact."

Adam knew he was onto something and stuck with it. "It speaks to motive, Your Honor. Mr. Grimm claims I blackmailed Mr. Montague into drawing up a false will and in forging my father's signature. Mr. Wain makes this supposition based on Mr. Montague's state of mind at the time the new will was drawn up. I assert Mr. Grimm came to that conclusion based on innuendo and rumor, nothing more. I also assert Mr. Montague would not confide in an employee and I had no evidence he corrupted any young women, much less used it against him."

But Wain would not give up so easily. "Your Honor, I'm sure we can produce other employees at the bank who can support Mr. Grimm's testimony."

"Yet you haven't," Adam said. "And I argue that any additional claims to Mr. Montague's state of mind could only be made because of influence by Mr. Grimm's testimony here today. A testimony, I might add, conspicuous in that it is the first time any of this has been brought into evidence despite the two trials that preceded this one."

Adam was glad to see Judge Littlejohn flustered. Brought in to slam the lid on the case in favor of the Hagen family, he had not planned on having a complicated case on his hands.

The judge addressed Grimm directly. "When did Mr.

Montague tell you he was being blackmailed by Adam Hagen?"

"I don't know," Grimm admitted. "I suppose it was around the time he asked me to draw up a revised will for Charles Hagen."

"Which was when?" Adam asked.

"I-I don't know," Grimm stammered. "I imagine it was on the same date as the will was dated. It was a very straightforward document and didn't take me much time at all to draw it up."

Adam smiled as he saw the first crack in Grimm's thin line of defense. "The date was left blank, Mr. Grimm. It was handwritten. Your Honor, I ask you to hand the document back to Mr. Grimm so he may verify that fact."

Littlejohn handed the document down to Grimm, whose mouth moved silently.

Adam saw his opening and pounced. "You claim the rest of the will was written in your hand. Would you say the date was written by another hand?"

Grimm blinked rapidly. "It appears that way. I can't remember the exact date I drew it up, but it was certainly around the time listed here."

Adam spoke over the sounds of surprise from the gallery. "And while you try to remember when you supposedly drew up the will, perhaps you could tell me how many copies of the will you made."

"How many?" Grimm repeated. "Two."

Adam leaned on the edge of the witness box. "Are you absolutely certain?"

"Yes," Grimm said. "I drew up two copies in my own hand."

Adam stepped away from the witness box, the very

picture of disappointment. "The one copy found at the Hagen residence and the one found in Mr. Montague's office. Is that correct?"

Grimm seemed relieved. "Exactly."

Adam reached into his coat pocket and produced a third copy of the will.

The gallery gasped.

Grimm's eyes went wide.

Adam smiled. "Then where did this third copy come from, Mr. Grimm?"

Adam handed it up to Judge Littlejohn. "As you will see, Your Honor, this is identical to the two other copies of the will already in evidence. Those were written not by Mr. Grimm but by the late Mr. Montague. I'm sure the court can find several samples of the deceased's handwriting to make an accurate comparison. You will note the copy now in your hand bears my father's signature, too." He turned to Wain. "His *real* signature, just like the other copies of the will already in evidence."

The gallery erupted as Judge Littlejohn banged his gavel demanding order. The deputies closed in and the ruckus died down.

Adam slowly walked back to his table, glad he'd had the presence of mind to create another copy in Montague's handwriting after learning about Grimm being called as a witness. Having a key to the bank had its privileges. "I submit to the court that if Mr. Grimm is unsure of how many copies of the will were produced, then his recollection of other events, including Mr. Montague's state of mind, must be called into question."

"Objection," Wain shouted. "Why is this the first time we are learning of a third copy of the will when previous court sessions have only discussed two?"

"For the same reason why Mr. Grimm was not called as a witness until today, Your Honor. The matter before the court concerned the validity of the signature, not the number of copies of the will. You'll also note the date corresponds to the same handwritten date on the other copies."

Caleb's face grew red beside Wain. "A forger producing another forged document isn't impossible."

Littlejohn banged his gavel. "Another outburst like that, Mr. Hagen, and you will be removed from this courtroom."

"Your Honor," Wain implored. "The sudden production of this new evidence is awfully convenient."

Adam held his tongue. The scales of justice had just tipped in his favor. He saw no reason to antagonize the judge with another outburst.

He addressed the judge instead. "May I be permitted to ask one final question of this witness, Your Honor?"

Littlejohn looked up from the will he had been handed. "I must advise you to be careful, Mr. Hagen. It might be wise for you to quit while you're ahead."

"My question speaks to another point Mr. Grimm mentioned earlier," Adam told him. "It concerns the possible reason for Mr. Montague's agitated state."

Littlejohn released a heavy breath. "Tread lightly, Mr. Hagen. This court already has much to consider."

Adam bowed. "I have only one short question, Your Honor." He looked at Grimm, who was wiping sweat from his brow with a shaking hand. "Mr. Grimm, you claimed you were closer to Mr. Montague than anyone else in his employ, did you not?"

"Well, as I said, it was a business relationship."

Adam was glad Grimm had made half of his point for him. "Were you aware of the state of his health?"

"He was always a healthy man as far as I could see," Grimm said.

"Yet he had taken to drinking heavier than normal in the days before his death, did he not?" Adam saw Wain standing to object and cut him off by clarifying, "Did you smell alcohol on his breath in the days before he took his own life. More so than normal, especially during business hours? Remember, you're under oath."

Grimm looked at Wain as if asking for permission to answer.

Littlejohn said, "Answer the question, Mr. Grimm."

"Yes, I remember he seemed a bit off in his final days," Grimm admitted. "But like I said earlier, I attributed it to—"

"Yes, we all know you thought it had to do with some fictitious blackmail scheme on my part," Adam said. "But were you aware he was being treated for a heart condition? A serious heart condition his doctor had recently told him would result in his premature death?"

The entire gallery, including the Hagen family, rose in an uproar, forcing Judge Littlejohn to summon Blake and the other deputies to clear them from the court. At the table, Wain had to restrain Caleb from attacking Adam.

Adam stood alone, head slightly bowed as he patiently waited for order to be restored. His trap had sprung nicely.

When the deputies had succeeded in clearing the court, the judge, his clerk, Wain, Caleb, and Adam remained. Grimm was practically cowering in the witness box.

Judge Littlejohn glowered down at Adam. "Now that it's just us, you'd better have a damned good explanation, Mr. Hagen. And evidence to support it."

Adam was glad he had one. "As I said earlier, Fred and

I were friends. He had seen how cruel my father had been to me all those years and took pity on me. He always managed to send me a little more money than my father allowed, a fact that I'm sure can be substantiated by my late father's business records. Mr. Montague's kindness saw me through many dark times in my life. I suppose I have him to thank for my father's change of heart in his last days. My father and I had reconciled. He even came to visit me when I was shot. I can produce witnesses to that statement should the court wish me to do so."

"Your Honor," Wain said. "I believe this court can do without the melodrama."

The judge agreed. "Get to the point, Mr. Hagen."

"Mr. Montague told me Dr. Moore gave him the sad news about his heart condition just before he took his own life. I suppose I should have kept a closer eye on him, but hindsight can be most cruel. I allowed the man to have his dignity and never thought he was capable of committing suicide. I know Dr. Moore will be willing to testify as to his medical condition here in court." *Or he will,* Adam thought, *when I tell him to.* "I only raised this detail because it speaks to the actual reason Mr. Montague was in a distressed state of mind before he took his own life, not some blackmail effort on my part."

Wain leapt into the uneasy silence that followed. "Your Honor, the respondent has entered two major items into evidence in a matter of minutes of each other. I humbly request we be given the opportunity to investigate these rather bold facts for ourselves."

The judge sat back in his chair and emitted another heavy breath. He looked at Grimm, who appeared to be on the verge of tears. "I take it Mr. Montague's condition is news to you, Mr. Grimm?"

The witness slowly shook his head. "I had no idea."

"Do you care to amend any of your earlier testimony in light of these new facts?"

"No, Your Honor," Grimm said, then added, "not really."

Wain dropped his head into his hands.

"You're excused, Mr. Grimm," Littlejohn told him.

As the little man scrambled from the witness box and dashed out of the courtroom, the judge said, "This court stands in recess until the day after tomorrow. We will have all of the facts at our disposal by then and rule accordingly." He banged the gavel and seemed as relieved to leave the room as Grimm had been.

The clerk quickly gathered up the judge's papers from the bench and darted after his boss into the chambers.

Caleb cut loose with a string of curses as he barged out of the courtroom. Wain slipped his papers into his satchel as Adam stood by the table, intent on allowing the young lawyer to either leave first or have the last word.

Wain chose the last word. "You know, your family warned me about you."

"You should have heeded them."

"Everyone ran you down except Elena," Wain said. "They all told me you were the devil incarnate, capable of anything, but not her. She's the only one of them who saw any goodness in you. That speaks more for her character than yours. But after what you did here today, I doubt even she will be able to speak on your behalf. I hope you're proud of yourself."

Adam knew if he had one weakness, it was his youngest sister's good opinion of him. And he resented this young pup using it against him. "Elena will never want for anything in this world. She can rest assured of that. God knows your career won't be worth much after what happened here today gets back to Philadelphia." He grinned at his brother-in-law. "An up-and-coming attorney being outshined by the black sheep of the family. The town drunk, no less." He shook his head. "Your firm won't make you partner now. But don't worry. I'll always have some work to throw your way. I'll keep you out of the gutter for Elena's sake. After you apologize to me, of course."

"Never!" Wain shut his case and stormed out of the courtroom.

Adam closed his eyes as the courtroom door slammed shut. The echo of it reverberated in his soul. Win or lose, at least they'd know they had been in a fight. Sometimes, that had to be enough.

He looked around the quiet room and smiled to himself. "You know, Adam. You could've made a pretty good lawyer at that."

CHAPTER 23

While the trial was just finishing up, Trammel was stuck in his office with Mayor Holm, and other leading citizens of the city. All of them were firing questions at him. None of them seemed to notice, much less care about the long white bandages that formed an *X* across the sheriff's face. His eyes, nose, and mouth were uncovered, but the gash Carson had stitched up was beginning to ache. He and Emily had pleaded with him to lie down and rest, but Trammel had no intention of resting with so much going on in his city.

Doc Carson and Emily stood on each side of his desk like guardians.

"Gentlemen," Carson said to the mayor and the others as he held up a hand to stop their questions. "I must ask you to appreciate our predicament. Most of our deputies are downstairs tending to the Hagen trial and Sheriff Trammel is recuperating from a severe wound to his face he suffered in apprehending the suspect in Rob's killing. He's still under the effects of an anesthetic and may not be able to speak with you for long. If he begins to feel poorly, I'll have no choice but to ask you all to leave." It was not a request, but a statement of fact.

All the men in the office seemed to take it as such.

"Well?" Mayor Holm asked no one in particular. "Did you catch the murderer, Trammel? Is he dead?"

Stanton's boot heel may have caught him only across the face, but his whole head ached. The painkillers Doc Carson had given him during the stitching had begun to wear off and his entire face began to throb. "The man we believe to be the killer of Marshal Rob Moran is dead."

Every man in the office began to breathe again. Some even shook hands with each other, as if they'd had something to do with catching the killer.

"I haven't been able to investigate the man's room personally," Trammel went on, "but I've had a deputy searching it all day. I think his name is Major John Stanton, but I don't know if that's accurate or if it's even his real name." He gently patted his bandages. "Just about the only thing I can tell you for certain is that he kicks like a mule."

Many of the men in the office laughed.

Mayor Holm did not. "You mean *kicked*, don't you, Sheriff? As in the past tense for he is most assuredly dead, correct?"

Trammel regretted meeting with these men while his brain was still in a fog, but he wanted to set the record straight before the Laramie rumor mill got busy working on the case. He just had to be sure not to slip up and accidentally tell them the truth about Stanton being alive. "Sorry for the poor choice of words, Mayor. I guess I'm still a bit out of it from Doc Carson's handiwork."

Mayor Holm made it clear he understood completely. "I think we've troubled the poor sheriff enough for one day." He looked at Doctor Carson and said, "Let's leave this man in peace and let us see the body. Mr. Stanton's body, that is."

Trammel was glad half of his face was crossed in bandages or the men in the office might have seen the look of surprise on his face.

The doctor stepped in. "I'd like to get a look at him myself, gentlemen. I've been too busy tending to the sheriff here to examine his corpse since Dr. Kelly had it pulled down from the roof. After I have had a chance to examine it, I'm sure we can arrange a time when you can see it."

"But I want to see it now," Holm said. "The man's dead, so looking at him shouldn't do much harm."

"No harm to him," Carson admitted, "but to yourselves is another matter entirely. Have you ever seen a body after it has fallen from a great height, Walt? I can assure you it's not a pretty sight. For the sakes of your stomachs and my examining room floor, it's best if I look him over first. When he's presentable, I'll invite you all to view the body."

The men began to protest, but Carson hushed them as he herded them toward the door. "The sheriff's been through quite an ordeal," the doctor told them as he encouraged them into the hall. "Let's give the man his rest. We don't want the wound he suffered to become infected. You, too, Mr. Mayor. Let's go and give this brave man the peace he deserves."

Trammel could tell Holm wanted to stay, but Carson did not give him the opportunity. The doctor pushed the last of the men out the door and closed it behind him.

Emily sat on the edge of Trammel's desk. "Doctor Carson's worth his weight in gold. He really knows how to handle them."

"He's been doing it long enough," Trammel said. "Don't forget to remind me to thank him when things calm down."

She winced as she stroked his hair. "You're in a lot of pain, aren't you?"

He tried to not touch his face. "Only when I breathe."

"There's only one thing that'll help with that, young man, and that's plenty of good old-fashioned rest. I'm taking you home right now. Doctor's orders."

Trammel knew his wife meant well, but rest was out of the question for a while. "I can't, Em. I've got the Hagen trial going on downstairs and a man searching Stanton's rooms. I'm the only one not doing anything. The least I can do is help where I can."

Emily pushed herself off the desk and put her hands on her hips. "I'd say you've done more than anyone could expect for one day. You single-handedly brought Rob Moran's killer to justice and saved the life of an innocent young woman all before noon. And you got your face cut open in the bargain. I'd say the City of Laramie got enough out of you for one day. Now, let's go, mister. Off to bed with you."

Trammel hated to disappoint her, but he was not ready to go anywhere near home yet. "You've got patients to tend to who need you more than I do. And I've got a deputy searching Stanton's place all alone. Clay's bound to be giving him grief. I'd best go see if I can help him any. After the trial breaks for today, I'll ask Blake if he needs any help. If I can come home then, I will." He even held up his right hand to show his sincerity. "I promise."

But she would not be persuaded by an oath she knew he would not keep. "Your cut is deep and serious, Buck. The only way it'll have any chance of healing is if you get plenty of rest so your body can heal. You may get an infection, and I'll be able to spot it easier if you're in bed instead of running around like you do. If you get an infection, you could die. It could go straight to your brain and, if that happens, no one on earth will be able to help you then."

Trammel did not know how he could convince her. "Damn it, Emily. We're shorthanded with a big trial underway and a killer who's supposed to be dead but isn't. I know I'm taking a risk, but it's a risk I have to take. I've got men out there risking their lives. I can't just rest while they're in danger. At least let me see how things are going. I'll rest a lot better knowing how things stand."

"Until tomorrow," Emily argued. "When you come up with another excuse to get out of bed."

"No. By then, I'll know what's going on in town. I'll have the men report to me at the house. I promise I'll rest as much as possible." He took her hand in his. "You wouldn't let me pull you from a sick patient, would you? Same thing here with me. Let me finish this part and I promise I'll let Blake and the others clean up the rest."

She did not pull her hand away, but did not look happy, either. "Did you see the way Mayor Holm looked when you talked about Stanton?"

Trammel was glad he had not been the only one who saw it. "Looked like he wanted to make sure the man was dead. Probably for Clay's sake."

"And he won't take kindly to you hiding Stanton from him."

"We'll let Carson worry about that on his own." Trammel smiled as he got up. "I'll be too busy resting, remember?"

She looked up at him before embracing him tightly. "I sure hope so."

Trammel ignored all the stares his bandages drew from the townspeople after he walked Emily back to her office.

In a short amount of time in town, many of the women in Laramie had decided to be treated by her instead of her male colleagues. He wanted her to worry about her patients instead of him. He had never been a man who enjoyed too much attention.

He was surprised to see a large crowd gathered in front of city hall as he walked back to check on Deputy Bush at Clay's saloon. He was there to search Stanton's rooms and take anything of interest.

But the crowd of people Trammel saw spilling out of the town hall troubled him. They were not in a panic, as if gunshots or a fire had broken out, but it was clear something had stirred them up.

He was glad to see Blake standing on the top step keeping an eye on the situation.

As he walked toward his chief deputy, he noticed a fair number of the crowd were members of the Hagen family. The gunmen they had brought with them had formed a loose circle around the family, separating them from the rest of the spectators.

Bartholomew saw Trammel and began to approach him, though his sister, Debora got there first. "I was wondering when you'd show up," she spat. "Come to help your friend steal our family fortune, have you?"

Bart followed up close behind her, though his glare softened when he saw the bandages crossing Trammel's face. "What in God's name happened to you?"

"Cut myself shaving," Trammel told him. "What are you all doing outside?"

"Judge Littlejohn had us thrown from the courtroom," Debora said. "Imagine that. Hagen men and women being cast out into the street like common rabble."

Trammel figured Adam had done something to cause

the judge to clear the court, but anything that took Debora down a couple of pegs was just fine in the sheriff's book. "Sounds like you folks have cause to ask for a refund. You're not paying him to treat you like that."

Trammel began to walk away, but Bart tried to cut him off. "Just wait a minute, Sheriff. You have no cause to talk to my sister like that."

Trammel did not stop walking when Bart stood in front of him, which gave the smaller man no choice but to back out of his way before he was knocked over. Sometimes, size was a benefit. He stood on the bottom step of city hall, making him eye level with Blake. "What happened?"

Blake kept eyeing the crowd as he said, "The judge kicked them out for causing a racket. It was all your friend Adam's doing. I've heard stories about him, but I don't think I know the half of it."

"You don't. What did he do?"

"Dropped some pretty hard facts on them," Blake said. "I don't think they were expecting that. Don't think they liked it much, either."

Knowing Adam as well as he did, Trammel was not surprised. "Adam's not one to allow something like a crooked judge stand in his way. Not when there's so much money at stake."

Blake glanced at Trammel. "You'll forgive me for saying so, but you don't look so good."

That reminded him of Bush and his search of Stanton's rooms over at the saloon. "Gary come back yet?"

"Just did," Blake said. "Lugged over a whole bunch of luggage with him, including Stanton's guns. And no, he didn't find a Sharps, but no one thought it would be that easy. He's going through what he found, then heading over to the livery to see if Stanton might've kept it on his saddle.

My guess is he ditched it in the swamp on the road to Blackstone. Or chucked it somewhere on his way back to town."

Trammel agreed. Most men would not get rid of a good rifle like that one, but most men had not used it to kill a federal marshal. Losing the murder weapon only made good sense. "Did Clay give Bush any trouble during the search?"

Blake shook his head. "Didn't come out of his room the entire time. One of the girls took to working the bar, so I'd wager you gave the barman quite a scare. The bouncer's back on the job, though. At least you didn't kill him."

Trammel felt his entire head begin to throb and the world swam before his eyes. The painkillers Doc Carson had given him were wearing off by the second. He figured he should get back home and in bed before he fell over face-first in the street. "Listen," he told Blake, "I'm in no shape to be out here, so I'm going to head home."

Before he could say anything further, Blake nodded. "I've already called in the night men to help keep an eye on things. I'll let Mrs. Trammel know if anything happens and I'll stall the mayor as much as possible. I'll also do whatever Doc Carson tells me to do about Stanton. Folks are already rumbling about wanting to see his body. I'll keep them at bay until you or the doc tell me otherwise."

Trammel was glad Blake had turned out to be as capable as Rob Moran had told him. "Thanks. I'll be home if you need me."

Chapter 24

From his rooms above the saloon, Lucien Clay parted a curtain and watched Sheriff Trammel walk away from Deputy Blake, perhaps heading for home. Clay did not know how the big man had earned the bandages that crossed his face but imagined his run-in with Stanton had something to do with it. He was glad the gunman had not gone down without a fight.

Clay, for his part, had never felt so helpless in his life.

He had allowed Trammel to barge into his place of business, knock out his bouncer, scare off his bartender, and kill one of his assassins.

All that after the night his saloon was laid siege to by a mob of angry protestors.

Clay was mindful of his agreement with the Hagen family, but the chaos could not be allowed to continue. In less than twenty-four hours, he had gone from one of the most feared men in the territory to a joke forced to hide in his rooms like a frightened widow. He had lived up to his end of his bargain with the Hagen clan. Trammel had not only been moved out of Blackstone, but he was bogged down in a murder investigation.

It was time for the Hagen family to live up to theirs.

Recovered from the pistol-whipping Trammel had given him, Clay ordered Oates to keep an eye out for Bernard Wain and bring him over to the saloon as soon as he left city hall. Given by what he could see of the Hagen family and spectators milling about on the street, Clay imagined Adam had managed to pull an ace from his sleeve. He had always been a resourceful man and had never been one to allow inconvenient facts to get in the way of what he wanted.

Clay had warned the family Adam would not go gently and judging from their frowns and ruffled expressions, they had not heeded his warning. Even crooked judges could not ignore all evidence, and he was sure Adam had uncovered something that turned the tide in his favor.

Clay was not simply a passive observer of what was happening right outside his window. His fortunes stood to rise or fall depending on their success against Adam. Either way, he would continue to have a piece of Blackstone, but how big a piece depended on how the judge ruled.

Stanton's death complicated things. Clay had not counted on having to sacrifice the mercenary so soon, certainly had not counted on anyone finding him on saloon property. A bit worried, Clay hoped Stanton had been true to his word and had managed to get rid of the big rifle. Without it, there would always be doubt about Stanton's guilt.

With it, Lucien Clay was as good as dead.

Either way, Trammel had turned out to be a far bigger obstacle than Clay had thought. Depending on how his conversation with young Bernard Wain turned out, Buck Trammel might not live to see another day.

Clay watched the street with renewed interest as he

saw Wain step out from city hall. He appeared every bit as flustered as his in-laws. He was glad to see Oates appear on the street and reach Wain just as the family flocked to him. The young attorney kissed his pretty wife on the cheek and patted her hand before handing his bag to Caleb and following Oates back to the saloon.

"Finally, something goes my way today," Clay said as he let the curtain fall back in place.

Knowing Deputy Bush had finished searching Stanton's rooms, Clay went down to his office without fear of questioning or arrest. Trammel and his men looked too busy with other matters for the moment to worry about him. Tomorrow might be different. For many reasons.

He opened his office door just as Oates brought Wain into the saloon. He beckoned the men to come toward him and took his seat behind the desk. Wain entered and sat down as Oates stood by the door waiting for orders.

"Go back outside and keep an eye on the street. And send someone to find Harry. I'm paying that louse to pour whiskey, not hide out somewhere. Tell him all is forgiven as long as he comes back right now."

Oates told him he would handle it and shut the door behind him.

Now that it was just the two of them, he could see how pale Wain was. His time in court must have gone worse than Clay had thought. The lawyer looked like a man who needed a drink.

But Clay did not give him one until he knew more. "Looks like Adam roughed you up pretty good in there."

"By lying." Wain's pink face reddened with rage. "He fabricated everything. A new copy of the will along with a fiction about Montague being depressed about some heart ailment no one knew about . . . until now."

The young lawyer was sharp, but he was only book smart. He did not have the years behind him to know life was about more than just knowledge.

Clay laughed. "You're threatening his future. You didn't expect him to roll over and let you rub his belly, did you?"

"I don't know what you're laughing about." Wain sneered. "You have as much to lose in this matter as we do. Perhaps more."

Clay imagined he did, but it was important to remind the youngster to know his place. If the family grew desperate, they might decide to forget their arrangement with Clay. He could not have that. Not when he looked vulnerable. Plenty of men in Laramie would not hesitate to move against him if he looked weak.

Keeping the young attorney in line would be a good place to start to reclaim his dominance. "I'm well aware of what I have to gain and lose by the trial, Mr. Wain. As long as you don't forget about our agreement, we'll be fine. Just make sure you don't lose. Do you think you can still rely on the judge to back you?"

"After the show Adam put on in there?" Wain shook his head. "I don't know. I do know court is in recess for the next day. I hope that gives my brother-in-law Ambrose enough time to remind the judge of where and by whom his bread is buttered."

"You'll probably have to pay him more," Clay said, "but that shouldn't be a problem for you. I can loan you the money if cash is a problem."

Wain appeared insulted. "It most certainly is not. My family is already indebted to you enough as it is. I have no intention of deepening our association."

"Just as long as you don't forget it runs pretty deep

already," Clay said. "Your family's good name won't be worth much if it gets tied to the murder of a local hero."

Wain sat stiffly in his chair and tried to put an edge in his voice. "Let me remind you, Mr. Clay—"

A series of hard knocks on the office door caused Clay to raise his hand to stop him from making a fool of himself. "What is it?"

"It's me. Oates," his bouncer said. "And it's important."

Before he had the chance to tell him to enter, the door opened and Oates staggered in. Adam Hagen entered closely behind him, a pistol aimed at Oates's back.

"You performed admirably, my good man." Hagen stepped aside and motioned toward the door. "Now go back outside and keep watching the street like a good dog." He kicked the door shut before Oates was barely through it.

He grinned at Clay and Wain, though there was no hint of humor in it. And kept his pistol in his hand. "Well, isn't this a cozy situation. My dear brother-in-law and my business partner together in conference. Hope I'm interrupting something important."

"You are." Clay remained calm. He knew it would only be a matter of time before Hagen learned of his betrayal . . . if he had not suspected it already. The man had many faults, but as he had warned Wain many times, Adam Hagen was no fool. "Grab a seat and make yourself at home." Clay gestured toward the small bar behind him. "Want a drink?"

Hagen shook his head as he tucked the pistol away and leaned against the door. "Always a gracious host. No thanks. I'm still relishing my victory over young Wain here. I don't want to dilute the feeling with liquor."

Wain had turned in his chair to face his in-law. "Relish it while you can, Adam. It won't last."

"That remains to be seen. Even you have to admit I made quite a compelling argument in there. Raising the Montague question without knowing all the facts was foolish on your part. That's what happens when my family sends a boy to do a man's job. I suppose handing the case over to you was Debora's idea. Probably thought she could save some money by keeping it in the family." He winked at Wain. "She's getting cheap in her old age . . . and she's getting what she paid for."

Hands balled into fists, Wain surprised Clay by getting to his feet and facing Hagen fully. For a moment, Clay wondered if the young man might strike Adam. That would be something to see. He doubted Adam would shoot him, but he would give Wain a beating he would not soon forget.

The back of the young lawyer's neck turn scarlet. "You're feeling awfully good about yourself right now, aren't you? Well remember this feeling, Adam. You'll need it in the days to come, especially when it comes out you're not really a Hagen."

"You wound me, sir." Adam's smile grew wider as he clutched his heart. "Is that your big secret? The cannon shot you hope will clear the field and win the day? My boy, I *am* a Hagen, by blood, if not by name. My mother was a Hagen, which is not in dispute. Neither is Charles's adoption of me by right if not by law. He raised me as his own and provided for me as such. I'd hoped a Philadelphia lawyer, even one as young as you, would know lineage plays no part in this case. The last will and testament of Charles Hagen leaves everything to me. Two judges have already ruled so."

"Your judges," Wain argued. "This one is different."

"I know. This one was bought and paid for by you, or should I say, the Forresters. But the law is the same. And if he does happen to rule against me, I can always launch an appeal of my own despite the governor's intervention on your behalf. I wouldn't be in too much of a hurry to make any changes to the ranch house, dear brother-in-law, for it will still belong to me long after Judge Littlejohn makes his ruling."

Wain slowly began to walk toward Adam.

Clay got to his feet to get a better angle on what might happen next. Whatever it was, it was bound to be entertaining.

As passively as if Wain were a spaniel sniffing the floor, Adam watched the lawyer approach. He remained leaning against the door as the young man spoke.

"When court reconvenes in two days, you'll see just what a Philadelphia lawyer can do."

"What a dramatic exit." Hagen pushed himself off the door and held it open. "Until then, good sir."

Wain stormed out.

Hagen laughed as he shut the door behind him. "What the boy lacks in acumen, he makes up for in enthusiasm, doesn't he?"

Disappointed, Clay resumed his seat. "Too bad enthusiasm doesn't win court cases."

"You'd be surprised. I think I'll take you up on that drink now." Hagen walked to the bar. "Will you have one?" He took the top from the decanter.

"No," Clay said. "I'm afraid of what you might put in it."

"Lucien, after all we've been through, do you think I'd reward your treachery with something as passive as poison?" Hagen chided. "Perish the thought." He poured himself a drink, replaced the top on the decanter, and put it back in place. "Though I must confess I'm curious. How much did they offer you to betray me?"

Clay decided there was no reason for honesty just yet. "What makes you think I betrayed you?"

"You've never been good at being coy, Lucien. I wouldn't recommend trying it now. Old dogs and all that." Adam took his drink and sat in the same chair Wain had occupied only a few moments before. "Ah, it's still warm from all of that indignation. I'll admit young Wain had thrown me for a loop for a moment. All those details he and Grimm laid out about my plans with Montague. That pup might be smart enough to ask the questions, but he hardly had the resources to find them on his own. And poor old Grimm certainly didn't know anything. I doubt they even knew he existed until you told them about him. Grimm was your man in Montague's bank, wasn't he?"

"Of course," Clay admitted. "I've got people in every major institution in this territory. The Bank of Blackstone is no different. You'd do well to remember that."

"I assumed as much." Adam toasted Clay with his whiskey. "Well played, by the way. Grimm is quite a forgettable fellow. He must've told you an awful lot over the years, but not about the will. That was all my doing. Me and Fred Montague alone. Only you knew the details, Lucien. You and me. That's how I knew you'd thrown in with my family against me."

Clay knew as much. "Too bad you can't use that argument in court. You can always call me as a witness if you'd like. I could tell him a couple of interesting things about our arrangement."

"Thank you for the kind offer, but you'll understand if I decline." Hagen sipped his drink. "Win or lose, I have more than enough for an appeal. Now, don't think I forgot about my original question. How much did they offer you to betray me?"

"Betray is an ugly word."

"But accurate in this instance. How much?"

"All of Blackstone," Clay told him. "Once you were ruined, of course."

"Oh, of course. One hundred percent of something is better than the fifty percent of our agreement."

"That was my thinking, too." Clay wondered if he could reach the pistol in the top drawer of his desk before Adam could draw. Unrivaled with a gun before Trammel had shattered his jaw, he imagined his reflexes were still good enough to cut down Adam if it came to that. "What tipped you off? Before Grimm, I mean."

"Trammel's rapid promotion. He's a good man, but not the first choice for running a city like Laramie. I knew such a move took political acumen my family doesn't currently possess. I would've heard about it if they had tried. I also would've been asked my opinion on the matter if the city fathers came up with the idea themselves. Moran may have put Buck's name forward for the job, but you're the only one who could've made it happen without my influence or knowledge."

It was Clay's turn to smile. "Like I've always said, Adam. You're no fool."

Ignoring the compliment, Hagen said, "Killing Moran was clumsy and unnecessary, though. Buck never would've helped me in Blackstone now that he has responsibilities here. He was too star-struck to allow himself to be distracted by my troubles."

"He's always had a knack for finding a way to save you before. Now, he couldn't do it even if he wanted to."

Hagen sipped his drink and thought about that for a moment. "Yes, I suppose you have a point. But no matter.

Events have been put in motion that cannot be undone, no matter how much we wish otherwise."

Clay had never sensed worry in Adam Hagen before, but he sensed it now. "Events seem to be unfolding just fine from where I sit." He watched Adam's eyes move over him.

As he finished the last of his whiskey, Hagen's eyes were not as passive as they had been watching Wain approach him. They looked Clay over as if seeing him for the first time. "Perhaps." Setting the glass on Clay's desk, he added, "For now," and stood up slowly, careful to keep his hands away from his sides.

It did not make Clay feel any easier. He shifted his chair just enough to be ready to go for the gun in his desk if he had to.

Hagen said, "I suppose it goes without saying that our previous arrangement is null and void. You're now the proud owner of a hundred percent of nothing."

Clay had been expecting that. "Well, like a wise man once said, 'Perhaps. For now.'"

Hagen bowed as he walked backward toward the door, pausing only once he placed his hand on the knob. "You know I'll have to kill you for this."

"Not if I kill you first."

"I'm glad we understand each other." Hagen touched the brim of his hat. "Until that glorious day, Lucien." He quietly shut the door behind him and left Clay alone in his office.

Clay's jaw began to ache, and he reached for the bottle of laudanum he kept in his pocket. He was about to drink it but stopped when he saw how much his hand shook from the effort. He had become too dependent on the stuff. He would have to wean himself off it. It was not the time to have the shakes. He would need steady hands for the deeds that lie ahead.

He called out for Oates, who rushed into his office. "I'm sorry about that, Mr. Clay, but he had a gun on me before I knew it and—"

"I need you to get a couple of boys together to do a job for me," Clay interrupted. He had not called the bouncer in to hear his excuses. "Good boys who can keep their mouths shut afterward and won't know they're working for me. Boys who haven't worked for me before. But you can't do it yourself. Understand?"

"Sure, boss," Oates said. "What do you need done?"

"To turn things in our favor for once."

Chapter 25

Trammel woke when he heard the creak of the stairs.

It was not the creak that bothered him, but the silence that followed. He raised his head from the pillow enough to look out the window and saw it was only beginning to get dark outside. Too early for Emily to be home from her patients yet.

It had to be someone else. Someone who had known he was home. Someone who figured he would be in no condition to hear them coming.

They were wrong.

He pulled the Peacemaker from beneath his pillow and quietly sat up in bed, listening.

Another creak on the stairs assured him it must be a stranger. Emily or a deputy would have announced themselves already. Anyone who knew him knew he did not like surprises.

Someone was intent on surprising him.

Trammel had other plans. He swung his bare feet out of the far side of the bed and crouched behind it. He knew the feather mattress would not offer protection from a bullet, but he did not intend to allow things to get that far.

Whoever was lurking in his house was already a dead man. He just did not know it yet.

Trammel ignored the pain webbing through his skull and blinked hard to keep his eyes clear, knowing it might be one of his deputies. He needed to be sure before he squeezed off a shot. He tensed when he heard the doorknob rattle before the intruder pushed the door inward.

A large, bearded man he did not recognize stepped halfway into the room, only to stop when he saw the bed was empty. His hands were empty, save for an overstuffed pillow Trammel recognized from the couch in the drawing room downstairs.

"Don't move," Trammel told him from behind the bed. "Drop what you're holding and throw up your hands."

The bearded stranger held the pillow with his left while he let go of it with his right. "Now, you just hold on there. This is all just a misunderstanding."

Trammel saw the man's right hand reach for something and the sheriff fired. The bullet burst through the pillow, sending feathers fluttering through the air.

The man cursed as he staggered back into the hall. He dropped the pillow and began to run down the stairs.

Trammel vaulted across the bed, hit the floor with his bare feet, and gave chase. The stranger turned and fired a shot that hit the wall to Trammel's left, causing him to duck. He heard the man reach the first floor and charged down the stairs after him.

As he reached the bottom step, he stole a quick glance around the wall. His front door was open. He saw the outline of a man crouched on his porch and ducked back just as a shotgun blast ripped through the wall.

Trammel stuck his pistol around the corner and fired.

A man yelped, followed by the unmistakable clatter of gunmetal on wood. He knew he had hit his mark.

Another quick glance proved no one was waiting for him outside, but he approached the doorway carefully. Two men were wounded, and they had tried to kill him twice. He did not want to make it easy for them.

The hall began to swim before him and, despite the pain, he blinked his eyes clear. He fell more than leaned against the side of the open doorway and raised his pistol. Although his vision had doubled, he could not see anyone waiting for him.

He felt himself begin to sink against the wall, no matter how much he willed himself to stay upright. Everything he saw tilted at a horrible angle and he felt his stomach lurch. The last thing he heard, over what sounded like Emily calling his name, was the sound of his own pistol hitting the floor.

Trammel woke with a start and felt two firm hands on his shoulders. "Easy, Buck. Easy. You're fine. Just weak is all."

Trammel shook his eyes clear and saw Adam Hagen smiling down at him. "Welcome back to the land of the living."

"If I'm seeing you," Trammel said, "I must be in the other place."

"If we were," Hagen said with a smile, "I can assure you we'd be having a much better time and your lovely bride wouldn't be with us."

Trammel struggled to raise himself enough to see Emily wringing out a cloth in a bowl on the dresser. Adam moved away so she could return to tend to her husband by placing that warm cloth on his head.

"You just had a nasty fall is all," Emily told him. "No new damage done. You're just exhausted and need rest."

He was beginning to think he might have dreamed up the part about the men who had snuck into his home. "There were men," he said before his mouth went dry. "Men who tried to hurt me."

"You hurt them first." Adam held up the pillow Trammel remembered shooting. "Couldn't do much for this old thing, I'm afraid." He tossed the pillow aside. "As for the two who came to kill you, I wouldn't worry too much about them."

The warm cloth Emily had placed on his head felt good. "Why?"

"Because judging by the amount of blood we've found, they won't be long for this world." Hagen laughed. "Good old Buck. Even with a face cut to ribbons and a busted skull, you still manage to put down your man. I'll chalk that up to just plain, old fashioned meanness."

Trammel was glad he had not dreamed the whole thing. "Luck is more like it. I couldn't see much. Where'd they go?"

"Got on their horses and rode out of town," Hagen told him. "Your deputies say it's too dark to track them now, not that it matters. Unless they've got a doctor waiting for them somewhere to stop all that bleeding, I don't think they'll make morning."

"Did you recognize them, Buck," Emily asked as she stroked his head, making his hair stick up.

"No," Trammel admitted. "They were just blurry shapes to me. I shot one up here and got lucky with the shotgunner covering him from the porch."

"I'll leave you two alone. I'll be here the rest of the night if their friends decide to come back."

Trammel's mind might have been foggy, but he remembered the trial was still going on. "Can't have that, Adam.

You've got enough going on and I can't appear to be partial. I'll have one of my deputies keep an eye on things."

"Like they kept an eye on you before?" Adam shook his head. "They're outside minding the street and the back alley. I'll be downstairs in the drawing room keeping vigil. You might need to appear impartial, but I don't." He left the bedroom before Trammel could argue with him.

Trammel was about to call after him, but Emily held a finger to his lips. "Don't fight him, Steve. He was awfully worried about you. Don't ask me how he did it, but he carried you upstairs all on his own. He laid into Blake something awful about not having a man watching you."

Trammel blamed himself for that. "I left when the trial was breaking up. Blake had other things on his mind. It's my fault for saying where I was going in front of folks. Should've been more careful about that, but—"

"But now, you need to rest," she told him. "Your stitches started bleeding again when you fell, and I've redressed them. That cut will get infected if you don't rest."

"If I have to hear about an infection one more time—"

"Then do what I tell you for once and *rest*. This isn't Blackstone. You don't have to carry the entire town on your back anymore. You have men for that. Let them earn their keep."

He held her hand as tightly as he dared as what really bothered him came to the surface. "I'm just glad they came at me before you were here. If they'd gotten hold of you, I was in no shape to do much about it."

She ran her free hand along the side of his face. "You don't have to worry about that. Blake's going to have a deputy with me at all times. You too. And don't go getting mad at him for not giving you regular reports. He's under strict orders from me to not bother you without talking to me first."

Trammel loved how protective she could be of him. "That so?"

She sat straight on the side of the bed. "It certainly is. This is my house and what I say goes."

"Yes, ma'am." He smiled despite the pain it caused him.

"Good." She pulled the sheets up to his neck and gave him a kiss on the cheek. "Now, you get busy resting and I'll get busy putting on a pot of coffee for the boys. I'll be back up here as soon as I can." She lowered the flame on the lamp and kissed him in the darkness. "I love you, Sheriff Trammel."

"Love you, too, Dr. Trammel."

Despite the darkness, he could tell she was smiling. "You say the most wonderful things sometimes."

By the time she got downstairs, Emily already smelled a pot of coffee brewing. She walked into the kitchen and found Adam Hagen at the stove. He not only had on her apron, but he was also frying some biscuits and bacon in a pan.

Emily laughed at the sight of Adam in the pink frilly apron Steve had bought her last Christmas. It was a gaudy thing, but she did not have the heart to tell him that. She wore it because she knew he thought she would like it.

Crossing her arms, she leaned against the doorway of her kitchen. "Why, Adam. I didn't know you were so domesticated."

Adam continued tending to his meal. "I'm a man of many talents, Emily. Learned how to do it in the army. We were out on patrol once and our cook ran off with a squaw we met on the trail. The sergeant who took over his duties damned near killed us with burnt bacon, undercooked biscuits, and coffee strong enough to polish brass. I took over the duties for the men and, I must say, we never had a more enjoyable patrol."

He held up one of the pink frills on the apron. "Can't say I'd imagine this is your style, though. I take it this was Buck's idea?"

"Oh, I know it's horrible, but don't tell him. He thinks it's pretty."

"Your secret is safe with me," he said, and she knew it was.

She looked at him as he stood at her stove. "You're a strange man, Adam Hagen. All these years and I still can't figure you out."

"Mystery is one of my few virtues. I like to keep people guessing."

She knew he meant to be funny, but she was not trying to joke. "I mean it. Steve spent a lot of time standing up against you in Blackstone. I couldn't blame you for resenting him for it. Yet here you are, in his house, guarding him and fixing a meal for his deputies."

Adam pushed the bacon around the pan with a spoon and flipped the biscuits. "Buck Trammel is my friend. That doesn't mean I have to be his. He didn't stand against me out of jealousy or greed. He did it because he was right. Opium is a terrible business. Believe it or not, I hate it. But my feelings on the subject don't matter a whit. Men will still buy it and smoke it. I wanted to win my family's fortune, so I used the only means at my disposal to make that happen. That takes money, and opium was the quickest way to get a lot of it. The poppy served its purpose.

Once I have my father's empire, I'll eradicate the stuff from Blackstone. On that, you have my word."

That did not lighten her spirits any. "Your trial is the talk of the town. My patients don't talk of anything else. I heard you put on quite a performance today."

Adam smiled as he tended to his cooking. "As I said, I'm full of surprises. Cooking's not the only thing I learned in the army. Picked up a thing or two about the law. Like cooking, it was out of necessity."

She had forgotten he had been an officer in the army. "You were brought up on charges?"

"More than once. The last time, even my own lawyer thought I was guilty. I had no choice but to take up my own defense."

"And?"

He held out his hands. "And I didn't hang. I guess that counts for something."

She watched him go back to cooking his meal and could not help but sense a certain sorrow in him. "People haven't always been kind to you, have they? Not even your own father."

"Charles Hagen killed my own father, as you know well, my good lady. The King raised me, though he resented it. I suppose that skewed my view of the world. I didn't have many friends because I didn't look for them. I learned early on that allegiance is best when it's bought, for at least then, you have some say in the outcome." He looked up at the ceiling. "Then that big lug upstairs came along and saved my life for no earthly reason than because it was the right thing to do."

"The way I heard it," Emily said, "Wyatt Earp didn't give him much choice in the matter."

"Buck got me out of Wichita," Hagen explained. "He

could've left me there while I was too sick to move. He didn't. That says more about him than it does of me."

Emily thought she was finally getting a glimpse behind the thick curtain Adam Hagen kept draped around himself. "And you've been paying him back for it ever since."

He looked at her. "Yes. In my own way, I suppose I have."

A shudder went through her. "I know you could've killed him if you'd wanted to. You're better with a gun than he is. Faster. More accurate. I'm glad you didn't, but I know you could've done it. In his own way, I think he knows it, too, though he'd never admit it."

She watched Adam take the pan from the oven and place it on top of towels he had piled onto the kitchen table. "When I was a boy, my father took me shooting once. I was ten years old, and he thought hunting would help me develop the killer instinct a man needed to have in order to survive out here. It wasn't my first time hunting. If anything, I'd brought down game he'd missed. Bookman, King Charles's right-hand man, too. Always brought them down with one shot, even when they were running away. I guess you could say I was born with a natural skill when it came to killing things. I remember this one particular autumn afternoon we came upon a buck atop a hill, a majestic sight. Framed perfectly against a clear blue sky. Its nose in the air, sniffing the wind. It would've been an easy shot for me, but I refused to take it. My father demanded that I take it. He even threatened to shoot me if I didn't."

Emily held herself even tighter. "What did you do?"

"What could I do? King Charles Hagen was not a man you defied, especially if you were ten. So, I aimed and fired and hit a rock in front of the stag's front hoof. The animal turned and ran along the other side of the hill.

My father knew I'd missed on purpose and berated me the rest of the day." Adam looked at Emily. "It was the most important lesson of my life. You don't kill just because you can. You kill because you have a reason. And some things are just too majestic to kill. The world is a better place with them in it."

Emily gasped when she remembered something. "You're the one who first called Steve *Buck*, aren't you?"

"I am," Hagen admitted. "Because of that story."

She was sad when she saw the look in his eyes change. The curtain closed again and Adam Hagen, robber baron and rake, returned. "Now, that's enough about the past. Besides, too much sentiment spoils the biscuits. Go on and read something. You've had a long day. I'll fix you a plate, then make sure the men are fed. I'll probably have to wake them up, but that's to be expected."

She could tell there was no sense in arguing with the man, as he'd already made up his mind. Besides, it was nice to have someone else do the cooking in her own house for once.

She had a feeling it might be the last comfort she enjoyed for quite some time.

Chapter 26

The next afternoon, Trammel woke with a start when he heard someone knocking on his bedroom door. He took the Peacemaker from beneath his pillow and aimed it at the door. "Who is it?"

"It's Blake," said the familiar voice. "I've got important news. Mrs. Trammel said it was all right for me to come up here personally."

Trammel recognized Blake's voice but did not lower his pistol. After what had happened yesterday, he and Emily had taken further precautions. "She tell you anything else?"

"Come to think of it, she did," Blake admitted. "She said I'm supposed to tell you the sky is blue, though I don't know why. It's been cloudy all day."

The phrase meant he had spoken with Emily and all was well. If he had said she told him to say the day was cloudy, Trammel would've blasted the next man through the door. As it was, Blake was telling the truth and Trammel lowered his pistol.

"Come in, then."

Blake opened the door slowly and popped his head inside. "You sure?"

Trammel laid back on his pillow. "I didn't shoot you, did I?"

Blake entered the bedroom and left the door open behind him. "How are you feeling?"

Trammel felt lousy. The painkillers Emily and Doc Carson had given him had thrown him for a loop. He felt groggy. His entire body hurt. His vision was blurry and the scar beneath the bandages felt raw. "I'm fine," he told his deputy. "What are you doing here?"

"Wanted to let you know how sorry I am about not having enough men watching you yesterday."

"Don't waste time apologizing. It doesn't do any good. You saw a mistake and corrected it. No harm done."

"Maybe not to you, but that's the other reason why I'm here. We think we found the two men who attacked you yesterday. Got them downstairs waiting for you in a wagon. Could help some if you were well enough to identify them."

Trammel felt a new energy course through him. He pointed to his clothes strewn along the chair across from the bed. "Give me my clothes. I'll get dressed and head down there with you."

Blake handed his boss the clothes and turned his back as the sheriff struggled to get dressed.

"They alive?" Trammel asked.

"Nope," Blake said. "But it's mighty complicated to explain how they got that way. Probably best if you see it for yourself."

Trammel grunted from the simple effort of getting dressed. "Sounds like they didn't die pretty."

"You can see for yourself. I'd say they had it coming, but I'll reserve judgment until you identify them if you can."

Trammel pulled his shirt over his head and got to his

feet. He pulled his pants up quickly and immediately felt dizzy from the effort. He leaned against the wall, holding up his britches until the wave passed.

Blake did not turn around. "You need any help, boss?"

"I've been dressing myself for a long time, Blake. I'll be fine."

Trammel moved past his deputy and opened the door. His braces were pulled up over his untucked shirt, but his shoulder holster was in the right place. "Let's go. I want to see what you brought me."

Blake followed him down the stairs. Trammel looked for any sign of Adam Hagen in the parlor but remembered Emily had said he had business to attend to that morning.

Trammel walked out onto his porch. A canvas had been thrown over the contents in the flatbed of the wagon. The four deputies around the wagon bade their sheriff a good morning.

"Blake here tells me you boys have something to show me."

Blake hopped up into the flatbed and took hold of the tarp. "You eat yet?"

"Hours ago. Why?"

"Because this is a mighty nasty sight, and I don't want you getting sick on me and passing out."

Trammel was beginning to lose patience. "Just let me see it."

Blake pulled aside the canvas. All four of the deputies besides Blake recoiled. Two of them got sick.

Trammel peered over the side of the wagon and looked at the carnage. He saw the bodies of two men who appeared to have been mauled to death. Judging by the stench, quite recently, too. Their faces were in horrible condition, but not enough to prevent Trammel from identifying them.

"These are the two who came after me." Trammel looked up at Blake. "Where'd you find them?"

"A freighter reported spotting them this morning on his way here. Said they were about half an hour west of here. Even told us were to look." Blake pointed down at the bodies. "Given their condition, I'd say a bear got to them. Maybe even a grizzly. Don't think it was wolves. We found them intact, so this looks like a bear to me. The blood from their wounds most likely drew it to them."

Trammel had not seen the results of many bear attacks, so he took Blake's word for it. "Think they were alive when they were attacked?"

"I'd say so," Blake said. "Why?"

"No reason. Just glad they suffered before the end is all. Run them over to Doc Carson for a final examination. When he's done with them, plant them somewhere and mark the graves in case they have loved ones who come later to claim them."

Blake threw the tarp over the bodies again. "Nobody'll be coming for these two, boss. I recognize them as a couple of drifters who blew into town about a month or so ago. Took odd jobs around town when they needed money to drink. Guess someone must've hired them to go after you."

"Never thought of myself as an odd job," Trammel said.

"No doubt they're working for the devil now." Blake hopped out of the wagon and stood next to the sheriff. He told the deputies, "Two of you run these over to Doc Carson like the sheriff told you. I want the other two to stay here to keep an eye on the house."

Trammel thanked the men and walked back inside.

Blake followed and closed the door behind him. "Boss, you sure they were the two who came after you?"

"Of course, I'm sure. I might be hurting, but I'm not feeble-minded. Their faces were in good enough shape for me to see who they were. Why?"

Blake took off his hat. "Those two were known to hang out in Clay's saloons is why. Kind of makes me think he might've put them up to it."

Trammel had never thought otherwise. "In Laramie, it's kind of hard for a man to walk into a saloon Clay doesn't own. But I don't doubt he probably hired them in the hope they might get lucky with me being in my present condition."

"Guess you proved them wrong," Blake said.

Trammel grinned through the pain it caused. "Yeah, I guess I did."

Both men jumped when they heard a knock at the door. The man announced himself as Deputy Bush.

Blake opened the door halfway. "What is it?"

"Sounds like trouble coming from the Tralee, boss. Word is that Clay's fixing to make some kind of speech. A crowd's already gathering in front."

Blake looked back at Trammel. "You get back to bed, boss. I'll handle this."

Trammel had already begun to unwind the bandages that crossed his face. "Like hell you will. If Clay's saying something, I intend on being there to hear it. Just give me a second to get this stuff off me."

"I don't think that's a good idea," Blake said. "You look about ready to fall over."

Trammel could feel the excitement and anger coursing through his body, pushing aside the pain and weariness. "I'll be fine as long as we walk slow. I'll prop myself up against a wall if I have to."

Blake did not look like he approved, but he did not argue with the big man.

Adam Hagen was glad to see the Laramie Hotel was doing a brisk business that early afternoon. Clay owned a sizable piece of the respectable enterprise and, per their agreement, so did Hagen.

Then he remembered he had declared their arrangement null and void the previous day, so none of the hotel's good fortune would benefit him.

The waiter he'd paid for information had told him Judge Littlejohn and his clerk were dining together in a private room in the back of the hotel's restaurant. Pulling apart the French doors of the room, he was glad to see the waiter had been right.

Judge Littlejohn had tucked a napkin into his collar as he sipped a spoonful of soup. His clerk did the same.

The judge glared up at him from behind the bowl. "You can't be here, Hagen."

"How inhospitable of you." Adam shut the doors behind him and leaned against them. "What was it the Bard said once? 'My wind cooling my broth would blow me to an ague when I thought what harm a wind too great might do at sea. I should not see the sandy hourglass run, for I should think of shallows and of flats and see my wealthy Andrew docked in sand, vailing her high top below her ribs to kiss her burial.'"

The judge's flat expression did not change. "I'm no Venetian merchant and I've no cause for ague save for your presence here." He returned to his soup. "Get out. I'm judging your case. We can't speak outside a court of law without Mr. Wain present."

Adam continued to lean against the door. "Nonsense. You haven't always held the honor of the court in such high esteem, so why start now?"

Littlejohn let his spoon drop into the bowl. "What the devil are you talking about?"

"I'll be more than happy to tell you in private." Hagen nodded at the clerk. "Tell the weasel to sup somewhere else. I don't talk in front of rodents."

The clerk continued to sip his soup, undeterred by the intrusion. "Weasels are mammals, not rodents. And I am no weasel, Mr. Hagen. You may rest assured of that."

The judge smirked. "So now that you've received your zoology lesson for today, get out."

"I don't think you want me to do that, Your Honor. I think you'll want to hear what I have to say in private."

Littlejohn sat back in his chair. "I'd threaten to call the sheriff to have you removed, but I doubt he'd do it, even if he was in any condition to do so."

"Buck Trammel has thrown me out of many places many times," Hagen told him. "He's his own man."

"Quite," Littlejohn said. "Well, since I can't make you leave, go ahead and say what you came here to say. But Mr. Hatch stays here. I have no secrets from him."

Hagen was sure the judge would regret that decision once he learned why his luncheon had been interrupted. "Fine. I want you to recuse yourself from the case."

"Recuse myself?" Littlejohn laughed. "Oh, that's rich, Mr. Hagen. Even coming from a brash man such as you. Why in the world would I want to do that?"

"So, you can save yourself the embarrassment of having your decision overturned in court."

Littlejohn folded his small hands across his stomach. "Upon what grounds would it be overturned?"

"Conflict of interest," Hagen said. "Last month, you became the godfather of one Jonathan Carrington, did you not?"

"I did. His father and I are old friends. What of it?"

"Mrs. Carrington used to be Miss Forrester," Hagen said. "I'd say that presents quite a conflict of interest, wouldn't you?"

The judge looked at him. He was silent, but his eyes were alive with a mixture of admiration and anger. "Your tentacles have a long reach, don't they, Mr. Hagen?"

"All it takes is money," Adam admitted, "and as you are a learned man, I'm sure I don't have to do anything so obvious as making a threat. I know you value your reputation, so I think we can come to something of a compromise."

Littlejohn's eyes narrowed. "Why do I have a feeling I already know what that might be?"

"Because it's a simple choice. You can either recuse yourself from the case due to a conflict of interest or have it overturned on appeal, unless, of course, you rule in my favor."

The judge drew in a deep breath. "If I took the rest of the afternoon, I doubt I'd have time to list all of the laws you've broken here today."

"The law of self-preservation is the law of the land," Hagen told him. "It's the one law from which not even judges are immune."

As he sipped at his soup, the clerk said, "Careful, Mr. Hagen. Playing lawyer in a courtroom is one thing. Threatening a judge is well out of your depth."

Hagen feigned shock. "I'm not threatening anyone. Think of me as something of a soothsayer of old. I'm simply predicting the future as I see it."

But Mr. Hatch could not be disturbed from his soup. "In that case, I'm something of a seer myself, which is why I can predict the future and save you from some possible embarrassment when court resumes tomorrow. Judges don't make rulings on their own. They make them based on the legal findings of their clerks. And since I happen to be the judge's clerk, that burden falls to me. You will lose your case, Mr. Hagen, not due to any conflict of interest on the judge's part, but because of a simple fact of law."

He looked up from his soup but held his spoon in place over it. "Neither you nor any of your lawyers in the two previous cases have disputed the first will of Charles Hagen. It is officially the will of record in the county office. This second will was written up shortly before the untimely deaths of Charles Hagen and his attorney, the late Mr. Montague. That being the case, the validity of the new will cannot be verified. You claim Mr. Montague died before he could file it with the county, but be that as it may, only one official document exists as far as the county is concerned. That is why Judge Littlejohn will be ruling against you and in favor of your family. You can attempt to overturn that ruling if you like, but you will lose. His judgment will be as final as it will be thorough."

Adam wanted to argue the point. To threaten. To say something, anything, but all words seemed to die at the back of his throat.

Mr. Hatch returned to his soup. "You can make a claim of conflict of interest should you wish, but as Judge Littlejohn was invited by the territorial governor to try this case, I think you'll find your claim will fall on deaf ears. The Forresters are already a wealthy family and have no need of your late father's estate. Furthermore, Mrs.

Carrington will not benefit directly from his ruling, so your case for a conflict of interest is weak." He sipped another spoonful of soup. "If I were you, I would be spending the remaining time you have gathering all of the money you can because, after tomorrow, you'll be a man without a town."

Adam did his best to find fault with anything Mr. Hatch had said but could not. "You really think I'll go that quietly?"

"Quite frankly," Mr. Hatch said after dabbing the corners of his mouth with his napkin, "we don't care what you do. You can burn Blackstone to the ground for all we care. That is a matter for you and your siblings to settle. Tomorrow, Judge Littlejohn will make his ruling and be on the next train back to Colorado. You might get lucky and find one of your cronies to hold up his ruling on appeal, but I doubt you'll find a jurist dumb enough to cross the governor's hand-picked man. You had a good run, Mr. Hagen, but it's over. You have lost Blackstone and the Hagen empire forever."

Adam felt the anger rise within him. "I haven't lost anything." He stumbled backward as a waiter pulled the doors open to bring in the rest of Littlejohn and the clerk's lunch.

"No, Mr. Hagen," the judge said. "You've not only just lost your balance, but you appear to have lost everything. I wouldn't be too worried about it, though. You seem to be an intelligent man. Unless I've missed my guess, you've probably made a small fortune from your illegal dealings in Blackstone. I'm confident you'll have no trouble finding another town to corrupt, just make sure it isn't in Colorado. You'll be arrested if you do, and I'd like nothing better than to see you dance at the end of a rope."

Adam stood there in the ruins of the dreams he'd had

while he watched the waiters clear away the soup bowls and replace them with plates full of steak and mashed potatoes.

"Now," the judge said, "unless you intend on standing there gawking at us while we lunch, I suggest you be on your way."

"Yes," agreed Mr. Hatch. "Conflict makes for poor indigestion."

Adam felt himself turn and walk through the dining room without saying another word. There was nothing more to say. He had been beaten.

He had lost.

Chapter 27

Not bothered by the reaction he drew from the citizens, Trammel walked along Main Street toward Clay's saloon. Blake walked beside him to prop him up if he felt dizzy.

Trammel was glad he had taken off the bandages that had crisscrossed his face. He not only looked less ridiculous, the air felt good on his skin. Still covered by a strip of bandage brown with blood from the stitching beneath it, his scar was already beginning to itch, which he took as a good sign of healing. He knew Doc Carson and Emily would give him grief over taking off the crisscrossing bandages, but he would remind them he had suffered many scrapes and scars from his childhood in Manhattan's Five Points slum. If he had not died then, he would not die now.

He wanted people to see what had happened to him the previous day. He wanted Clay to see it, too. He wanted whatever crowd gathered to hear the criminal speak to see their sheriff's ruined face. They might have laughed at his bandages. They would not laugh at the sight of his scar.

"You still feeling spry?" Blake asked him from the corner of his mouth.

The walk was making Trammel feel better. "As long as we don't have to run, I'll be fine."

"Just don't keel over on me," Blake said. "You're too big for me to pick up on my own."

"I'll keep it in mind."

They rounded the corner and found a good-sized crowd had gathered in front of Clay's place. Deputies held back half the crowd, who were shouting Clay's name as they called for his arrest. The other half were drunks and saloon girls Clay had undoubtedly turned out to shout down the protesters.

Others were regular civilians who had stopped in front of the saloon to see what all the fuss was about.

Trammel noticed Brillheart across the street on the roof of city hall, cradling a rifle. He nodded in that direction and told Blake, "Good thinking putting him up there."

"Pays to be careful," Blake said. "I figured he can watch over us while we hear Clay from city hall."

"I'm not going to city hall," Trammel said as he began to push his way through the crowd. People objected and cursed at first, but when they saw who it was, they quickly got out of the way. Trammel did not stop until he was in front of the saloon. He imagined he blocked the view of the people behind him, but he was not in the mood to care.

Blake followed him. "Boss, if you get weak, there's nowhere for you to lean."

"Don't worry. I'll be fine."

Clay leaned on his walking stick as he hobbled out of the Rose of Tralee Saloon. The crowd grew even louder. Pushing and shoving broke out between both groups, but stopped when Clay raised his hands and asked them to be quiet.

He pointed his walking stick at Trammel. "I see our

esteemed sheriff has climbed out of his sick bed to join us this afternoon. I'm glad to see you up and about despite your wounds."

"I'll just bet you are," Trammel said, which caused a ripple of laughter in the crowd.

"I'm glad you're here," Clay went on, "as part of what I have to say pertains to you." He looked out over the crowd. "Fellow citizens of Laramie, I ask you give me a few moments of your time to allow me to answer some of the scandalous and baseless rumors that have circulated about me for the past couple of days. We are all still mourning the loss of Rob Moran, the finest lawman Laramie has ever had. I know some of you have been led to believe I had something to do with his assassination. Given the nature of my business interests, it's understandable some of you might think I was involved in this horrific deed. I appear before you all today to assure you that neither I nor any of my associates had anything to do with it."

Half the crowd cheered. The other half booed and shouted he was guilty.

Clay raised his hands again to quiet them. "A general sense of lawlessness has descended on this town since Rob Moran's passing. A lawlessness Sheriff Trammel and his deputies seem unable to stop. The blame does not entirely fall on their shoulders. They are human beings, and the loss of Marshal Moran has affected us all. We cannot continue to depend on the law to keep us safe during these lawless times. That is why I am proposing the formation of a new group that will be able to do the job Buck Trammel seems unable to do with the resources at hand. That is why The Laramie Vigilance Committee is being formed to combat the ugly element that has seeped into our fair city."

Trammel had not been expecting this. He supposed

Clay thought up this idea when the men he had sent to kill him wound up dead.

"I am merely assisting with the committee's formation. I will not play a role in how it conducts itself. I don't have to, for we have the full backing of the Laramie Businessman's Association, as shown by Mr. Williamson's attendance here with me today. Come on out and let the people get a look at you, Howard."

Trammel watched Howard Williamson step out from the saloon like a man expecting gunpoint. He raised his hat to the crowd, but there was no happiness in it. The crowd responded with a mixture of cheers and boos.

Clay continued. "With the support of the Businessman's Association, I am confident the Laramie Vigilance Committee will be able to . . ." His voice trailed off as Trammel stepped forward and began climbing the steps to the saloon. Clay backed away before Trammel pushed him over.

An uneasy silence fell over the crowd as the sheriff turned to face them. He let them look at him, take in his size compared to Clay and the others. He wanted them to see his mangled face.

And to hear his words.

"There will be no Vigilance Committee or any other kind of committee in Laramie. I don't care who backs it, not even the president himself. We have law in Laramie. We have order. It's up to me and my men to enforce it, which is exactly what we're doing. Yesterday, we caught Rob Moran's killer and we'll prove it before a judge. You'll be able to come and hear the facts for yourselves. Until then, you can ask me any question about the Moran case or any other matter concerning the law."

He nodded toward city hall across the thoroughfare. "My office is right over there, and my door is always open.

But anyone"—he looked over at Williamson, who did not meet his gaze—"and I do mean *anyone* who takes the law into their own hands will be breaking the very law they think they're upholding. You'll be arrested like any criminal and treated accordingly. We will not allow a vigilante mob to run loose doling out whatever justice they see fit at the moment. That's up to a judge, not us."

A skinny old man in overalls at the edge of the crowd called out, "How about you start by arresting Clay right now, Sheriff? We all know he's guilty."

Half the crowd cheered while the other half booed.

A scuffle broke out but died down as soon as Trammel said, "Me and my men are still looking into Clay's involvement in Rob Moran's death. If we have enough evidence, we'll arrest him. Until then, we've got no reason to hold him for anything." He looked over the crowd and the crowd looked back. "Now it's time for all of you to go home or be about your business. The show's over." He looked at Blake. "Deputy, help these good people on their way."

Blake called for everyone to disburse as he threaded his way through the crowd. Both sides grumbled, but none of them held their ground, not even the protesters.

Using his size to his full advantage, Trammel turned to face Clay, who came up to just under Trammel's chin. "You're getting in the habit of making public displays of yourself."

Clay looked up at him. "You've left me no choice. Your antics have made me look weak in front of my enemies. These speeches of mine reassert my power. You might hate me as much as I hate you, but I serve a purpose. I keep the underbelly of this city at bay. If I fall, you'll see a scramble for control that will make the streets of this city run red with blood."

Trammel was in no mood for a debate. "If you pull another stunt like that again, I'll have you locked up for inciting a riot."

Clay did not back up but craned his neck to look Trammel straight in the eye. "The riot will follow my arrest."

"Don't worry," Trammel assured him. "The next time I come for you will be the last time you breathe free air."

Clay's eyes moved over Trammel's ruined face as he sucked his teeth. "It's a shame what you've been through since moving to Laramie, Sheriff. I heard there was an attempt on your life last night."

"You more than heard about it," Trammel said. "You sent them."

"At least Mrs. Trammel wasn't home," Clay went on. "Perhaps next time, she won't be as lucky."

Williamson quickly moved between them before Trammel could grab hold of Clay. "I think we've all had enough excitement for one day, gentlemen. Why don't we break this up now before something happens that we'll all regret? There's still a sizable crowd out here. We wouldn't want to encourage them to act out."

Clay sneered as he walked backward into the saloon. "Good thing you were already ugly before the scar, Buck. It might improve your looks."

The two men went inside, but Williamson remained blocking Trammel's path. "Don't do it, Buck. I know you want to hurt him, and I won't be able to stop you, but I'm begging you to let him go."

Trammel turned his attention to the much shorter businessman. "Guess you wouldn't want your friend to get hurt, would you, Williamson?"

The older man sighed as he turned his hat in his hands. "I'd have expected you to understand my relationship with

Clay better than anyone. If I don't pay off to him, my members' windows get smashed. If you crack down on him, my cattle pens will be burned to the ground or worse, my customers' livestock will come down with a sickness. Not everyone has a sheriff's star to protect them, Buck. Some of us have to find a way to live here. Clay's a bad sort, but I've seen worse. I have a feeling you have, too."

Trammel had, but that was in the past. Laramie was his present and his future. "What I said to Clay goes for you, too, Howard. Any of that Vigilance Committee nonsense comes to pass, you'll be in the same cell as Clay. Understand?"

Williamson put his hat back on his head. "I understand, Buck. I just hope you get around to understanding some things yourself. A man in your position would do well to have a broader view. The kind Rob Moran had." Williamson bid him good day and stepped away to join the disbursing crowd.

Trammel placed his hands on his hips and looked out over the city he now called home. Unlike Blackstone, he could not see all of it from the front steps of the saloon. It was a city with large streets and side streets and alleyways and vacant lots. It had commerce and wagons loaded with passengers and goods going to and coming from all points on the map.

Blackstone had a lot of moving parts, too, but at least he could see them all from one place. In Laramie, it was impossible to know what was going on everywhere at all times. That troubled him and he began to wonder if he had made a mistake leaving Blackstone.

Maybe Adam Hagen had been right when he'd told him to reconsider accepting the position. Trammel realized he had been pushed into it too quickly and he finally knew why. The Hagen family had wanted chaos while their trial went on in town. They wanted Buck Trammel out of Blackstone when they moved to take the town away from Adam. It was a brash, bold move but it had worked. They had set a gilded trap for him and he had been foolish enough to walk right into it.

He thought about turning in his star and going back where he belonged. Back to Blackstone. The town had changed in the past year, but he still considered it home.

He could protect Emily there, if not himself.

Still pondering his options, he saw Adam Hagen storming along the thoroughfare straight toward the saloon. Trammel had seen that look in his eye and that straight gait before. He knew men usually died soon afterward. He stepped off the boardwalk and moved to block his friend's path.

Adam kept coming. "Get out of my way, Buck. I've got business to attend to."

Trammel didn't move. "Not before you calm down."

"Like hell I will," Hagen said as he tried to push past the sheriff.

Trammel held his ground. "Tell me what happened."

"Damn it, Buck," Hagen yelled. "I said get out of my way!" His right hand went for the pistol on his hip.

The sheriff grabbed Adam's hand before it got there and held it in place.

Hagen looked up at him, his eyes wild. "Let go of me."

"Not until you tell me what happened." Trammel's grip on Hagen's arm tightened. "You know I'll break your arm if I have to. That would be a shame, after all the hard work you put in to getting it working again."

Trammel sensed Hagen's arm go slack as his eyes grew

wet. He had never seen Adam like this, not even at his lowest point.

Hagen ducked his head. "I'm ruined, Buck. Flat out ruined."

Trammel let go of Adam's arm and turned him toward city hall. "Let's get inside where we can talk about this in private. There are too many eyes and ears on the street for my liking."

Chapter 28

After hearing about Adam's failure with Judge Littlejohn, Trammel regretted he had not replaced the empty bottle of whiskey in the bottom drawer of his desk. Liquor was the only way he could think to restore his friend's sunken spirits. "Sounds like the judge has made up his mind, doesn't it?"

Adam slumped in the chair across from him. "It certainly does."

Trammel was torn. The lawman in him was happy to see one less criminal in the territory, especially one as successful as Adam Hagen. But he could see the loss of the family fortune was tough for his friend to take and tried to put a shine on it. "You're not hurting for money, are you?"

"No," Adam admitted. "All of my holdings in Blackstone are my own property and built with my own money. I'm not poor, but that was never the game of it. I was looking for power and legitimacy. Both of those will be gone after the judge's ruling tomorrow. And Clay will have free rein over the territory now that Moran's dead and no one has been named to replace him as territorial marshal. He'll do his best to cut me out of the opium trade, which should make you feel better."

"I was never fond of the practice," Trammel admitted. "You know that."

"But I kept it respectable," Adam noted. "He won't. He'll flood Wyoming with the stuff and won't care who he hurts. His alliance with my family and Moran's death has served him well."

Trammel had an idea. One he thought might actually work. "What if I put my name forward to take Moran's spot as U.S. marshal?"

Adam shook his head as he smiled wearily. "Why would they give it to you? You're the one who let Moran get killed, remember? You're responsible for all the lawlessness that has gripped this town since you got here. Williamson so much as said so himself by aligning himself with that ridiculous Vigilance Committee." He let out a deep breath and closed his eyes.

"No, my friend. I'm afraid they've painted you into the same corner as they've painted me. And they've done a wonderfully elegant job of it." He opened his eyes and looked up at the ceiling. "I wonder which member of my family came up with the idea first. Caleb is certainly capable of it. Bart's never been able to get out of his own way, so I doubt it came from him. Debora's got the spite, but not the acumen, though I've no doubt she's at the heart of all this. And Elena. My poor Elena. She's the only one of the bunch worth a damn and yet, her husband finished me off. I suppose it's fitting the husband of the one sibling I love played a role in my downfall. Young Mr. Wain proved a worthier adversary than I'd first believed."

Trammel knew he might not have whiskey on hand to brighten his friend's spirits, but he had something that might come close. "You still good at keeping secrets?"

"Like the grave. Why?"

Trammel stood up and put his hat on his head. "Come with me. There's something I'd like to show you."

Adam stood as well. "Sounds intriguing."

Trammel opened the office door for him. "You don't know the half of it."

Hagen followed Trammel down the stairs to the basement of city hall where the jail cells were, but they did not visit the prisoners. They walked along the hall to an iron door behind which Doc Carson kept his office as coroner.

Trammel knocked on the door three times and said, "It's Trammel. Open up."

A latch was thrown, and Doc Carson peered out from the other side. He looked at Hagen. "What's he doing here?"

"He's with me," Trammel said, stating the obvious. "It's all right, Doc. Let us in."

Carson kept the door half-open. "Buck, I'm not in the practice of defying you, but that's not a good idea." He looked at Hagen. "That man's nothing but trouble."

"I'll take full responsibility. Now open up."

The coroner clearly did not approve, but pulled the heavy door open anyway, only to quickly shut it as soon as Hagen followed Trammel inside.

It was a dimly lit room with curtains blocking out most of the sunlight. Oil lamps burned on wall sconces and on tables throughout. The place had the sharp smell of chemicals and death. A single door led out to the back courtyard of the building where bodies could be brought in and taken out away from the public eye.

Trammel led Hagen to an area curtained off from the

rest of the room and pulled aside the curtain, revealing Major John Stanton in a hospital bed.

Hagen gasped.

The gunman's entire body, save for his head and right arm, was covered in plaster. His eyes were redder than bloodshot and his head was heavily wrapped in bandages.

But his eyes were open, and it was clear he was very much alive.

Adam Hagen looked over the man's broken body. "I thought he was dead."

"So does everyone else," Doc Carson said. "That's what we want them to think. For now, anyway."

Hagen looked up at Trammel. "But the fall. How could he have survived?"

"He almost didn't," the sheriff said. "Saving his life was all the doc's doing. Seems like he has a knack for the living and the dead."

"He's worse than he looks," Doc Carson admitted, "and he ain't exactly pretty. His knees are shattered and most of his ribs are either cracked or broken. His left arm was broken in three places and he's suffering from cranial fractures. I think he's paralyzed from the waist down, but I won't know that until the plaster comes off in a few weeks. By some miracle, he's still conscious and his right arm is fine. In fact, I think that's the only reason why the sheriff here wants him alive."

From the bed, Major Stanton laughed as best he could. "You should've let me die, Trammel. I'm as good as dead as far as you're concerned. You'll never get anything out of me."

Trammel ignored him and spoke to the doctor instead. "What do you think his chances are, Doc?"

"Of surviving? I didn't think he'd live this long. He

fights the soup Emily and Dr. Kelly pour into him each day, but he takes it."

"Emily?" Hagen asked. "She knows about this?"

Doc Carson nodded. "It was thanks to her that he's still among the living. She worked his heart when he started to fade and brought him back to life. Old Stanton there is a regular Lazarus if you don't mind a shade of blasphemy. He'll never walk normal again, if at all. He'll probably be in a wheelchair for the rest of his life. But if he's lived this long, I imagine he'll live a bit longer if only out of pure meanness and habit."

"I'll live long enough to repay my debt to you, Trammel," Stanton said. "I'm counting the days."

Trammel gestured to the paper on the table beside the bed. "He sign it yet?"

"Nope," Carson told him. "Won't sign it for me or for Emily, neither. He tries to spit at it from time to time, but his lungs aren't strong enough to reach it."

Trammel had expected that. "You look tired, Doc. How about you give us a couple of minutes alone with him? There are some things we have to talk about you're better off not hearing."

But Doc Carson did not move. "Hearing's one thing. Knowing is something else. I know he's alive now. I expect him to be that way when I get back. Anything you do to him is nothing short of murder, Buck. I won't be part of that, sheriff or no sheriff."

"He'll be alive when you get back," Trammel told him. "You have my word."

Doc Carson looked Hagen up and down. "He staying with you?"

"He is, but he won't hurt Stanton, either. You've got my word on that, too. We won't touch a hair on his head."

The doctor grumbled as he went out the back door of the office and into the courtyard.

Stanton sneered at Trammel and Hagen. "Looks like it's just the three of us now, boys. Do your worst. I won't tell you anything."

Hagen remained at the foot of the bed while Trammel moved to the left side. He looked down at the broken man. "You're in a bad way, Stanton. Just about the worst I've ever seen."

"The idea of killing you one day is the only thing keeping me alive."

"Can't blame you, but that's going to take a long time. Longer than even a tough man like you can stand. Lying flat on your back like this won't get any easier and that ceiling you're staring up at will only get closer and closer with every day that passes."

"Maybe," Stanton said, "but it'll be worth it."

"Killing me won't make you any less of a cripple," Trammel reminded him. "You're a broken man. Your pride is gone. You can't even relieve yourself without someone tending to you like a baby. That's got to be burning you worse than any hate you've got for me."

Stanton gritted his teeth. "Don't be so sure, Trammel. Every indignity only makes me want to kill you even more."

Adam said, "I know all about that kind of hate. Unless you find somewhere for that fire to go, it'll burn right through you. It'll cook you alive right there in that cast."

Stanton grabbed for Trammel with his right hand, but the sheriff was just out of reach. The hired killer cursed with impotent rage.

Trammel remained unmoved. "Right now, all you've got is words, Stanton." He picked up the piece of paper from the table and held it up for the patient to read.

Stanton looked away as if the mere sight of it scalded him.

"This paper is your quickest way out," Trammel went on. "A full confession that says Clay hired you to kill Rob Moran. Sign it and I can promise the judge will go easy on you. Commit you to a sanitarium where you can get all the care you need for however long you live. But if you don't sign it, it's no skin off my hide. I've already got enough to try you for Rob Moran's murder. You'll be convicted and, seeing as how Rob was a U.S. marshal when you killed him, you'll spend the rest of your life in a federal penitentiary. I don't have to tell you they don't treat men in your condition too well in places like that. The guards won't like that you killed one of their own."

Stanton turned his head to face Trammel. "If you had anything on me, you'd have brought me before a judge by now. Instead, you're keeping me squirreled away down here. Why?"

Trammel shook the paper. "This is why. I want you to sign this so I can lay my hands on Clay once and for all. All you did was squeeze the trigger. I want the man who put a target on Rob Moran's back. I want him to admit in open court why he did it."

Stanton's eyes moved from Trammel to the man standing at the foot of his bed. "I know you from somewhere, don't I?"

"Probably," Adam said. "New Orleans, I think."

"Yeah." Stanton's mouth drew into a crooked smile. "Adam Hagen. The card sharp. I thought you were familiar. I was supposed to be hired to kill you once, but another gun got there before me and took the job. Guess he wasn't very good."

Adam shrugged. "He was good. I just happened to be better."

"I was going to get another crack at you," Stanton told him. "Clay didn't want to trust a crooked judge, so he ordered me to kill you. I was in the process of planning it out when your big friend here kicked in my door and came after me."

"That's a shame," Adam said. "If you'd come after me, you'd be dead already. I'm a bit more experienced than poor Sheriff Hauk."

Trammel didn't care about their past history, only the present. "Your gunning days are over any way you slice it, Stanton. You don't have a reputation to protect anymore and any twisted loyalty you had to Clay is canceled. If he were in your position, he'd have signed that paper days ago and you know it."

Stanton's eyes snapped back to Trammel. "I don't care what Clay is. I know what I am, and I don't take a man's money only to stab him in the back later. Whatever he does is his own business."

Trammel slowly lowered the piece of paper. "There's also a third choice here."

Stanton tried to look stoic, but the light of interest in his red eyes was obvious. "And just what might that be?"

"I could give you an easy way out of all this," Trammel offered. "A way to spare yourself years of suffering and pain. A way to go out on your own terms like a man . . . if you wanted it."

Stanton jutted out his jaw as he swallowed hard. "How?"

"The doc's not here all the time," Trammel said. "It could be arranged for you to have a bottle of laudanum at your disposal. In your condition, it'd be enough to finish the job. You'd just drift off to sleep and never wake up again."

"And let me guess," Stanton said. "You'd supply the bottle if I sign that paper."

Trammel nodded once. "You have my word."

Hagen added, "And it would be considered a dying declaration. It would hold up in any court in the land."

Stanton's eyes moved back and forth between the two men, before finally stopping on Trammel. "And all I have to do is sign that paper?"

"That's all. The laudanum is yours if you want it."

Stanton licked his lips. The idea had taken root in his mind and was growing fast. "Can you get your hands on a bottle?"

Hagen laughed. "Oh, I think I know where I can find one or two."

Stanton looked at the paper for the first time. "Give me the laudanum now and I'll sign it."

Trammel shook his head. "Sign it first. Time is of the essence. Adam will come back after the doc leaves tonight with all the laudanum you can drink."

Hagen added, "You have my word, too, for as much as it counts."

Stanton had clearly made up his mind. "Give me a pen and something I can write on."

Hagen went to a bookshelf and removed a heavy book. Trammel noticed it was a Bible.

Adam grinned. "I figured it was apt under the circumstances."

Taking the Bible from him, Trammel placed the paper on top, held them both upright on Stanton's chest, and handed him the pen from Carson's inkwell.

Stanton's hand shook a bit as he took hold of the pen. "Why does it feel like I'm signing my own death warrant?"

"Think of it as a train ticket to freedom," Hagen said. "Why be morbid?"

Stanton looked the men over one more time and signed the confession.

Chapter 29

To keep pace with Trammel, Hagen had to take the stairs two at a time. "He signed it. By God, you actually got him to sign the damn thing."

"Learned it from Emily," Trammel said without breaking his stride. "If you can't appeal to a man's sense, appeal to his dignity."

"Smart woman, that Emily."

When they reached the first landing, Hagen grabbed the sheriff by the arm. "What are you going to do now?"

Trammel held up the confession. "I'm going to use this to get Judge Spicer to issue a warrant for Clay's arrest. Then I'm going to arrest Lucien Clay and put him where he belongs once and for all." He took the next set of stairs.

Hagen scrambled in front of him. "Wait, Buck. Do you know what this could mean? If you can get Lucien to admit my family paid him to kill Moran—"

"I just might be able to save you from the poor house," Trammel said as he moved around Hagen and walked up to the courtroom. "That's nice if it happens, but arresting Clay is all I care about. I doubt it'll happen in time to do you much good. Clay won't crack so easy."

"We'll do more than crack him, my friend. We'll break him into a thousand pieces!"

Trammel stopped when he got to the top of the stairs. "*We're* not going to do anything. Clay's my business, not yours. I need you to head over to Emily's office. I want you keeping an eye on her until I say otherwise. Clay's friends aren't going to take kindly to me arresting him and someone's liable to try to use her against me."

"She'll be as safe as if she were shielded by Gabriel's wings." Adam began running down the stairs before he turned. "Thank you for this, Buck. I mean that."

Trammel had no time for gratitude. "We'll talk about that later. Just get over to Emily's place now."

Lucien Clay took some comfort in the pretty girl's tears.

As belted his robe around himself as he watched her pick up her clothes from the floor. He found her weeping had served to dull the constant pain in his jaw. He was reminded of how another's indignity could be a tonic for him. She was not as dramatic as Delilah had been, but in time, he would make her a fine whipping post.

He had already begun to wean himself off the laudanum since his run-in with Hagen the day before. And although it had only been a day, he found his hands shook less, and his pain was only mildly worse. His mind was clearer than it had been in months. That was good. He would need all his wits about him once he went against Adam Hagen for control of the territory's underworld.

After the family's judge ruled against Hagen the next day, Wyoming would belong to Clay. Every official who had pledged loyalty to Adam would soon be knocking at Clay's door, their hands out and their minds open to whatever he commanded. He would make them crawl at first, of course, but within a month, he imagined his reach would extend throughout the territory and beyond. Men in power would be eager to forget they ever knew anyone named Adam Hagen.

Clay walked over to the bar as he watched the young woman, now dressed, limp toward the door. He picked up a decanter of whiskey, pulled out the top, and poured himself a drink.

"Don't forget to close the door behind you, darling. A man needs his privacy, you know."

He had just replaced the decanter on the bar when he heard the girl cry out.

Clay turned with the decanter top in his hand, intent on teaching her a lesson, when he saw Buck Trammel standing in the doorway. His Peacemaker was aimed straight at Clay's head.

Clay rolled his eyes. "Not this again. Don't you ever get tired of your own games, Trammel? What is it this time? A ticket for spitting on the boardwalk?"

Keeping his pistol trained on the saloon owner, Trammel reached into his coat pocket and tossed a folded document at him. "Lucien Clay, I'm here to place you under arrest for the murder of United States Marshal Robert Moran."

Clay dropped the decanter top and barely heard it hit the carpet. "This must be some kind of joke."

But the scowl on Trammel's broad face told him it was no joke. "Read it for yourself, Clay. Just reach for it real slow. We wouldn't want you doing anything that might get you shot."

Clay picked up the warrant from the seat of the chair where it landed and slowly opened it. He was surprised to see that it was not only authentic, but it had been signed by Judge Spicer.

He looked up from the warrant. "On what evidence? I'm entitled to know that much."

"Based on the confession of your accomplice Major John Stanton."

"But that's impossible," Clay yelled. "He's dead!"

Trammel's thin smile was enough to turn Clay's blood cold. "I said he fell from the roof. No one ever said it killed him. He's alive and he's talking. Can sign his name pretty good, too." The smile disappeared as quickly as it had appeared. "Now get your hands up and walk toward me. The judge wants to see you . . . right now."

Clay felt everything beginning to slip away from him. Dreams that had been tangible only seconds earlier slipped through his fingers like so much sand. "Wait just a minute, Trammel. Let's talk this over."

The sheriff thumbed back the hammer of his pistol. "I said move. Now."

Clay held up his hands. "I'm not armed and I'm not fighting you. I just need you to know this is bigger than me. Much bigger."

"Tell it to the judge," Trammel said. "Don't make me come over there and drag you out of here, Clay. You won't like that."

"What if I told you it wasn't my idea? That I was paid to do it. Would that make a difference to you?"

The Peacemaker did not move. "It might if I knew who it was."

"It was Wain who hired me to do it." Clay was speaking quickly. "Bernard Wain, that fancy lawyer out of Philadelphia. He's married to the Hagen girl, Elena. He's the one who paid me to do it. He wanted you tied up in knots while he and the family went after Adam. I think he's cooking up something else, too. Something up in Blackstone. I don't know what it is, but I'd bet it's something big. I can find out for you, Buck. I can find out for you right quick if you let me go."

"The only place you're going is jail. The only question is for how long. You put down what you just told me in writing, and it'll put Judge Spicer in a better frame of mind. Now move!"

Two hours later, Trammel and Doc Carson were sharing a bottle of whiskey in Trammel's office. The events of a busy day had settled heavily upon their shoulders and whiskey was the best way either man could think of to offer some measure of relief.

"Well, at least it's all out in the open now," Carson declared as he crossed his feet on Trammel's desk. "No more secrets. I don't know about you, Buck, but I hate secrets. They can eat at a man's innards worse than cancer. At least, that's the way I feel about it."

Trammel could not disagree with the older man. "Never had much use for them myself. Keeping them gets to become like a job. At least we're done with all of that nonsense for now."

Carson looked at him from across the desk. "Do you really think so, Buck? Do you really think Stanton's and Clay's confessions will be enough to end all of this? The Hagens and the Forresters are mighty powerful families."

"Power like that only helps if you've got friends in the right places," Trammel reminded him. "Once word spreads about what they've done, I'd wager those friends will be in an awful hurry to cross to the other side of the street when they see them coming."

Doc Carson did not seem so sure. "I've seen men who killed in front of a street full of witnesses walk free when it came time to say so in court and none of them had a pea's worth of clout like those families do. Besides, the confessions of a couple of murderers like Stanton and Clay won't amount to much up against good families."

"Time will tell, Doc," Trammel said. "All I can do is arrest them." He tapped the warrants Judge Spicer had issued for Bernard Wain and Caleb Hagen on his desk. "Got my men spread out all over town trying to hunt them up. I'll feel a lot better when they're locked in cells across from Clay."

Doc Carson looked at the glass of whiskey he held against his flat stomach. "That all you've got your men doing tonight, Sheriff?"

Trammel had hoped the conversation would not get around to that. "Meaning?"

The doctor frowned. "What was that you were just saying about keeping secrets? You think I don't know why you invited me up here for this friendly drink? I know it wasn't on account of my charming personality. You've got Adam Hagen down in my office right now feeding Stanton some laudanum, don't you?"

Trammel frowned, ashamed of himself. "How'd you know?"

"Iron door into my office and an iron door out to the courtyard," Carson says. "Tough for a man to break through. Impossible for a man to see through. But as for hearing, it's a fine device for eavesdropping. Had my ear to the door the entire time you and Hagen were working on Stanton. I've got to say, you boys made a mighty convincing case."

Trammel set his glass on his desk. He remembered Carson's threat before he left them alone with Stanton. He needed to know what he thought of it now. "And what do you plan to do about it?"

The doctor shrugged. "I told you if you killed him, it would be murder. I meant it. Now, if he happens to drink a couple of bottles of laudanum on his own, that's his doing. His choice. As long as I don't see any signs of a struggle, there's no reason why I wouldn't write it up as a suicide." He swirled his whiskey in his glass. "Hell, it's almost legal." He drank the swallow down and motioned for Trammel to pour him another one.

Trammel did, then poured one for himself. "Stanton dying under your care will put you in a bad light with the mayor and the governor."

Carson laughed as he took his scotch and recrossed his legs on Trammel's desk. "I wouldn't worry too much about me. I'm an old man long past retirement anyway. Besides, the mayor won't touch me. The governor's my nephew." He raised his glass and winked at Trammel. "The Hagens and the Forresters aren't the only people in this territory with connections."

Trammel laughed, too. If Wyoming had taught him anything, it was that family was a funny thing. Sometimes he was grateful he was an orphan.

He looked up when he heard a knock at the door and told whoever it was to come in. He was surprised to see Adam Hagen standing there with the most curious look on his face.

And two full bottles of laudanum in his hands.

"What happened?" Trammel asked as Hagen came in.

Adam placed both bottles on Trammel's desk before sitting down next to Carson. "He wouldn't drink them."

Doc Carson took his feet off the desk and turned to face Adam. "He what?"

"I offered the bottle to him and he flat out refused. Told me he'd had time to think about it and changed his mind. Said he likes that offer you gave him about a sanitarium. He plans on using it to help himself get better so, one day, he can roll up on you in his wheelchair and blow your brains out, Buck. His words, not mine."

Doc Carson shook his head. "Well, if that don't beat all. Guess there's something to be said for the power of hate."

"A topic I know well." Adam nodded at the bottle of whiskey. "You wouldn't happen to have an extra glass around here somewhere, would you?"

"Take mine." Trammel shoved his glass across the desk and Hagen caught it. "I probably shouldn't be drinking anyway. And you shouldn't be here at all. My boys ought to be bringing in your brother and brother-in-law any minute now. Judge Spicer signed their arrest warrants about an hour ago."

Adam took the glass with him as he sat back in the chair. "No, Buck, I'm afraid your men won't. Hagen family has skipped town."

Trammel sat up straight in his chair. "They what?"

"They high-tailed it out of here when they heard you'd arrested Clay. Guess they figured they couldn't count on Lucien's discretion any longer. The whole lot of them tried to commandeer my train to leave for Blackstone ahead of schedule. When my crews refused, they hit the trail on horseback and buggy. Took their gunmen with them, too."

Trammel had not been expecting that. He thought he had moved fast enough to outsmart them.

Adam clearly saw the look of disappointment and anger on Trammel's face. "My family is a lot of things, Buck, but they're not stupid. They know you've got paper on them here in Laramie, but that paper doesn't extend beyond the city limits. I'd say they've got a three-hour head start on you back to Blackstone. The trail being as clear as it is, I imagine they'll reach Blackstone just after midnight. They'll hole up in the ranch house and their men will keep you at bay. The place is built like a fortress. Believe me, I know."

Trammel felt his neck begin to redden. "Why didn't you tell me before?"

Adam grinned at him from behind his whiskey glass. "Because I had a prisoner to poison, remember? Besides, there's no real danger. We know where they're going. I've already wired ahead to my boys in town. They'll be waiting to give them a proper homecoming." He drank his whiskey and winked at Trammel. "I've even arranged for Big Ben to have the home fire lit for them upon their return."

But Trammel did not want that. He had seen what Hagen's men could do. He had also seen what the hired hands of the family could do. He knew Hawkeye would be caught in the middle of two different bands of thugs who would not care if innocent people got in their way.

He knew Hagen was right about the family being able to defend the hilltop. Hawkeye could take every deputy he had and still find himself outgunned from a higher position.

The family had been right to run. They were smart. Blackstone was well outside Trammel's jurisdiction.

As the effects of the whiskey faded from his mind, or perhaps because of it, an idea came to him. To Adam, he said, "You think we can take your train to Blackstone?"

"I know we can," Hagen said. "Why?"

That part could wait.

Trammel asked Doc Carson, "You think you might be able to get me a meeting with your nephew?"

"I don't see why not. But why would I want to?"

"Because depending on his mood, he might help keep a lot of innocent people from getting killed. And he's the only man I can think of who can stop it with the stroke of a pen."

Chapter 30

Stan turned in the saddle when he heard the train whistle echo behind him in the darkness. He knew Adam Hagen must be on his way back to Blackstone.

Stan had gotten the family out of Laramie as fast as he could. Even if Lucien Clay managed to spill his guts and tell Trammel everything he knew, no arrest warrant could reach them there. Perhaps if the sheriff had a federal marshal on the books, but since he did not, Stan was not worried.

He had been worried, however, that his employers would not have been able to endure the harsh conditions of a fast ride back to Blackstone. They were city people, after all. Refined people not accustomed to being jostled around the bumpy, winding road to Blackstone. But he had not heard a single complaint from them the entire trek north. He imagined some of them were asleep by now. He also imagined they preferred the cramped confines of the coach to the cold conditions of a cell in the city jail.

As they rounded the last bend in the road leading straight to Blackstone, Stan and his horse noted something in the air that gave them pause. The odd light in the distant clouds along the horizon should not be there. He had taken this road several times at night and had never seen it before.

He knew it could not be the moon. It was not supposed to be visible that night. He had once worked on a cattle ranch and still kept track of such things.

That light was not coming from above the distant clouds, and it was not lightning. It was coming from below them, as if something were shining up at them from beneath.

Something that didn't belong.

Stan rode back to his man who was driving the coach. The lamps lit on either side of the coach provided a fair amount of light around them and the team of horses. "I'm going to ride ahead to make sure it's all clear for us. Keep them moving. I'll let off a shot if I see something."

The driver told him he understood, and Stan dug his heels into his horse, sending it into a fast gallop. Normally, he did not like traveling so fast in the dark, but the road was straight, and he knew his mount could see just fine. He raced along the road for about ten minutes until reaching the outskirts of Blackstone, then slowed his horse as he reached the mill and brought her onto Main Street at a trot.

He could see the reason for the odd lights in the sky but seeing it did not make it any easier to believe.

On the hill high atop the town, the Hagen ranch house was engulfed in flames. Tongues of fire shot up from the windows to the roof and toward the sky through holes in the roof. From that distance he could not see if ranch hands were trying to put out the fire, but he knew it was no use. The house was already gone. And so were a fair amount of his employers' worldly possessions.

The house was gone, and with it, his only way to keep

the Hagen family safe. They still needed a place to stay. A place he and his men could protect. He snapped the reins and rode it over to the Occidental Hotel. Several of his men were out front, watching the ranch house burn in the distance.

"Mr. Stan," one of them called out when they spotted him approaching in the darkness. "Good thing you're here. We just noticed the house is on fire and don't know what to do."

Stan knew there was no time to lose. "I want you to clear out the top floor of rooms for the Hagen family. I don't care if you have to pull people out of bed, just do it."

The train whistle sounded again, nearer. He imagined that meant even worse news than the loss of his employers' home and possessions. "I want every available man we've got down here in the lobby, making sure no one comes in or out from now on. If any constable gets in your way, shoot him. Kill them all if you have to. We need to keep the family and the rest of us safe. I want men inside keeping an eye on the outside. They see anyone approaching with a torch or even a lit match, put them down. I don't want anyone trying to burn us out of here, too. Understand?"

The gunman said he did and began barking out orders to all the men around him and inside the hotel.

Stan brought his horse around and rode back to the family. They needed to know what was going on and what would be expected of them as soon as they reached town. He found them at the spot where he had first spotted the odd lights against the clouds and was glad to see the small group was still moving at a good clip.

He pulled up his horse beside the moving carriage and knocked on the door. Caleb Hagen raised the shade. He had a pistol in his hand. "What is it, Stan? We've seen the lights."

"Your ranch house is burning to the ground, Mr. Hagen." Stan spoke on over the gasps and curses the news caused. "Me and my men have already secured you a place to stay in the Occidental. We're going to pull the coach right up to the place and have you folks run inside. My men will take you up to your rooms. I'll come up and let you know what's happening as soon as everything is settled."

Caleb's pale face turned red. "This is Adam's doing, damn him. Probably had that Negro of his do it just to spite us."

"But all my things, Caleb," his sister Debora said from the darkness of the coach. "My finery is in there."

Caleb waved her to be quiet while he spoke to Stan. "Have you been into town? Have you seen any sign of Adam's thugs?"

"Not yet," Stan told them, "but you've heard that train whistle as clear as I have. They probably know he's on his way as we speak, so there might be a whole bunch of them around the hotel when we get there. My boys will clear them out if it comes to that. For now, all I need you folks to do is run out the far side of the coach as soon as it stops."

Caleb gripped his pistol tightly. "We'll be ready, Stan. And thank you."

The shade dropped again and Stan rode to the back of the line to tell the other men what was happening. He had them ride up and form a wall of horseflesh around the wagon. He did not know who or what might be waiting for them when they got back to Blackstone and he wanted to be ready for anything.

He had worked hard to secure his reputation as a gun

hand and bodyguard. He would not let Adam Hagen or his friends put that in jeopardy.

It had already been a long day, but something told him that his troubles were just beginning.

Adam Hagen clapped his hands and grinned from ear to ear as his train approached Blackstone Station.

"Would you look at the sight of it, Buck? The damned place is burning beautifully. Why, if Francis Scott Key were here, he would be inspired to write a poem to celebrate it."

Trammel looked out the window and saw the flames poking through the ruined roof of the ranch house in the distance. "Just looks like a waste to me."

"Nonsense," Hagen chided. "Don't be so literal. It's a symbol of my return to power. And no matter what happens, no Hagen will ever rest their head beneath that accursed roof again."

Trammel watched his friend press his face against the window of his private car.

"A lot of evil happened in that house," Adam said. "It's only fitting that fire takes it now. My only regret is that my dear old father did not live long enough to see it."

Trammel felt the train slow to a crawl as it approached the station. "The man saw enough while he was alive." He took hold of his Winchester and patted his pockets for the countless time, taking comfort in feeling all the ammunition he had jammed into them. "I just hope this doesn't end up turning bloody."

"I do." Hagen looked away from the fire and at the sheriff. "You're sure my family will continue on to Blackstone once they see the fire? They won't head back to Laramie, will they? Or keep riding on?"

Trammel was almost sure of it. "They won't risk riding into my jurisdiction. And their horses are probably just about played out. Stan's no fool. He'll get them to cover and fast. My money's on the Occidental. It's closest to the station and he can keep them reasonably safe there, so long as your boys don't start something beforehand."

"I already wired ahead and told them to remain at town hall," Adam said. "They won't defy my orders."

For everyone's sake, Trammel hoped Adam was right. If things turned messy, so be it, but Trammel did not want to be the cause of it. He was already risking his reputation as it was. He did not want Hagen's henchmen starting a shooting war he and Hawkeye would have to finish.

The documents he had brought from Laramie were just pieces of paper, even if one of them sported the governor's signature. His newfound authority would be easier to enforce if the air were not full of lead.

The train jerked to a halt and a long plume of steam shot out from the smokestack, blocking their view from the windows for a moment.

Hagen checked his pistol was loaded one final time before he, too, grabbed his rifle and walked toward the back of the car. Despite the dim light of the private car, his eyes were shining. "Let the festivities begin!"

Chapter 31

Hawkeye remained in front of the jail, unsure of what he should do next.

Someone had set fire to the Hagen ranch house. That much was certain. With the family in Laramie, the place was empty, so he doubted it was an accident. It probably had been torched by Big Ben London on Adam's orders. It was the kind of thing Adam would do to spite his kin.

Hawkeye knew he had a bad mess on his hands. The street in front of town hall was thick with constables. Their blue tunics and brass buttons caught the light from the oil lamps in front of the hall. Every one of them was wearing a gun belt. Every one of them was holding a rifle, too. Thirty armed men with guns massing just across the thoroughfare from him and he was powerless to do anything about it.

Jesse, the head constable, was barking out orders to the men to get in line while Big Ben stood with his back to them. Looking toward the station where the train had just pulled in, he was probably waiting for some kind of signal from Adam, who was undoubtedly on the approaching train.

Hawkeye found himself wishing Buck were there. Not out of fear, for Hawkeye was not afraid, but out of not knowing what he should do next. The constables were forming themselves into two lines that spread the width of Main Street. Up the street, he could see the Hagen family's gun hands scrambling into the Occidental, probably turning the hotel into some kind of fort against Hagen's constables.

Hawkeye knew he could not do much against the constables. Technically he was the sheriff and outranked them, but no man stood much of a chance against thirty armed men. Not even Buck would stand up well against those odds.

He also knew there were civilians in the Occidental. Innocent men and women and even some children were being pushed around by Hagen family men while he just stood there and watched. If he had a role to play in any of this, it had to be up at the hotel. To protect the innocent, even if the odds up there remained thirty against one.

His duty defined he keep his rifle at his side and his pace steady as he began the long walk along the boardwalk to the Occidental. As he drew closer to the hotel, he saw a man in every window of the lobby and imagined more were covering the back. Adam Hagen had already arranged for one building to be torched that night. The Hagen family's men would make sure the Occidental was not another one.

Hawkeye began crossing the thoroughfare to the hotel when he felt the ground begin to tremble. A lot of horses were heading his way in a hurry.

He walked quickly—but did not run—and hopped up onto the boardwalk of the hotel.

One of the Hagen gun hands named Bill saw him coming and went for his gun.

Hawkeye raised his rifle and Bill stopped cold.

"I'm here to find out what's going on," Hawkeye told him. "That's all."

Bill moved his hand away from his gun and pointed at the direction of the burning ranch house. "Don't you have eyes in your head, boy? Adam's men are fixing to kill some Hagens tonight and we're not going to let that happen."

"Neither am I," Hawkeye said as he lowered his rifle. "Sounds like the family's on their way back from Laramie."

"They sure are." Bill turned to look in that direction. "And if you've got any sense, you'll clear out of here. We don't need any of Adam's men sneaking around causing trouble."

"I'm nobody's man." Hawkeye stood right next to him. "The family deserves protection just like anyone else in town. I'm here to help in any way I can."

Bill did not seem impressed. "Can't see as how one boy with a rifle can make much of a difference here."

"The rifle doesn't make much of a difference," Hawkeye agreed, "but this star makes it legal."

Bill looked like he had more to say but forgot it when he saw the Hagen family's coach race onto Main Street and take a sharp turn toward the hotel.

Hawkeye cringed at the sight of the lather on the horses' hides and the foam coming from their mouths. The poor animals had been ridden half to death and came to an immediate stop when the driver pulled the reins and threw the hand brake.

Bill opened the door of the coach and helped Debora

Forrester down first and rushed her into the relative safety of the hotel.

Hawkeye held out his hand for Elena to take, which she did, and he ushered her into the lobby, where Bill guided her over to her sister and took both women upstairs.

Mr. Forrester, Caleb, Bart, and Bernard Wain walked into the hotel with the gunmen they had taken to Laramie.

Caleb stopped when he saw Hawkeye standing before them. "What do you think you're doing here, boy? I don't want any of Adam's men around here. Get out."

"I'm enforcing the law, Mr. Hagen," Hawkeye told him, "and you'd do best to follow the women upstairs. You'll all be safer upstairs."

Bart Hagen and Ambrose Forrester did not protest and walked around them to follow the women upstairs.

Stan tugged on Caleb's arm. "He's right, Mr. Hagen. Best if you stay with the women to keep them calm. We'll be able to keep an eye on you better that way. You'll be protected, I promise you. My men are watching every inch of this place. Just make sure everyone stays away from the windows."

Hawkeye had not expected Bernard Wain to protest. He noticed the lawyer had a gun on his hip.

"I'm not going anywhere until Adam is dead!" the lawyer yelled. "He's responsible for all of this. He's ruined everything. Everything! I'll kill him the first chance I get."

"Don't talk nonsense," Caleb told him. "He'd kill you before you even thought about going for your gun."

"Well, that's just what he's going to have to do," Wain said. "I never bought into all that nonsense about him being good with a gun anyway. People out here are easily impressed." He pointed at his brother-in-law. "And don't you go writing me off as just some upstart pup. I can take care of myself."

Stan got between Caleb and Wain. "No one's calling you a coward, Mr. Wain. I've got my doubts about how bad a man Adam Hagen is, same as you. But your wife is upstairs, and she needs you a whole lot more than Adam needs a bullet. Go to her, sir. We'll take care of things down here."

Hawkeye watched Wain scowl as he stormed off toward the staircase like a boy who had just been sent to his room without supper.

Caleb said, "Thank you for that, Stan. He's been talking about killing Adam ever since we left Laramie."

"Go on upstairs, sir," Stan answered him. "I'll be up in a while to let you know how things stand."

Caleb complied with much more dignity than his brother-in-law had shown.

Stan looked at Hawkeye. "You mean all that business just now about enforcing the law, or was that just talk?"

Hawkeye met his glare. "I meant it. Every word."

"Good." Stan rubbed his mouth with the back of his hand. "Very good. If you're serious, it might help if you stood out front right now. I'm paid to keep the Hagens alive, and I can't do that if this turns into a shooting match. You might be able to stop that from happening by keeping those constables away."

Hawkeye had already decided to do exactly that. "Just make sure your men don't do anything to spark it off, Stan. I can't do much if this turns into a shooting match." The sheriff walked outside and leaned against the porch post. Bathed in oil lamplight as he was, his star was clear for anyone to see.

He looked up the street. Hagen's constables were still

in two lines spanning the thoroughfare. Hawkeye did not want to go up against them if he did not have to. He then looked toward the station as the engine emitted a large plume of smoke from its smokestack. Evidently Adam Hagen and only God knew who else had arrived in town. Still leaning against the post, he decided to keep his eyes on the station, for when trouble started, it would no doubt start there.

CHAPTER 32

Trammel and Hagen walked from the station in darkness.

The oil lamps around town flickered, revealing the boardwalks were unusually quiet. The lights in all the saloons blazed brightly, but none of the usual drinking sounds came from any of them. It was as if the entire town was holding its breath as it waited to see what happened next.

Spotting the double line of constables in front of town hall, Trammel saw Big Ben London standing in front of them, no doubt looking to Hagen for orders. "I'd appreciate it if you left those boys where they are. Things are apt to go a whole lot better without them poking the bear."

Adam laughed in the darkness. "Take a look at the home fire I had set for Caleb and the rest, Buck. I'd say the bear's already been poked plenty and is mighty ornery. But never let it be said Adam Hagen isn't a man of peace. I'll let you have a crack at being civil. If that fails, we'll do this my way."

"We'll do this the law's way, Adam," Trammel said. "I'd order you away from here if I thought you'd go. I just don't want to give you the pleasure of laughing in my face."

"That's not why you don't order me away," Adam said

as they drew closer to the Occidental. "We both know you could knock me cold with one punch if you chose to. You want me here so you can keep an eye on me. And you're right to do that."

Sometimes Trammel forgot Adam was smarter than he was. He only hoped he was not too smart for his own good.

As they walked closer to the hotel, Trammel spotted Hawkeye leaning against the porch post. He kept himself from calling out to him from the darkness just in case he fired off a shot out of an abundance of caution.

He watched his former deputy straighten as he heard them approaching, then saw the look of relief on his face when he saw who it was.

"Buck!" he called out. "Thank God."

"And no thanks for my presence?" Adam answered. "I'm offended, Sheriff."

Hawkeye ignored him. "I'm sure glad you're here, boss. Things are mighty tense at the moment."

"I can see that." Trammel stopped in front of the hotel and looked inside. "The Hagens and their men in there?"

"They are and they're itching for a fight," Hawkeye told him. "Why didn't you wire ahead and tell me you were coming?"

"Things happened too fast for that. Come on over here and I'll tell you all about it."

He was surprised when Hawkeye refused to move. "Afraid I can't do that, Buck. I'm here to keep the peace, even from you and Adam."

"Hawkeye—"

"Your last words to me were that I wasn't your deputy anymore," his former deputy cut him off. I'm sheriff of Blackstone now and I'm charged with keeping this town safe. I'd have thought you could appreciate that more than anyone."

"I do." Trammel reached into his coat pocket and saw Hawkeye tense.

He had become his own man since Trammel had left for Laramie.

The former sheriff opened his coat slowly to show he was only reaching for his inside pocket. "Your reading get any better since I left?"

"Practice it every day by readin' *The Bugle*." Hawkeye eyed Trammel's coat. "Why?"

"On account of I have some bad news for you." Trammel pinched the paper between his fingers and handed it out to the sheriff. "You're no longer the sheriff of Blackstone. You're my deputy again."

Hawkeye reached out and took the paper without stepping from the boardwalk. He opened the document and held it up to the oil lamp. His lips moved as he tried to read it.

"Mind the flame, Sheriff Hauk," Adam said. "It's a rather important document you're holding."

Trammel was not sure how much of the letter Hawkeye could understand, but the look on his face told him Hawkeye understood enough to get the gist of it. He looked up at Trammel. "This say what I think it says?"

He was glad to see some of the wonder of the old Hawkeye return. "That depends on what you think it says."

Trammel and Adam tensed as Stan led three other gun hands out onto the boardwalk with Caleb Hagen and Wain in tow. The attorney had a gun on his hip, which Trammel took as a bad sign.

Caleb snatched the document from Hawkeye before

the young man could protest. Holding it at his side, he sneered at the two men standing in the street. "Well, isn't this predictable. Buck Trammel and Adam Hagen side by side again. You know, you almost had me believing your law-and-order bit back in Laramie, Trammel. Almost, but not quite."

"Guess that's why you tucked your tail between your legs and ran back here to Blackstone."

"A prudent measure under the advice of my attorney." He inclined his head toward Wain. "Your blind loyalty to my brother aside, he assures me you are currently out of your jurisdiction. Your warrant has no merit here."

"Quite out of your jurisdiction," Wain agreed. He was speaking to Trammel, but his eyes were fixed on Adam.

"How about you read that paper you're holding?" Trammel said. "And don't bother burning it after you're done. It's already been filed in Laramie. Wouldn't want destruction of public property added to your charges, would you?"

Caleb shook the letter open and held it at a distance so his aging eyes could focus in the dim light. Wain looked on beside him.

Trammel enjoyed the surprise on their faces as they reached the good part.

Caleb allowed Wain to take the document and turned on Trammel. "This is impossible. A forgery! My brother must've helped you do it. He's good at that sort of thing."

"The stamp's not a forgery," Trammel told him. "Neither is the territorial seal. It's legal. As of nine o'clock this evening, the governor has decreed that the Town of Blackstone has been incorporated into the City of Laramie." He waited for Wain to reach the same conclusion then stated the obvious. "That means you're in my jurisdiction after all, Caleb."

Caleb paled, evident even in the weak light of the oil lamp. "On whose testimony?"

"Lucien Clay," Trammel told him. "And Major John Stanton."

Hawkeye stepped down from the boardwalk and stood beside Trammel and Adam. Trammel flexed his right hand until the bones popped.

The gunmen behind Caleb and Wain tensed.

Trammel was glad to say the words he had waited so long to say. "Caleb Hagen and Bernard Wain, under the authority vested in me as the Sheriff of the City of Laramie, I hereby place you under arrest for the murder of United States Marshal Rob Moran."

Caleb took a couple of steps backward toward the hotel. The four hired gunmen inched closer to him.

Trammel took his Winchester in both hands. "Don't try to run, Caleb. You won't get very far. You either, Bernard."

From Caleb's left side, Stan said, "This is all news to us, Trammel. Let's wait the night and clear this up in the morning. No one's going anywhere till then anyway."

Trammel said, "I'll agree to that, but I'm taking these two with me to jail tonight. Don't want them getting any ideas about sneaking out a window or worse."

Before Stan could respond, Wain surprised everyone by dropping the document and standing in front of Caleb. His hand was dangerously close to the gun on his hip.

Trammel pointed at him as Hawkeye raised his Winchester to his shoulder. "Don't do anything stupid, Bernard. You'll get your day in court."

"Court." Wain's eyes burned bright in the lamplight.

"You think the only justice to be had can be found in a court?" He lowered his head as he glared at Adam. "You. You did this. You ruined everything you miserable cur."

Trammel felt Adam grow perfectly still.

"Careful now," the gambler said.

"I've been careful!" Wain roared. "I'm sick and tired of being careful and plotting and being coy when it comes to you. You have no decency, no honor. You killed their father and tried to steal their money. You're the lowest form of life there is, and you always manage to find a rock to hide under, don't you? You murdering coward."

Trammel turned when he heard the thirty constables begin marching down Main Street. Big Ben London was out in front. Adam must have given them some kind of signal while Wain's rant distracted him.

"Mind your words, boy," Adam cautioned. "I'll indulge your youth for only so long for the sake of my sister."

"Your *sister*," Wain spat. "You don't care about your sister. She's not even your sister. She's your cousin at best and everyone knows it except her. That will is as phony as your reputation and I'll be damned before I wind up in jail while you live to torment her any further."

"Keep talking like that," Adam said, "and you just might get your wish."

Trammel saw the final spark of hate flair in Wain's eyes. "Bernard! Don't!" But it was too late.

The lawyer slapped at his gun handle and began to pull.

Adam drew and put two rounds into Wain's chest before his Colt cleared leather. A shot from Hawkeye's rifle hit him in the forehead half a second later, sending him sprawling backward.

Trammel figured he was dead before he hit the boardwalk.

From somewhere inside, a woman screamed. Trammel looked inside and saw it was Elena.

"Elena!" Adam called out. "Elena, forgive me!"

Caleb looked down at his brother-in-law's body, then slowly raised his eyes. They did not have the same spark of anger Wain's had held. They held fear. "My God," he whispered. "What have you done?"

Stan grabbed Caleb by the collar and pushed him inside the hotel as the three remaining gunmen raised their rifles as they fled inside. One of them cracked off a shot in Trammel's direction before Hawkeye cut him down.

Adam put a shoulder into Trammel and pushed him to take cover on the other side of the street as the air filled with breaking windows and gunshots. The sound of gunfire erupted all around them as Trammel, Adam, and Hawkeye dove behind the sparse cover of a water trough in front of the mill's warehouse.

Trammel held on to his rifle as he tried to make himself as flat as possible while bullets bit into the wooden box of water. "I didn't want this!" he shouted above the gunfire.

"Neither did I," Adam said as he ducked a bullet that came too close for comfort, "but we've got it now."

Trammel looked up Main Street and saw the lines of constables had broken into a mob. Some spilled through the side streets to the back of the hotel while the rest of them began returning fire into the hotel.

Women screamed from inside the Occidental as bullets shattered the few remaining windows. The gunmen in the hotel shifted their aim to the constables in the street and Trammel watched several men in blue tunics crumple to the ground as the survivors took cover in the shadows of the boardwalk.

A new round of gunfire echoed from behind the hotel as the Hagen men covering the back found targets to shoot at.

Trammel clenched his rifle tighter as Hawkeye and Adam continued to fire at the men in the lobby of the Occidental.

It was turning into a slaughter. Tensions that had been building for weeks had come to a boil and, if he did not do something to stop it, more innocents would be killed.

It was not about the law. It was about hate and he had to end it somehow.

He pushed Hawkeye's rifle aside before the deputy could crack off another shot. "Stop firing."

Adam had flipped over onto his back and was feeding more rounds into his rifle. Trammel snatched the Winchester from him and threw it into the street. "I said stop firing."

Adam reached for the rifle, but a bullet sent him back behind the cover of the trough. He grabbed hold of Trammel's coat. "Have you lost your blasted mind?"

"I'm about the only one in this whole mess who hasn't." Trammel pulled his coat free of Adam's grip. "Get over to your men and tell them to keep cover and stop firing. Do it now."

"Stop firing?" Adam repeated. "But why?"

"Because I'm ending this, right now." He took Adam by the arm and threw him onto the boardwalk. The effort made his face ache, but he pushed the pain aside. "Now go!"

Adam cursed him as he drew his pistol and ran toward his men who had taken cover in the darker sections of the boardwalk.

Hawkeye held his rifle against his chest as he looked at Trammel. "What do we do now, boss?"

"Cover me. I'm going in." Before Hawkeye could stop

him, Trammel dropped his Winchester and pulled his Peacemaker as he ran around the water trough and bolted for the front door of the Occidental. He expected to feel the sting of a bullet with every step he took, but the men in the hotel were too occupied with shooting at the constables to pay him any mind.

Trammel leapt over Wain's corpse and crashed through the front door.

Every rifleman in the lobby looked at him.

He spotted Caleb Hagen crouched beside a sofa and dove for him just as some of the men began to turn and fire at him.

He tackled Caleb and landed with the man on top of him.

Stan, who had also taken cover next to his boss, turned to aim his gun at Trammel.

But Trammel held Caleb close against him. And had the barrel of his Peacemaker against Caleb's temple.

"Let him go," Stan ordered, "or you die."

"Lower your guns or your boss dies." Trammel thumbed back the hammer of his pistol. "I mean it."

Gunfire echoed all around them as the two men stared at each other.

"What about them outside?" Stan asked without lowering his gun. "Will they stop firing, too?"

"Tell your men to stop shooting and take cover. Find out for yourself."

Stan hesitated before shouting for his men to stop firing. He moved to the side of the grand staircase and yelled the same thing to the men stationed at the rear of the hotel, then slowly stood up as the sound of rifle fire began to die down all around them.

Adam had gotten his men to obey.

"See?" Trammel said. "I told you I'm a man of my word."

"So am I." Stan thumbed back the hammer of the pistol and kept it aimed at Trammel's head. "And I gave that man right there my word I'd keep him safe."

"You lived up to your word," Trammel told him. "He's safe. And he's going to be safe. With me. In jail. Tonight."

Stan shook his head and renewed his aim as he stepped closer. "No way. There's no way you take him out of here."

Trammel jammed the barrel of the Peacemaker against Caleb's temple until the man cried out. "How about you ask your boss?"

"Enough!" Caleb shouted. "Stan, lower your gun. All of you, lower your guns. It's over."

Trammel heard hammers being eased down throughout the lobby of the hotel.

All of them except for Stan's.

Trammel tightened his grip around Caleb's neck. "You heard the man. Put it down."

"Then what?" Stan asked. "That bunch out there comes in here and arrests us?"

"Only one man's going to jail tonight," Trammel told him. "I've already got him in custody. You and your men have the hotel. You have good cover. None of you is going to jail tonight. And probably not tomorrow, either. We can write off this whole mess as a misunderstanding that got out of hand. But nothing's going to happen until I walk out of here with him. You've got my word on that, too."

Stan's pistol quivered before he thumbed the hammer down and slid the pistol back into its holster.

Trammel was glad the man had finally seen reason.

"Step back over to the stairway while we get to our feet. Any sudden moves and you'll have to try to get paid by a dead man."

Stan backed away and rested both hands on the stair railing.

Pulling Caleb up with him, Trammel got to his feet, the barrel of his Peacemaker never moving from the man's temple. He held Caleb close as they backed out of the hotel.

"I'm right here, boss," Hawkeye said from the street. "Just keep on coming. I've got you covered."

Trammel stopped when he saw the governor's order on the boardwalk where Wain had dropped it. He let Caleb go just long enough to pick it up then wrapped his left arm under his prisoner's chin. "Wouldn't want anything to happen to this, would we?"

Hawkeye walked out from behind the trough and met them in the middle of the thoroughfare.

Stan stepped out onto the boardwalk and watched the three men walk away. "I'll be seeing you, Sheriff. I'll be seeing you real soon."

Trammel did not doubt it. "I'll be around."

He turned Caleb around and grabbed hold of him by the collar as he marched him past the constables to jail. *His* jail, not Hagen's. Hawkeye walked backward, his Winchester trained on Stan until they were well out of rifle range.

Adam Hagen stepped closer and doffed his hat as they passed by. "I bid you a good evening, brother, and pleasant dreams."

Caleb struggled against Trammel's grip, but the sheriff kept him walking.

The prisoner said, "You're a dead man, Trammel. You'll die for what you've done to me."

Trammel took a quick glance at the burning house high on the hill. The flames were still going strong but appeared to be dying down. "Maybe. But not tonight."

Chapter 33

One week later, Trammel kissed Emily's hand after she set a plate of chicken and beans in front of him. "If you keep this up, Mrs. Trammel, I'm going to get fat."

"Good. I want you fat and slow. Maybe that way, you'll stop trying to get yourself shot."

Trammel doubted there'd be much chance of anyone trying to shoot him in the near future. Things had quieted down in Laramie as quickly as they had fired up. Lucien Clay was in a cell in the basement of city hall waiting for his trial to start the following week. He had already arranged a plea deal with the judge, who'd promised to give him only five years of hard labor for his cooperation in the Moran case.

Stanton's good arm was shackled to his bed while he waited for his broken limbs to heal. He would be transferred to a hospital and kept under guard while he recovered. The judge had agreed to allow him to serve his time in a sanitarium if he remained a cripple. If he recovered, he would serve out the rest of his ten-year sentence in a penitentiary.

Due to their cooperation with the court, neither man would hang.

Things also promised to remain quiet because Adam Hagen was out of the picture. Judge Littlejohn had been true to his word and ruled the only will recognized by the court was King Charles's earlier, uncontested will. With Bernard Wain dead and Caleb Hagen awaiting trial, the judge had granted full control of the estate to Debora Hagen Forrester and her husband Ambrose.

The ink had hardly been dry on the judge's decision before Debora's new attorneys served Adam with an eviction notice, telling him he had less than a week to clear out of his rooms at the Phoenix Hotel, which was, of course, Hagen family property.

"I never thought I'd say this," Emily said as she sat at the dining table beside Trammel, "but I'm actually going to miss having Adam around."

Trammel set down his fork before he dropped it. "You're kidding."

"I'm serious. Although he almost got you killed any number of times, he was still a friend. And you have to admit he was charming in his own way."

Trammel saw it differently. "I've had just about enough of his charm to last me the rest of my life. Besides, I'll be stretched pretty thin between here and Blackstone now that it's been incorporated into the city. Just because Hawkeye will be staying on there doesn't mean I can ignore the place. I won't have any time for Adam's nonsense." He could still see the sadness in his wife's eyes. "I thought you'd be happy to see him go."

"He was always loyal to you," she noted. "He stood by you whenever it counted. I'll always be grateful to him for that, and I won't apologize for it, either."

"Well, I'm grateful he's going." Trammel meant it, too. "What with Debora running Blackstone now, it'll be good for him to put down roots somewhere else. Give himself a fresh start. He needs that. And so do I."

They both looked up when they heard a loud knock at the front door.

Emily frowned as she got up to answer it. "For heaven's sake, Steve. Can't they leave you alone? Today is your first real day off since we got here."

Trammel eased her back into her chair. Ever since two men had broken into their home with the intent to kill him, he preferred to answer the door himself. "You keep eating. I'll see who it is and send them on their way." He walked to the front door.

Draped over the newel post where he had left it the night before, he pulled the Peacemaker from his shoulder holster and held the pistol at the door. "Who is it?"

"Only your favorite vagabond in the whole wide world."

Trammel shut his eyes and sighed. It was Adam.

He kept the pistol at his side as he opened the door.

Adam Hagen stood there, dressed in a dark suit and a loud red brocade vest. His flat-brimmed hat was tilted at a rakish angle and his beard trimmed into a fashionable Vandyke. The gambler glanced at the Peacemaker at Trammel's side. "Is that how you greet an old friend down on his luck?"

"You're just about the best dressed poor man I've ever seen." Trammel looked behind Adam at the wagon loaded with goods from the various saloons he had once owned in Blackstone. The sign from the Pot of Gold was most prominent. "Stopped by to say goodbye on your way out of town?"

Hagen frowned. "My, you have gotten maudlin since Wichita, haven't you? I'd have thought your newfound success would've served to brighten your outlook on life.

Your foes bested, either in the ground or rotting in jail. Your status as a bona fide Western hero affirmed. Why, one would be forgiven for expecting you to be somewhat happy."

Trammel was beginning to get a bad feeling in his belly. Hagen only talked like this when he was about to tell him something unpleasant. "What are you working up to, Adam?"

"I'm not working up to anything except to put your mind at ease. For I didn't come here to say goodbye. I'm here to say hello again."

Trammel looked at the wagon, then back at Hagen again. "What are you talking about? All your stuff is packed and loaded."

"Indeed." He turned to the driver and waved him on. The freighter released the brake and cracked the whip, sending the team of mules on their way. "It's soon to be unloaded at the place formerly known as the Rose of Tralee. Never liked that name anyway. I think the Pot of Gold sounds much nicer. Besides, it would be a shame to let a perfectly good sign go to waste. My sister would only burn it out of spite."

Trammel felt himself grip the Peacemaker tighter. "You're what?"

"Good heavens. City life has made you dull, hasn't it?" Adam smiled. "I've moved out of Blackstone only to take up residence here in Laramie." He patted Trammel on the left shoulder. "Isn't that great news? I thought you'd be happy."

"Happy?" Trammel had heard the words, but they did not make sense to him. "But you and Clay broke off your partnership. How—"

"Oh, that," Hagen said. "Well, it was a verbal dissolution, but old Lucien never got around to filing the proper papers with the county or the city. So, legally, I own it all. As my family taught me well, such legal details do matter. I may have lost the Hagen empire, at least for now, but I've gained control of Clay's businesses. Saloons, hotels, and all of the other unmentionables we won't talk about now." He tried another smile. "We're going to be working together again, Buck. I thought you'd be pleased by this."

Trammel was flooded with a lot of emotions, but none of them came close to being pleased. He'd thought he was finally rid of Adam Hagen and the storm clouds that followed him wherever he went. But he was not rid of him. Nothing had changed except the name of the town.

Adam obviously saw Trammel's disappointment. "This isn't Blackstone, Steve. That part of my life is over. No more getting even with my family. No father to fight. No scores to settle. No enemies to fend off. Clay kept a tight lid on this city, and I will make it tighter. You can count on that."

Trammel felt his neck begin to redden as he finally looked Hagen in the eye. "And you can count on this, Adam. You're right about this not being Blackstone. Laramie's three times as big which gives you more power than you've ever had before. I stood against you when I had to up north and the same goes for down here. Every time you step over the line, I'll be right there to push you back where you belong. Understand?"

Adam's smile dimmed a bit. "Yes, Sheriff. I'm afraid I understand all too well." He touched the brim of his hat as he stepped away. "I bid you and Dr. Trammel a pleasant day."

Trammel shut the door and leaned against it. He looked toward the ceiling, maybe even to Heaven itself, and wondered what he had to do to rid himself of Adam Hagen once and for all.

He did not know how long he had been standing there when he felt Emily frowning at him from the other end of the hall.

"I guess I should've known better than to expect our troubles to be over," she said.

"Over?" He remembered the Peacemaker in his hand and shoved it back into its holster. He knew he would need it before long. "I think our troubles are just beginning."

TURN THE PAGE
FOR AN EXCITING PREVIEW!

Johnstone Country. Locked and Loaded.
Marshal Dan Caine is sworn to uphold the law. But sometimes justice isn't served. Sometimes killers go free. And sometimes a lawman has to take off his badge to make those killers pay—the old-fashioned way. . . .

They broke into the cabin of a harmless old man. First, they tortured him to find out where he hid his tin pan gold. Then, they murdered him—brutally, viciously—when the man insisted he had no gold. Afterward, the three killers got drunk and laughed over the old coot's screams of agony. By the time Marshal Dan Caine heard about it, the trial was already over. The victim was none other than Dick Meadows, the cranky old cuss who'd raised Caine as an orphan. The suspects were the sons of a filthy rich cattle baron who'd used his money and power to intimidate the jury. The verdict was unanimous: not guilty. And so the killers walked free. . . .

As a lawman, Caine has to respect the court's decision. But as a man who believes in justice, he has a moral obligation to step outside the law, climb onto his horse, and avenge the murder of his oldest friend.
No judge. No jury. Just one executioner. . . .

National Bestselling Authors
William W. Johnstone
and J.A. Johnstone

RAISING CAINE

A Guns of the Vigilantes Novel

On sale now!

www.williamjohnstone.net

Chapter One

Sheriff Dan Caine looked out of his office window into the dusty main drag of Broken Back, a Texas cow town precariously perched on the crumbling edge of nowhere.

Across the street, outside John Taylor's mercantile, Mrs. Jean McCann and Mrs. Blanche Baxter were in deep conversation, though what they found to talk about was beyond Dan's comprehension since a burg as small as Broken Back generated little gossip. Mrs. McCann was pregnant again. What was it, her third or fourth? Dan had lost count. He watched Frank Lawson, the local gambler, dressed in his usual black frock coat, white shirt, and string tie, touch his hat as he passed the ladies and then continue on his way to Ma's Kitchen where he breakfasted every morning on coffee and three fingers of bourbon. Lawson had once worked the Mississippi riverboats, but that was a dozen years ago and he'd fallen on hard times since then, fallen so far and so fast in fact that he'd landed with a thud in Broken Back where the stakes were low, and he counted his winnings in nickels and dimes. Lawson carried a silver-plated Remington derringer and the talk was that across the card tables he'd killed several men with it. But he'd never drawn down on anybody in Dan's town. Just as well. Dan Caine had little tolerance for shootists, especially homicidal, washed-up gamblers.

Mrs. McCann and Mrs. Baxter's conference had drawn to a close and they hugged and went their separate ways. A dust devil spun in the street and then collapsed in a puff of dust, and the risen sun burned away the shadows and opened a furnace door that blasted waves of dry heat over the town.

Dan Caine sighed and reread the letter again. It was from Toby Reynolds, a rancher who'd once hired a much-younger Caine as a puncher and had kept up a desultory correspondence with him for years. The missive was badly spelled, painstakingly written in block letters, and the news it imparted was straight to the point and all bad.

> DEER DAN. I HAVE BAD NOOS ABOUT YOUR FREND DICK MEDOWS. HOW IT CAME UP HE WAS MURDERED AFTER NOOS GOT AROUND THAT HE HAD STRUK IT RICH AND HIS CABIN WAS FILLED WITH GOLD. AS WE BOTH NO DICK NEVER HIT PAYDIRT IN HIS LIFE. THREE MEN WAS ARRESTED FOR HIS MURDER THE SONS OF THE BIG RANCHER BARTON CLAY. BUT THANKS TO THEIR PA HAVIN MONEY AND INTIMIDATIN THE JURY THEY WAS FOUND NOT GILTY. DAN, THEM THREE BOYS CELEBRATED IN THE SALOON AND LAFFED ABOUT HOW DICK HOLLERED WHEN THEY HELD HIS TOES TO THE FIRE. FOLKS AROUND THESE PARTS NO THE CLAY BOYS GOT AWAY WITH MURDER BUT THEIR PA HAS HIRED RUBEN

WEBB THE TEXAS DRAW FITER TO KEEP OUR TOWN AND USELESS CITY MARSHAL IN LINE. THE MARSHAL IS A DARN FOOL. CLAY RANCH IS EAST OF TUCSON AT THE FOOT OF THE RINCON SKY MOUNTINS. I JUST THOT YOU WOULD WANT TO NO.
—TOBY REYNOLDS ESQ.

Dan dropped the letter and his eyes went to the street again. Nothing stirred except for John Taylor's yellow dog that flopped down outside the mercantile's door and glared balefully at Sophie, Dan's calico cat who was sunning herself on the boardwalk. That dog, his name was Ranger, had chased Sophie seven times, caught her once, and never tried it again.

Dan's attention went back to the letter and its disturbing contents. He built a cigarette, thumbed a lucifer into flame, and smoked as he remembered . . .

Snake River Dick Meadows was not by any stretch of the imagination a nice old man. He was rattlesnake mean, cranky, violent in drink, and he hated people with a passion, avoiding them in the same way ordinary folks walked wide around skunks.

But when Dan Caine was just six years old, Meadows had saved his life. He'd found the boy alone, hungry, and frightened in a ramshackle cabin in the New Mexico Territory, clinging to the body of his mother who'd been dead for three days, casually killed, along with his father, by a passing Apache war band.

The old man made a meager living as a tin pan and wandered far and wide, but he called a small stone cabin in the Arizona Territory's Mogollon Rim country his home not-so-sweet home. His attitude to Dan was one of indifference, once staking the boy out to call in a grizz that had been prowling too near his workings. But Meadows kept the growing youngster fed and taught Dan how to hunt, fish, and shoot, including tutoring him in the ways of the Colt revolver.

Dan struck out on his own when he was sixteen, mounted on a ten-dollar horse, carrying a Springfield carbine, Model of 1877 in .45-70 caliber that he could shoot ten times in a minute with accuracy. He and Meadows shook hands and promised to keep in touch, but they never did.

Until the letter came.

Dan's deputy, a half-Scottish, half-Apache breed, walked into the office from his bunk in one of the cells. His father had taken his offspring's name from a bourbon bottle and called him Old Crow, though Dan just called him Crow. Suffering from the effects of last night's overindulgence at James Logan's saloon, Crow wore only fire engine red long johns and, a holdover from his early days as a drover, his battered hat, the front brim curled up and secured with a pin he'd received from the Women's Temperance Guild of Kansas. Crow had been drunk at the time and could never remember which of the ladies had given it to him, but nonetheless it was a prized possession. He stood beside Dan's desk, scratched his belly, and yawned.

"Speak, thou dreadful specter," Dan said.

"Coffee," Crow said, his voice breaking on the word.

"You know where it is," Dan said.

Crow shook his head and held up two shaking hands. "Get it for me, Dan."

"Who was it this time?" Dan said, rising to his feet.

"Same as usual," Crow said. He sat gingerly on the chair opposite the sheriff's desk. "Eleanor Martine."

Dan poured coffee into a thick white cup. "Eleanor Martine . . . her real name's Ellen Martin," he said.

"Gimme . . . gimme . . ." Crow said, reaching out with both hands for the cup.

"What was the drink?" Dan said. "Or can't you recollect?"

"Champagne," Crow said. He tested the coffee. "Ow . . . ow . . . hot."

"What kind of champagne?"

"French, from France. Oh, my head. Frog . . . fail . . . fall . . . how come when I say a word starting with f my head hurts worse?"

"Try fake, false, fraud . . . like the French champagne you guzzled last night. It's made in Fort Worth out of raw alcohol, ginger ale, and apple juice, and Logan buys it by the barrel, bottles it himself, and charges top dollar."

"But Eleanor drank it."

"No, she didn't. When you weren't looking, she poured it out, and you were too drunk to notice."

Crow groaned. "Three dollars a bottle and we drank about nine or ten. A month's wages gone. Pffft! Just like that."

"Was she worth it?"

"Who?"

"Ellen Martin."

"I don't know."

"You were too drunk to know."

"I woke up in my bunk. I've no idea how I got there." He held his head in both hands and groaned. "Dan, put me out of my misery. Just shoot me."

"Sure, I will, but later. In the meantime, I've got something I want you to read."

"Read? What time is it?"

"It's just gone nine."

"In the morning?"

"Seems like."

"Nobody reads at nine in the morning. It ain't Christian."

"You will." Dan tossed Toby Reynolds's letter across the desk. "Wrap your eyeballs around that."

"Do I have to?"

"Only if you want to keep your job."

Crow picked up the letter. "You're a hard-hearted man, Dan Caine."

"And you're one complaining Injun."

"It's only the white part of me that complains, not the Injun half."

"And if you don't eyeball the letter right now, both halves of you will be out of work."

"I'd shake my head at you if it didn't hurt so much," Crow said.

He read the letter, rubbed sleep from his eyes, and read it again. Then he said, "Dan, I'm sorry."

"Don't be. Snake River Dick Meadows was a disgusting human being, and I owe him nothing but my life. But I reckon that's enough."

"Enough for what?"

"Enough for me to head to the Arizona Territory's rim country and see that the three men who murdered Meadows pay for what they did. I want them to hang."

"Dan, a rich man's sons are gallows-proof, you know that," Crow said. "Money talks in a courtroom. The hundred-dollar bill is the West's best defense lawyer, and that's a natural fact."

"Then I'll find another way to punish them. I'll be wearing a gun."

"Ah . . . then you haven't heard of Ruben Webb, the

Amarillo drawfighter that Reynolds mentions in his letter, huh?"

"You're correct, I haven't had that pleasure."

"Well, the talk is that when he was seventeen, he put the crawl on John Wesley Hardin."

"The loose talk in the saloon?"

"Yeah, from men who . . ."

"Heard it from other men who heard it in another saloon."

"Something like that. Dan, I know you set store by Wes Hardin."

"Yes, and I still do. As you know, I did some hard time in Huntsville with him and I can tell you this . . . Wes never backed down from anyone, even Wild Bill Hickok. And if a two-bit, wannabe gunman like Webb says otherwise then he's a damned liar."

"All right, I'll try a different tack. Have you told the fair Helen about Dick Meadows?" Crow said.

"Some of it," Dan said.

"How long have you been married?"

"Six months."

"And now you're going to leave her and lay your life on the line in the Arizona Territory?"

"That's how it shapes up," Dan said. "What I aim to do has to be done. To do otherwise would mean I could never again hold my head high in the company of men."

"Maybe, and probably only in the Arizona Territory, nowhere else." Crow said. "Dan, you can't go up against those Clay boys as a lawman. Your sheriff's star won't shine in that neck of the woods."

"Then I'll go as a vigilante and do what the law should've done in the first place."

"You're bucking a stacked deck. Taking on a big rancher with three sons and who knows how many punchers riding for his brand are mighty long odds." Crow held his head and whimpered. "Oh, dear God, even thinking about it is making my white-man headache worse."

"White-man headache?" Dan said.

"An Apache doesn't get headaches. Didn't you know that?"

"Well, I guess they don't get them often, unless like you, they drink too much tiswin." Dan got to his feet. "Hold the fort," he said. "I have to speak with Helen."

"She doesn't know about the letter?"

"No. The Patterson stage pulled in early this morning and Buttons Muldoon and Red Ryan brought it to me. Helen doesn't know about it yet."

"When do we leave?" Crow said.

"You're not leaving," Dan said. "This is a job I'll handle by myself."

"That's a hell of a thing to say to me, Dan," Crow said. "You're the sheriff of Broken Back and I'm your shadow. That's how it's been since you first pinned a badge on me. You head for the Territory and I'll be right behind you." Dan opened his mouth to speak, and Crow held up a silencing hand. Dan thought he looked like a cigar store Indian in long johns. "Besides . . . oh my poor head . . . I know the country south of the Mogollon Rim, well some of it at least."

"How come?" Dan said.

"You don't want me to answer that. It happened a couple of years ago before I got civilized."

"Tell me," Dan said.

"You won't like it. It ain't about what you would call churchgoing folks."

"Go ahead. I'll try my best to bear it."

"Are you sure?"

"Sure, I'm sure. Have at it."

"Well, it was some years after my father died when I was living on the San Carlos with my ma and her new Chiricahua husband. She was a nice lady and last year I heard that she'd died way too young of the cholera."

"I remember that," Dan said. "And I was right sorry."

"Anyway, how the Mogollon Rim thing came up, me and a couple of other young Chiricahuas, Tarak and Delshay, nice fellers, heard that an army payroll wagon had left the reservation on its way north to Fort Apache, so we planned on robbing it. You sure you want to hear this? It ain't respectable."

"Yeah, I'm sure. Now get to the exciting part."

"There is no exciting part. Unbeknownst to us, the wagon was met with a cavalry patrol from the fort and they cut loose on us. Tarak got a thumb blown off and Delshay took a bullet to his left leg, broke the knee that later left him with a limp. At least that's what I heard."

"And you didn't get hit?" Dan said.

"No. Maybe them soldiers thought I was a white man. Well, anyway, when we got back to the reservation old Geronimo, a nice enough feller but death on Mexicans, asked me to join his war band, but right there and then I decided to leave the Apaches behind me and walk the white man's path."

"You do look like a white man, you know," Dan said.

"Yellow hair and green eyes, how could I look like anything else?"

"Back in the day you must've seemed a mighty strange kind of Apache to ol' Geronimo and them. Hell, what am

I talking about? You even look like some mighty strange kind of white man."

And that was true.

Crow's straight, fair hair fell over his shoulders except for two braids that framed his face. He'd inherited his wide and high cheekbones from his Apache mother and his six-foot-two height and stubborn chin from his Scottish father.

And he was being stubborn now.

"Sheriff Caine, I'm a very sick man this morning, close to death, but you're not going to the Arizona Territory without me, so put that in your pipe and smoke it."

"Who can I leave in charge of law and order in this wild and wooly town?"

"John Taylor."

"He's a grocer, for God's sake."

"A grocer who'd like nothing better than to get out from behind his counter and strut around town with a star on his chest."

"Now I study on it, maybe you're right. At town meetings Taylor's a man who likes to puff out his chest and talk and brag, all the time poking holes in the air with his finger."

"A banty rooster boasting on a dung heap," Crow said.

"I'll talk to him," Dan said.

"What are you going to tell him?"

"That you and I are going on a hunting trip into the Arizona Territory after mule deer."

"He'll want to load you up with cartridges."

"That's all right. Where we're going, we'll probably need them."

Chapter Two

His cat tucked under his arm, Dan Caine crossed the sunbaked street and took the alley between the mercantile and a land office that led to open ground and a small limestone cabin with a wood shingle roof and wraparound porch. Dan bought the cabin from a dentist who'd called it quits, closed his practice, and headed for Austin where there were more folks with bad teeth than in Broken Back.

That summer Dan Caine was in his early thirties, a brown-eyed, broad-shouldered, good-looking man with jet black hair and eyebrows that were slightly too heavy for his lean face. He had a wide, expressive mouth and good teeth, and women, respectable and otherwise, liked him just fine. Dan Caine looked a man right in the eye, holding nothing back, and most times he had a stillness about him, a calm, but of the uncertain sort that had the brooding potential to suddenly burst into a moment of hellfire action. He seldom talked about himself, but as a young man he'd served three years in Huntsville for an attempted train robbery. He'd spent the first four months of his sentence in the penitentiary's infirmary for a bullet wound to the chest he'd taken during the hold-up. At some point during that time, probably in the spring of 1880 according to most historians, he was befriended by John Wesley Hardin. Prison life had tempered Hardin's wild ways, and Wes convinced the young Caine to quit the outlaw trail and live by the law. Released early in the summer of 1882, Dan Caine drifted for a couple of years, doing whatever work he could find. He arrived in Montana in January 1884, the year the citizenry, irritated by the amount of crime in the Territory, appointed hundreds of vigilantes to enforce the law. Hard-eyed hemp posses dutifully strung up thirty-five cattle and horse thieves and an even dozen of just plain nuisances. Dan didn't think Montana a good place to loiter, and in the fall of 1885 owning only his horse, saddle, rifle, Colt revolver, and the clothes he stood up in, he rode into the town of Thunder Creek, missing his last six meals. The sheriff, Chance Hurd, a former outlaw himself, liked the tough, confident look of the young man, fed him steak and eggs, and gave him a job as a twenty-a-month deputy. Now Hurd was dead, and Dan had moved on to Broken Back where he was offered the job of town sheriff.

Dreading what he was about to tell his bride, he stepped into the cabin and Helen greeted him with a wide smile. Dan was again struck by how pretty she was and how lucky he was that she'd consented to marry him. Helen was teaching a class that day, eight kids between the ages of six and twelve crammed into a tiny cabin reserved for that purpose by the town fathers, and she was dressed for work, wearing a plain, brown cotton dress with white collar and cuffs, her dark hair pulled back in what she called a "schoolmarm's bun."

Dan set down Sophie and returned his wife's smile. "You look as pretty as a field of bluebonnets," he said. "And that's a natural fact."

Helen dropped a little curtsy. "Why thank you, kind sir," she said. "There's coffee in the pot and some leftover yellow cake in the cupboard. And now tell me why you're back here so early in the morning. It seems that you just left."

Dan held out the letter. "The Patterson stage just delivered this, Helen. I think you should read it."

A frown wrinkle appeared between the woman's eyes, and she said, "Dan, you're such a man of mystery." She took the letter from his hand, read it, read it again, and then said, "You told me about Dick Meadows. He was not a nice man and sometimes he treated you cruelly, but I guess I should be sorry he's dead."

"He saved my life, Helen. I owe him."

"I think you paid back what you owed him many times over. Judging by what you told me, he treated you like a slave."

"I would've died in my folks' cabin. It was cold and there was no food and I was six years old and I'd been trying to wake my dead mother for three days. Dick took me out of there and gave me a home." He hesitated and then added, "Of a sort."

"Well, I'll mention him in my prayers tonight," Helen said. A pile of blue covered textbooks under her arm, she said, "Now I must get to school." She moved toward the door, stopped, kissed Dan on the cheek, and then said, "See you later, husband. Don't forget the cake and take a slice to Deputy Crow."

"Helen, wait," Dan said. "We have to talk about this."

"Talk about what? The cake?"

"No, about the men who murdered Dick Meadows."

"I don't want to talk about that," Helen said. A gleam of irritation lit up her eyes. "The old man who saved your life and then abused you is dead. Well, it's sad. Now let it go."

"I can't. I want to see that the men who killed and then escaped justice are punished. I owe him that much."

"And what do you owe me, Dan?" Helen said. "What do you owe your wife?"

She was angry. Dan saw her body stiffen, white knuckling the hand holding her textbooks. It was the first time Dan had seen Helen angry, and it shocked him. She was ready to pit her bird and he needed to step carefully.

"I love you, Helen," he said. "And I want to spend the rest of my life with you."

"A life that could be cut short in the Arizona Territory . . . and all for a dead old man you didn't even like. Is he really worth dying for? Dan, you're not making any sense. It's as though you're talking nonsense to me in a foreign tongue, Mandarin Chinese maybe, and I can't understand a word you're saying."

"Helen, the dead can't cry out for justice, only the living can do that. I'll get Dick Meadows the justice that was denied him."

"Why? For heaven's sake, why?"

"Because it's my duty. It's that simple. Helen. Duty calls and I can't turn my back on it."

"Dan, the star on your chest means that your duty is to this town."

"And if I showed yellow and didn't do what has to be done, I could never wear this star or any other ever again." Dan touched his wife lightly on the cheek and said, "If you can't understand why I'm doing this thing, at least tell me you'll stand by me."

"I can't do that, Dan," Helen said. "I can promise you nothing." She shook her head. "I think you're a fool, and I think you're throwing our marriage away like you'd throw away dirty dishwater. Yes, dirty dishwater, Dan. That's what our marriage means to you."

"Miz Caine, are you all right?"

The voice outside belonged to twelve-year-old Nat Campbell, Helen's star student.

"Yes, I'm just fine. Go back to school, Nat," she called out. "I'll be right there."

"You ain't sick, ma'am?"

"No, Nat, I'm not sick. Now go back to school like I told you."

"Yes, ma'am."

Helen opened the door and said, her voice like melting ice, "When will you leave, Dan?"

"As soon as me and Crow saddle up. I expect we'll head for San Antone and catch a train to the territory."

"Dan, I'll tell you one thing you shouldn't expect," Helen said. "Don't expect me to be here when you get back. If you get back."

"Helen, wait . . ." Dan said.

But his wife was gone, striding, back stiff, toward her waiting class.